Forget Me Not

A Wayward Inclination

Forget Me Not

A Wayward Inclination

by Daniel Lee Mansell

Forget Me Not

A Wayward Inclination

© Daniel Lee Mansell 2018

Published by
Lighthouse Christian Publishing
SAN 257-4330
5531 Dufferin Drive
Savage, Minnesota, 55378
United States of America

www.lighthousechristianpublishing.com

Prelude

"Dear Jesus," a little girl, no older than eight began to pray as she knelt beside her bed. Her little hands were clasped together in a traditional sense and her head was bowed in reverence to her God. The moonlight beaming in through the slightly opened window illuminated her small, country cottage-style bedroom. Dolls, horses, and teddy bears adorned the white dresser tops on the other side. Hand-painted letters made of wood and adorned with ribbons hung on one wall, spelling out the girl's name, "MADISON". A swift breeze occasionally rolled in through the window, causing the lace curtains to rise and fall as the little girl continued to pray.

"Please forgive me for punching Luke's leg in the car on the way home from church today. He started it, but I know I shouldn't have hit him, and I'm sorry. Daddy says that it was a sin no matter what and that I should talk to You about it. I know that Luke is very young but he sure does get on my nerves sometimes. That doesn't matter I guess. I'm older and I shouldn't have hit him. So I'm sorry. Also, please forgive me for not minding Mommy when it was time to get up this morning. Luke was worse than me, but I'm still sorry. I should have minded Mommy no matter what. Daddy said that too. Daddy's pretty smart I guess."

Outside the window, it was a quiet night. So quiet you could hear the little girl's voice all the way to the road, which was a few hundred feet from the house. Her window was on the second floor of her family's two story white-framed farm house. An assortment of flowers and shrubs surrounded the base of the home, complimented by a neatly trimmed, healthy lawn. The light outside the front door was still on, revealing a wrap-around porch complete with bench swings and large ferns hanging just a few feet from each other. Various other lights in the house were still on as well, as the rest of the family settled in for bed.

"Thank You for my Mommy and Daddy and Luke," the little girl continued. "Yes, Luke, too. Also thank You for my friend Haley, and my teacher, Mrs. Taylor. And thank You for Buster and Max, my two doggies, and of course, Tinker, the cat. I pray that she has her kittens soon so she doesn't bust like Daddy says. Also, thank You for Frank, the frog, who mommy and Daddy don't know I have yet."

Another gust of wind, this one stronger than the rest, blew through the window, causing the curtains to flutter. This did not seem to startle the little girl, as she continued to pray. "Most of all God, thank You so much for sending Your Son to die on the cross for my sins."

Suddenly on the roof of the house, just above the little girl's window, appeared the silhouette of a man. He was perched on the rooftop in a still pose and patrolled the night air with sharp senses and determined anticipation. Over his white clothing he wore a long, white robe that hung over his body. One either side of his head, the collars from his outfit were raised, casting a shadow over his face. Jet black hair hung over his eyes and face, down to his mouth, further obscuring the man's features and identity. His eyes began to open, ever so slightly, as the little girl continued…

"Thank You for raising Jesus from the dead so that we can all go to Heaven to be with You one day."

The man's eyes opened wider. They were a bright blue color that pierced into the night sky like a knife. He remained motionless, ready, as if awaiting something.

"Oh yea, and God please send Your angels to protect my family and friends and animals tonight and help us all to get a good night sleep."

Suddenly, in the distance, appeared a red ball of flames. It was several miles away at first, but gaining fast, headed in the direction of the house. The ball of fire screamed as it tore across the landscape, hurling a long trail of black smoke behind.

"Amen," the little girl finished, as she stood up and climbed into bed, grabbing a hold of her favorite teddy bear.

"Amen," the man said with a slight grin as he stood from his position, the furious ball of fire approaching quickly in the reflection of his eyes. "Sleep well, child of God," he proclaimed as he pulled two long, flaming blades from behind his back and readied himself to attack. "Tonight, you sleep in the company of angels."

I

The middle-aged man sitting in the back row did not sit well with Andrew, who was seated in his normal place, three rows up from the back. The man sat emotionless in a brown overcoat keeping his hands buried in his deep pockets except to look at his watch occasionally. His expression and overall appearance was peculiar, to say the least, though not so that it drew the attention of anyone else in the congregation. Andrew, however, was the youngest in this particular setting, still in his early thirties. He was also the newest member, making him the most likely of candidates to be overly suspicious of anything out of place in these times. Being led to the Lord by his father when he was young was what Andrew had considered to be the most significant achievement of his life thus far, but it wasn't until recently that he really began to understand and fully appreciate his relationship with Christ. His recent decision to renew his commitment to God was nothing less than a cause for celebration, as it proved to be the missing link in Andrew's life since the loss of his father as a teenager.

After the election of President Jimmy Tolston, Andrew's celebration of his new life in Christ was brought to a close, almost as quickly as it began. It seemed impossible to think that Christians would one day have to join the dark world of alleyways and underground meeting places in order to continue to worship God together the same way that they and their ancestors had done for well over two hundred years as free Americans.

Since the law banning the public practice of Christianity as a religion had been passed by Congress several months ago, church congregations all over the nation had been forced to either disband or take the risk of worshipping God together in secret. Although the now underground religion still thrived, numbers of practicing Christians had been on a steady and steep decline since the law was put into place. There were no signs of improving or even steadying anytime soon. Initially, a handful of politicians had put forth a considerable opposition to the law; however, their incredible efforts were beginning to be proved in vain. Many political experts were beginning to suggest that within the next year, it would become illegal to worship privately as well. Within the next two years, it was predicted that it would be against the law for someone to claim himself a Christian at all.

President Tolston and his running mate hinted towards these changes during their hard-fought campaign, claiming that religion in general had caused a great deal of division in American society over the centuries, leading to what they described as an "imminent downfall and ultimate demise of our great country." For the most part, the President delivered these types of ideas very subtly to the American people, fearing that making his case ultimately against Christians too strongly would keep him out of office. It was obvious now that Tolston had been planning an anti-religion agenda for years that only now people were beginning to buy in to. Some remained hopeful that the changes would not last long, but for most, especially new Christians, hope had left the picture long ago. Although Andrew was still fairly new to the fold, he was determined not to be deterred from his new found faith in God.

Andrew tried to keep an eye on the man in the back row without drawing any unwanted attention in return. Once again, the man lifted his arm to look at the time, then placed his hand deep back into his pocket. The building was very old and the lighting was bad, but even though they were in a room no bigger than a fast food restaurant, Andrew couldn't make out any features other than what could be vaguely seen. The man had light skin, wore sunglasses, and had dark hair.

The congregation, which had been dubbed *Lux Ex Tenebris,* Latin for "Light in Darkness," had just heard another sermon from their leader and were beginning to pray. The man in the back row suddenly rose to his feet and ran out of the back of the room, leaving the door to the only entrance into and out of the room wide open. This roused the other fifty or so members just enough to cause a brief moment of silence. Andrew watched the doorway cautiously. Something wasn't right, and he knew it, despite the others' seeming lack of concern.

"Our Heavenly Father," the pastor began, closing his eyes and lifting his arms with his Bible in hand. The congregation bowed their heads unanimously, some raising their hands with the pastor. Andrew's attention remained fixed on the open door, occasionally looking around at the others and wondering why they weren't more concerned by the suspicious man's behavior. Slowly, he began to creep towards the middle of the room, enabling him to better see through the door. He knew that if something were there, the pastor would have noticed it before he began to pray; however, the pastor's eyes were closed now as he continued to pray.

"Thank You, Jesus, for allowing us to come together in Your glorious name," the pastor continued. "Thank You for giving us freedom in You, oh God, the freedom to choose to serve You and love You and accept You as our Lord and Savior. We come to You this day to ask for Your forgiveness and mercy, as well as for Your guidance during this, our troubled time. We ask that You would grant mercy upon the leaders of this great country, the black sheep who have led Your people astray. These menacing devils continue to torment Your people by forcing them to worship You in secret."

Andrew inched closer to the center of the room where the steel chairs were divided to form a row going up the middle of the room to the front where the pastor stood. He moved slowly and cautiously so as to investigate the still open door without disturbing the prayer.

For months now, services just like this one were being shut down and good people just like those in this very congregation were being placed in prison with common criminals. Every single day, another previous pastor was being tried by the courts for his part in maintaining hidden, yet public places of worship. The sentences being handed down were not only unjust, but ruthless as well. It was as if the nation's law enforcement had shifted its entire emphasis on bringing down Christianity wherever it bloomed.

Things were getting worse, and Andrew suddenly had a very bad feeling that *Lux Ex Tenebris* was the next target. If this were indeed the case, there was no escape. The only entrance to and exit from the old abandoned storage room was in the back, and was now opened to the empty and decaying factory building outside of it. Any number of men could be lying in wait outside that door, either waiting to come in or waiting for the members of the church to come out. Andrew had not noticed anyone or anything out of place when he arrived, and obviously nobody else had either, but it certainly was not ridiculous to think that people could be hiding out there, not by a long shot. Meeting secretly like this also meant exposing yourself to the possibility of a few surprises from the opposition, if you were found.

"God we praise Your holy name; we lift You up to the highest of places," the pastor continued, accompanied by the occasional "amen" coming from the congregation. "We submit to You Lord, everything that we are and everything that we ever will be."

Without warning, a loud bang emerged from the open doorway accompanied by a bright flash of light and a puff of thick, white smoke. Andrew, who had inched nearly to the open row in the middle of the room, jumped back, nearly falling over a chair behind him. Smoke began to enter the room in chunks as another loud bang accompanied by a flash of light went off. Curiosity turned to panic as Andrew quickly picked himself up and began to back up towards his original seat on the outer edge of the room. He looked around to find himself the only person in the room to react to what was going on. Even the pastor, who was still standing in front of the room with his eyes closed and his arms raised, seemed unmoved by the disturbance. He continued to pray.

"God, we ask that You deliver us from the clutches of evil as we boldly claim our seats at the table of our enemy." The pastor's voice began to rise in volume as he continued. "We ask that You grant us the wisdom and the courage to continually go forward, seeking nothing less than glory for Your name and the opportunity to spend eternity in Your holy presence."

Andrew was nothing less than astonished by the lack of reaction by not just the pastor, but also the entire congregation, all of whom remained perfectly still with their eyes closed and their heads bowed in reverence to God. From the back of room, figures dressed in black began to move through the smoke, swiftly and robotically. Men dressed in what appeared to be some sort of riot gear carrying automatic rifles filed into the make-shift church and took positions around the outer walls of the room, eventually surrounding the entire congregation. Red lasers beaming from the scopes of the soldiers' weapons interlaced through the transparent smoke that now filled the room, each of them fixed on the foreheads and chests of each of the church members.

Unsure of what to do or where to go, Andrew soon found himself frozen in fear. All he could do at this point was to remain still, save for the uncontrollable trembling that had taken over his entire body. He did not so much as blink as a bead of sweat made its way downward past the outside edge of his eye. Although fear kept him from investigating it further, it did not seem to him as if any of the lasers were pointed in his direction.

"God, You are…" the preacher suddenly gasped and then fell to the floor unconscious. Andrew quickly turned his attention towards the front of the room, where a tall man in a black suit had taken the place of the congregation's leader, who now lay on the floor. He had appeared quite literally out of nowhere. Andrew had all but blinked his eyes throughout the entire invasion and had not seen him come in through the door at any time. There were no vents, no windows, or no passages of any sort that could have allowed him to suddenly appear in front of the room, taking even the preacher by surprise.

The man wore a long black jacket over his suit and a fedora hat that was situated to cover his eyes and shadow his face. His eyes seemed to glimmer a fiery orange color through the shadow against no known source of light over an evil, malicious smile. With his slim and bony fingers joined at their tips he began to speak in a low and somewhat gargled, yet distinguished tone that quickly gathered everyone's attention. He hissed in obvious delight as he spoke.

"This…" he began. "This gathering, as you already know, is in direct violation of the law." The man began to walk forward slowly into the middle aisle, moving his head back and forth as he walked. He made it a point to briefly gaze into the eyes of every member of the congregation as he passed. The members sometimes let out a slight gasp in horror, while others just remained as still and as quiet as possible. Slowly he made his way towards the back, where Andrew was still standing.

"And as you all know," the man continued. "The penalty for breaking the law in this, our great country, can be quite…stiff." Andrew was at least four or five rows behind everyone else in the congregation. He knew that once the man had made his way to him, he would be the primary focus of the man's attention.

Escape had not yet left his mind, but he worried about being taken down by one of the soldiers' weapons. He wasn't sure whether or not they would actually shoot him, seeing as how the penalty for breaking the public practice of religion law did not even come close to warranting death or serious injury. By the looks of things and the strange disposition of the man walking towards him, however, he was not sure if he was willing to gamble on it. Then suddenly, upon reaching the members seated closest to Andrew, the man turned and began to make his way back towards the front of the room.

Andrew seemed confused by the lack of attention he seemed to be receiving by both the soldiers and the strange man pacing the room. Now the one thing keeping him from planning a way out was the thought of running away like a coward while the rest of the congregation had to remain and face their punishment. It wasn't like him to be selfish in any way, but this wasn't your normal every day bust either. Something about this was out of place, even wicked, and Andrew was feeling more uncomfortable and afraid by the second. The man was now nearing the front of the room once again, this time with his hands behind his back and his head down. He was quiet for a moment, in thought, as if he was planning his methods before carrying them out. Upon reaching the front, where the preacher remained unconscious on the floor, he turned and looked at the congregation once again.

"It's really quite simple," the man continued, still smiling crookedly. "You break the law, you pay the consequences. You will be happy to know, however, that

I am not here to collect your debt to society." The man now focused his full attention on the entire congregation. The evil radiating from his expression seemed to gaze into the very souls of everyone in the room, except the soldiers, whose tinted masks protruding from their helmets hid any hint of emotion. Suddenly, the entire wall behind the dark figure burst into flames, causing panic among the church members. Andrew flinched and ducked in obvious shock. The man, who could not have been standing more than a few feet away from the wall, seemed unmoved by the flames behind him. He raised his hands above his head, the fire intensifying in unison, and began to speak in a language entirely unknown to Andrew.

The door in the back of the room slammed shut as the ceiling began to take on flames. Within seconds, all four walls and the entire ceiling were engulfed in rolling flames. The church members were crouching in their places and praying, some of them aloud and clinging to each other in fear. The man at the front of the room continued to speak in a foreign tongue, nothing that Andrew had ever heard before. Through the smoke that was now beginning to fill the room, Andrew began to be able to make out the more distinct facial features of the man, who no longer seemed to be a man at all. His face was devilish, looking as if it was part lizard, part man.

Andrew realized that his sole option now was to get to the door and get it open. He quickly made his move, making his way through the thick smoke and chaotic environment. The door handle was hot, by no surprise, but did not deter Andrew from his mission. He had to get the door open and try to get everyone else's attention as quickly as possible before the whole place went up in flames. Oddly, the fire seemed constricted to the walls and ceilings for now, but the heat was rising and people were already coughing uncontrollably from the smoke.

Andrew, using his shirt sleeve as a glove, turned the handle of the door and pulled. The door would not budge. It was a heavy, steel door but it had never locked and there was really no reason for it to not open. Andrew pulled again, and again, to no avail. His desperation had now peaked as he began to ram his shoulder into the door to try and loosen whatever was holding it closed. The scene behind him intensified and it was obvious that time was slipping away. He soon found himself slipping to the floor, banging on the door in desperation.

Suddenly, from the room behind him, Andrew could hear music. It was familiar but out of place. He slowly turned to find that all of the fire and chaos had gone and been replaced by the quiet and calm of his one bedroom apartment. Using the door handle on his front door, he picked himself up off the floor, then dried his eyes with the sleeve of his shirt. It had all been a dream. It was one of many, in fact, that had plagued him for months. This time he had somehow managed to make it out of his bedroom and all the way to the front door.

Andrew's alarm clock, which was set to play a different playlist each morning on his mp3 player, was going off in his bedroom, just a few steps away. He walked to the small window over the sink in his kitchen and opened it enough to breath in the morning air just as the sun was coming over the horizon outside, then splashed some water on his face in the sink. This was slowly becoming a new routine for Andrew, who had never experienced nightmares like the ones he had been having recently. Despite months of therapy, both from a licensed therapist and his pastor at church, the dreams were getting worse and more real with time. It was even beginning to affect his work and social life.

The phone rang, startling Andrew as he stood in front of the sink pondering what he had experienced the night before. It was too early for phone calls. Normally, if it was work related, he would have received the call on his cell phone, but this was his home phone, so it must have been a friend or family member. After letting it ring a couple of times, Andrew picked up his cordless phone from the counter across from him and answered.

"What?" he asked. He knew that he had been asleep because of his dream, yet he felt as if he hadn't slept at all. He stood up straight in an attempt to wake up. "Are you serious?" He paused for a moment. "But why in the world didn't…?" Andrew began shuffling through drawers to find a paper and pen. "Uh huh…" He reached over to flip on the light switch in the kitchen and began to scribble on the back of a receipt with a pencil. "And what channel did you say that was on?"

II

The sun seemed enormous during that one flaring moment when it readied to make its half-way journey over the rolling hills and fields of southwest Texas. The same energy that moments ago had manifested itself in glowing orange behind the silhouettes of trees was now casting thick beams of light onto a dew-filled landscape. The fall had brought with it an array of beautiful colors and leaves falling from the trees. It was mid-autumn and the grassy areas were now a golden wheat color.

Andrew drove along the bending and curving highway in his small SUV with haste, as he juggled his cell phone and a hot cup of hot chocolate. Chocolate and caffeine were his greatest allies since the migraines began to plague him just after the death of his father at age 15. So far everyone that he had spoken with from his cell phone knew nothing more of the incident other than what had been reported on the news a few minutes earlier.

Andrew might not have known anything to this point himself had his mother not seen the report on the television earlier that morning. Apparently a news team from channel seven had been in town that morning to do a follow-up story on a previously alleged scandal involving the town's mayor when they heard about what happened on a police scanner and rushed immediately to the scene. Word was that they had arrived even before any paramedics were on the scene. According to what Andrew had gathered so far, it appeared as if the bus had somehow caught fire, but only in the front.

As he made his way out of the city limits, Andrew's mother called him on his cell phone. "I'm not there yet mom," he said immediately after placing the phone to his ear.

"Are you sure that's his route?" his mother asked.

"That's been Jim's route for the entire five years that I've been here, but I'm sure he's okay mom. I don't think there was enough damage done to the bus to hurt him." He knew that this was a lie as soon as he told it. In fact, if somebody did get hurt, it would have certainly been the driver. Still, he had to remain optimistic.

James Davis, or Jim as he was called, had been a deacon for David Engel at the First Baptist Church of Adjacent Cove, where Mr. Engel had been the pastor for seven years, until his untimely death. David Engel was Andrew's father and had died of bone cancer at a young age. Jim had been Brother Engel's best friend for many years. Jim had spent more time at the hospital than anyone other than Andrew and his mother, Barbara. He was there through every surgery and every treatment. Ever since Brother Engel's death, Jim did everything within his power to take good care of Andrew and his mother. This was a promise that he had made to Brother Engel on his death bed, and it was one that he would stop at nothing to keep. Being a teenager without a father was obviously difficult for Andrew, but Jim did the best that he could to step in as the positive male role model in his life. According to Andrew, it was this very gesture that kept him going.

Being a teacher in Adjacent Cove for over thirty years, Jim had been instrumental in getting Andrew his position at the junior high. They ate lunch together every school day for three years during Jim's off period and talked about everything from their faith to Andrew's father. Even after Jim retired from teaching, he and Andrew still met at least twice a week for lunch. This time was especially good for Andrew. Not only did he enjoy hearing the stories about his father over and over again, but he also needed the spiritual mentorship that Jim provided. Although he was nearing his thirty-first birthday, Andrew felt as if he was still a fairly immature Christian.

Jim's wife, Cindy, was initially not crazy about the idea of him keeping his bus route because she had been looking forward to him being at home all the time. She finally warmed up to the idea after she saw how happy it made Jim to continue working with kids in some capacity. The children loved him almost as much as he loved them. Jim's tall stature and tough appearance was no match for his reputation of being a big teddy bear.

"Well I still can't get Cindy on her cell," Barbara continued. "I just hope he's alright. Do you think you should go to the hospital instead?"

"I don't really know," he replied. "For some reason I feel like I need to go out to the bus first. Jim's phone isn't even turned on, I don't think. I have a feeling he's okay, though. I'll call you as soon as I find something out, I promise. In the meantime, keep trying Cindy."

Andrew pushed down the gas pedal a little more in order to pick up the pace. The idea of Jim being somehow badly injured lingered heavily on his mind. Still, he tried to remain positive. He wondered to himself if perhaps he should have gone to the hospital first, as his mother had mentioned, but something was telling him that he needed to go and see the bus first, before it was towed away and possibly repaired. The sun had been up for several minutes now and cars began to fill the country roads as people started making their way to school and work.

Despite being a small town of roughly 23,000, Adjacent Cove was not immune to traffic delay in the morning and evening times. Being located just 32 miles northwest of Austin and right on a major highway had caused traffic issues to rise every year for multiple decades. As more quality jobs became available in the Austin and San Antonio areas, commuters from other small towns surrounding Adjacent Cove had to go directly through downtown in order to gain access to the highway. City officials had introduced several cost-efficient methods over the years that could theoretically solve the problem, but nothing seemed to be working. Traffic was now beginning to affect bus routes and cause roads next to schools to be dangerously busy before and after school, and residents were calling for a bypass to be built around the city as a permanent solution.

Three Fork Road, the discreet dirt road to the right surrounded by old oak and maple trees could not have come into view sooner for Andrew, who was growing more concerned by the moment. Ignoring his blinker, he quickly turned onto the road and hit a large tire crater causing him to spill hot chocolate onto his lap. At the time, however, this was the least of his concerns. He ignored the mess and continued down the old road in negative anticipation of what he might encounter. His mother had told him that all she had been able to see was a bus turned up on its side and burnt at the front.

Within a couple of minutes, Andrew could see the flashing red and blue light atop a fire engine over the hill in front of him. Upon nearing the scene, he also noticed two city police squad cars from Adjacent Cove and at least three county sheriff's office vehicles. A Trenton County Sheriff's deputy, who wore an orange vest and could be seen from several yards back, was insuring the safe passage of vehicles traveling in each direction along the road. Only a few small houses existed out this way, but the accident had drawn lots of attention so far, causing the road to have much more traffic than it could obviously accommodate. The surrounding fields provided the only parking spaces for the ten or twelve vehicles that were there for various reasons.

Andrew's heart sank as he was first able to make out the back door of the long yellow school bus, which was tilted nearly to its side in a small ditch running along the left side of the road. From the back, it was impossible to make out the extent of the damage to the bus, but the fact that it was almost lying on its side meant something bad had happened. The more severe damage became easier to see as he slowly approached and then passed.

At this point Jim was nowhere to be found and Andrew wondered if he shouldn't just keep driving and go on to the hospital. At the same time, he wanted to take a closer look at the front of the bus and ask anyone if they knew where Jim was. Trying to survey the damage from his truck proved to be too difficult with people in the way; so, he pulled off the road on the same side of the wrecked bus and stepped out from the car. Upon turning around, he was somewhat startled by the condition of the front of the bus leading up to the front windows.

Andrew walked closer to the bus to get a better look. The front end was charred so that not even a hint of the original yellow paint remained. The grill had melted away, save for a small deformed section in the lower right corner of where it was once assembled. The engine covering was wrinkled as if it were a rug that had been pushed into a corner, exposing about half of the cracked and blackened engine. The two large windows in front of the driver and the entranceway had begun to melt and were warped and cracked in places. The window closest to the door had popped almost completely out of its frame. On the dirt road were marks indicating where the front tires of the bus had blown just a few feet back before it started towards the ditch.

Andrew stood there with his hands in his pockets, perplexed at what could have generated so much heat so quickly and without drawing Jim's early attention. An explosion was not consistent with the type of damage that had been done in this case. In fact, if something had exploded, more of the bus would have been exposed to fire other than just the front. Something had erupted toward the bus from a very close range, rather than exploding out of it. Andrew was not a detective, but he knew that there was something odd about what had happened there earlier that morning.

"I'm afraid you're going to have to step back sir," a police officer said as he placed his arm in front of Andrew and began to push him back. Andrew ignored him, staring at the damage to the bus. The officer was strong, but at six feet five inches and 245 pounds, Andrew was no pushover.

"Drew?" Andrew heard a familiar voice coming from the back of the bus. His real name was Andrew, but everyone called him Drew for short. The officer lowered his arm and stepped away. "A bit raggedy today are we?" she continued as she approached.

Instead of the usual dress pants and shirt and tie that co-workers were accustomed to seeing, Drew was wearing jeans and a long sleeve rugby shirt. His straight brown hair that hung just past his ears was brushed, but in a way that made him look more like a skateboarder than a school counselor. He had already left a message for the principal that morning saying that he would either be late or absent, depending on whether or not Jim was okay. Drew had never missed or been tardy for a single day of work at that school; so, he wasn't worried about it being a problem.

"Michelle," He finally answered, looking up at the short, but slender, Hispanic woman approaching him. Michelle Ortiz was the school district's public relations director and appeared to be the only school administrator there. "Sorry, it's, this is just crazy, right?"

"I know," she responded.

"It's not that it's overly dramatic; well, it really is, but it's just on this one part of the bus. It's just strange, you know? Any ideas?"

"I don't know, who knows what could've done it. I guess it just caught on fire somehow. We're just going to have to leave it to the experts. Luckily, there weren't any kids on it though. Could've been much worse ya' know?"

"And what about Jim" A lump filled Drew's throat as he asked the question that he had been dreading.

"They were putting him in the ambulance when I got here," she answered. "From what I was told he doesn't look like he was burned significantly or anything but they couldn't really get anything out of him."

Drew was immediately relieved by the news that Jim seemed okay. "What do you mean they couldn't get anything out of him?"

"Well he wouldn't talk. He was like, in shock or something. They said that he had passed out in his seat and that's where they found him. His seat belt was the sole thing that kept him from falling out when the bus went into the ditch and tilted over."

"Passed out? I wonder why?" Drew asked as his concern changed to curiosity.

"They don't know," Michelle said. "They got him to come to, but he just wouldn't talk. I saw his hand shaking when they were loading him up. I swore I heard him mumbling too, but I may have just been hearing things."

Drew turned his attention back to the bus, his curiosity growing with every new development. He started slowly towards the charred front end with Michelle walking behind, then bent down to take a closer look underneath the side of the bus, which was lifted from the ground from being tilted almost completely over. The rubber from both front tires was completely gone leaving shredded pieces along the deep tracks left in the dirt road that were left by the naked rims. Evidently, Jim had continued to drive on them after the fire had already started, melting away the rubber.

"Was the fire still going when the police first got here?" Drew asked Michelle while still staring at the damage.

"Um, I don't think so because I heard one of the firemen telling a reporter or somebody that there was nothing to put out when they got here. I know that the sheriff's deputy got here first." She leaned over to try to see what Drew was looking at.

"Did he use the fire extinguisher to put it out himself or did someone else put it out?"

"I honestly don't know who put it out, but it wasn't him because the fire extinguisher is still full. He must've grabbed it because it fell out onto the ground when they opened the door, but it still had the pin in it."

Drew stood and walked around to the other side of the bus, which was just a couple of feet from the ground. The door had been opened somehow but was not damaged. It was possible that it could have not been locked into place, making it easy for someone to swing open from the outside. The seat belt was cleanly cut leaving two straps hanging from the seat. The small fire extinguisher that would have been under the dashboard and within Jim's reach was left standing on the ground next to the bus. Just as Michelle had said, the pin was still in the handle. The plastic inspection tag was also still in place, proving further that Jim, in fact, did not use the extinguisher. This meant that either he passed out before he could use it or the fire was put out some other way before he needed to.

"Why do you ask?" asked Michelle.

"Oh, it's nothing," Drew responded after a brief moment. "I was just curious. I'm no detective."

"Well, luckily you don't have to be one Drew," Michelle said. "That's what those guys are for."

"I guess they'll take it back to the bus garage to get a better look at everything huh?"

"My understanding is that they're going to take it to that old warehouse next to the police station. I believe the tow truck is on its way now, but they want to get plenty of pictures and comb over the scene several times and all that before taking it away. I think the police department and the sheriff's office are both going to be working on it once it's at the warehouse."

Both agencies were initially involved because the incident involved an independent school district vehicle and happened outside the city limits. Ultimately, the sheriff would handle any kind of foul play that might have occurred with the Adjacent Cove Police Department assisting, if necessary. If it was just an accident, then obviously it would be the responsibility of the school district to take care of everything. Without having received any kind of statement from Jim, authorities could rely exclusively on findings from initial and further investigation of the bus and accident site. The fact that Jim was in shock could mean any number of things at this point, and nobody was willing to speculate in the slightest bit as to what exactly had occurred there that morning.

"Wel,l I know they have it under control," Drew said as he reached out to shake Michelle's hand. "I'm just really worried about Jim right now."

"He's at the hospital by now," Michelle answered as she grabbed Drew's hand. "And don't worry Drew, I'm sure he's okay, just a little shook up," she added reassuringly. Drew smiled in gratitude and turned to make his way back to his truck. Michelle turned her attention back to the media, who stood by to hear any more news as it developed. The television news crew had already headed back towards town to cover its original story.

Almost the entire administrative staff knew about the friendship that was shared between Jim and Drew. Jim's lengthy service and devotion to the school district had made him quite popular, especially to those who had been there for several years themselves. Jim was the type of teacher who could be called on by the school's administration and board for just about anything. Drew was already known among a number of the staff before he started working for the school district because he had attended its schools for many years up until he graduated. Most people were also aware of his father's death during his time as a student and how Jim had stepped up to help.

Upon reentering his vehicle, Drew noticed that he had left his cell phone in the passenger seat. His mother had called four times while he was away. He put his key in the ignition, shut the door, and rolled up his window before opening his flip phone to call her back.

"Oh, boy." he thought to himself as he pressed the speed dial and placed the phone to his ear.

"What did you find out?" his mother asked immediately upon answering.

"He's gonna' be fine mom, it's okay," Drew answered calmly. "They took him to the hospital to check him out. There's probably no more than a couple scrapes and bruises, if that."

"So what happened?" she inquired.

"There was a small fire and I guess it caused the bus to go off the road. It's not a big deal, don't worry." Obviously, Drew felt that there was much more to it than that at that point, but he did not want to worry his mother or anyone else for that matter. "Have you gotten a hold of Cindy yet?" he asked.

"No, not yet. Are you going to the hospital now?"

"Yes mom, I'll call you after I find something out okay?"

Barbara was unable to drive because of knee surgery the previous week. She had injured her knee in a car accident many years back and had elected not to have surgery against her doctor's advice. Over the years, the condition of the knee deteriorated so that finally she had to have complete knee replacement. She had just gotten home from the hospital a few days ago with strict orders to stay off of the knee and to stay at home until the doctor told her otherwise.

As he circled back, Drew had briefly glanced down the seemingly endless dirt road when he noticed a man standing in the middle of the road about a hundred yards away. The road was clear at the time and the weather conditions were sunny and clear, making it impossible to miss the man. However, the distance between them ruled out the possibility of making any kind of accurate description. All Drew could tell was that the man was wearing dark clothes with a long, black overcoat and that he had straight, snow white hair that hung down a few inches past his shoulders. The mysterious man stood motionless on the road with his arms crossed, looking in the bus's direction. Drew's concern for Jim was the one thing enough to drown out his surprisingly strong instincts, which produced a rather strong and immediate uneasy feeling about the man.

"What's this guy's deal?" Drew asked himself. Upon turning completely around, Drew took one more look with his rear view mirror but the man had gone.

Drew had noticed many things at the scene that lent to the idea that this was not an everyday accident by any stretch of the imagination. Perhaps that is why Jim had passed out and was now in some sort of shock according to what Drew was told. Perhaps that is why Michelle had seen Jim's hand shaking while they put him in the ambulance. Drew began to feel that it was possible and even likely that whatever happened had frightened Jim so badly that it caused these very reactions, reactions that were unlike the man in any other setting.

Drew wondered if anyone else, especially the authorities on the scene, had felt the same thing that he did. He wondered if they would give it the same amount of attention that he would. He wondered if they would insure, if necessary, that justice was fairly served. If somebody or something had done this, any friend or family member would have wanted to see justice done and for Drew it was no different. That was the part that was easy to explain. What he couldn't explain was the passion he was feeling beyond the most typical of emotions, the sudden and uncontrollable drive to know exactly what happened and why. There was a bigger picture to all of this, just not one Drew could fully understand at the moment.

"This is silly," he thought to himself, laughing quietly. "Since when did I become a cop?"

III

The weather forecast coming in from Adjacent Cove's own KACE 1370 AM was predicting a major cold front to be coming in from the north in the latter part of the week. Apparently, it would be bringing with it highs in the upper forties and lows well past the freezing point. This was a rare weather occurrence for the first week of November in this part of the country, but certainly not one that had never been seen before. Still, it was only Monday, and this was just the latest prediction. Weather patterns in Texas were known to change as they approached and passed, sometimes more than once.

Trenton County Hospital had two locations, one in the neighboring town of Grant, about twenty miles away and one in Adjacent Cove, the county seat. It was an old hospital but the construction of a new facility just down the street was set to begin early the next year. Plans were also in place to build a third location in Oak Hill on the other side of the county. The area had grown so much in recent years, and the two hospitals in existence were finding it more and more difficult to take on the growing number of patients needing treatment in any capacity.

Drew sighed as he parked his truck in the emergency room parking lot and turned off the engine. The bus incident was being mentioned one more time on the news and weather update.

"It appears that everything is going to be wrapped up here, Don," said the reporter. "Uh…they have managed to tilt to the bus back onto its tires and it looks like they're just trying to figure out how to get the tow truck in front of it without tipping over in the ditch itself."

"So, still no word on what caused this fire?" the DJ asked.

"Nothing yet, Don. I've approached both city and school officials and neither of them have been able to provide any information other than what we already know. I do know, however, that the bus will be taken to a secure facility in Adjacent Cove so that a further investigation can be done. I think that right now the biggest question on all our minds is whether or not this was indeed foul play as it seems to appear to some, but we won't know anything further until we either receive a full report on the damage or hear from Jim Davis, who was driving the bus when this happened. Back to you, Don."

"Okay, thank you Tom. There you have it, a bus fire happening in the wee hours of the morning. Still no word on what caused the fire, but luckily, no children were on board when it happened and it appears at this point that the driver is okay as well. We'll keep you updated, of course, along with your weather and traffic reports here on KACE 1370."

Drew pulled his keys from the ignition and opened his door. Just before stepping out, he stopped for a moment, and then sat back in his seat with one leg still hanging out of the door. He stared into the dashboard, pondering, without so much as a blink. His father had taught him to pray when he was faced with a situation that made him uncomfortable or uneasy in any way. Before his father's death, Drew had learned to pray automatically in these types of situations. He prayed before tests, during any kind of conflict with another person, even before football games. The last time that he had prayed that way without even thinking about whether or not he should was the night before his father died.

The wind outside suddenly began to gust, startling Drew. All around him, the trees were perfectly still and there were no trash or leaves blowing around, but the gusts in the immediate area of his truck were rocking the vehicle back and forth. The door was pressing towards his leg with great force, trying to close. Drew pushed the door open and stepped outside with his arm in front of his face to block the wind. His door slammed shut behind him. After taking just two steps, the wind stopped just as suddenly as it had started. He slowly lowered his arm and straightened his body, wondering what in the world had happened. The wind was gone now, even from around his truck. It had simply vanished. Even on somewhat windy days small whirlwinds nicknamed "Dirt Devils" were known to pop up from time to time and kick up a bit of dirt. What he had just experienced had been much more powerful and there was no other wind outside.

After surveying the area for a moment and finding nothing, Drew fixed his hair and started walking towards the hospital. He turned and looked over his shoulder from time to time to see if anything else happened, but nothing ever did. As he approached the emergency room entrance to the hospital, he turned a look one last time, still perplexed and a bit shaken by what had just happened.

Upon entering the hospital, Drew immediately noticed a man sitting in the waiting room. It was the same peculiar man that he had seen just a few minutes earlier on the dirt road as he turned his truck around. Although he had seen him from a distance before, he knew that this was the same person.

"How in the world did he do that?" Drew asked himself. He had driven straight to the hospital and had not noticed the man walking in before him. He would have had to go pretty fast and possibly even take a faster route in order to beat Drew there.

This time Drew could make out the man's features, as he was merely a few feet away. He wore the same dark clothing with black pants and a long black overcoat. His long, white hair was straight and hung well below his shoulders, just as he had thought. His face was abnormally pale and his skin, aged and leathery. His face was thin, revealing high cheek bones and a pointy chin. A small glimmer from around the pupils of his eyes was all that could be seen through the dark lenses of his sunglasses. The man sat motionless in the chair with one leg crossed over the other and his hands joined in his lap. It did not seem to bother him that Drew was now staring at him from across the room.

"Can I help you, sir?" the nurse behind the front desk asked.

Drew acted as if he had not even heard the woman. He continued to look at the man and wonder who he was and how he had gotten there so fast.

"Sir?" the nurse asked one more time, this time startling Drew a bit.

"Oh yes, sorry," he responded as he turned around. "I'm here to see my friend," he continued, occasionally looking back at the man. "Dim Javis."

"I'm sorry, who?" the nurse asked.

"I meant Jim Davis, sorry again". The man had made Drew nervous. He wasn't sure if it was the fact that he was both at the scene and now here or the fact that he got here so fast or his appearance in general that made him feel uncomfortable. "H-he was brought here earlier."

The nurse sat at the desk and began typing on her computer. She then pressed a button on the wall next to her, opening the large double doors next to the desk. "Room seven, all the way down this hall and to your right," she said.

"Thank you," he responded as he proceeded through the doors and took one more glance towards the waiting room. He continued down the hall as instructed until he came upon room seven.

Jim lay in the hospital bed with his eyes closed as if he were sleeping. His wife Cindy was on the other side of the bed talking on the hospital phone. After Cindy waved him in, Drew entered quietly so as not to disturb his friend and mentor.

"Your son just walked in," Cindy said to Barbara, who was on the other line.

For a moment, Drew just stood at the foot of the bed with his hands in his pockets. Everything appeared to be okay. A tube ran under Jim's nose which provided oxygen so that he could breathe easier, but other than that he wasn't connected to any machines or anything.

"Drew," Cindy said. "Your mother wants you to check your cell phone. She says she's been trying to get a hold of you but it keeps going to voicemail."

Drew pulled his cell phone from his pocket to find that it was not even turned on. He opened it and pressed a couple of buttons, including the power button, but received no response.

"It's dead," Drew answered. "I don't know why though, I charged it on the way here 'cause I wasn't sure how long I'd be here."

"Huh, that's weird," Cindy said. "Well, at least you brought yours. I left the house in such a hurry I forgot mine." Cindy relayed the information to Drew's mother then picked up where she had left off in the conversation. She stopped and looked back at Drew as she suddenly remembered something.

"Ya' know, now that I think about it, Jim's phone is dead too," she said. "Must be somethin' in the hospital drainin' the batteries."

"Must be," responded Drew. Without thinking too much more about it, he placed his cell phone back in his pocket and turned his attention back to Jim. As Cindy continued talking to Barbara, Drew grabbed a chair from the back of the room and placed it next to the bed. He sat down and placed his hand on the bed next to Jim's. He began listening to what Cindy was telling his mother on the phone.

"He was in some sort of shock when they picked him up but the officer told me that he was awake," Cindy explained. "By the time they got him here, he was unconscious again." She paused for a moment while Barbara spoke and then continued. "I don't know, they said that he is fine. No heart attack, no stroke, nothing like that. He's just unconscious. The doctor's running some tests just to make sure, but he seems to be okay. Still, something has to have caused him to pass out, right? He wouldn't even talk to anybody about it when he was awake."

Drew stared at Jim. As far as he could tell, it just seemed like he was asleep. If he had been in shock, then something must have frightened him. Until Jim woke up and told everyone what had happened, all anyone could do was speculate. Cindy had just mentioned that they were running more tests, which made Drew a bit nervous, but he remained confident. He felt that was the best that he could do right now. He placed his hand on the bed next to Jim and closed his eyes and began to pray silently.

"Drew?"

Drew lifted his head to see Jim looking at him with his eyes half open. The room was suddenly completely quiet. Cindy stood from her chair, forgetting that she still had the phone in her hand.

"Let me call you back Barb," Cindy said before hanging the phone up on the wall.

"Jim?" said Drew, as he leaned towards him.

"Sweetie?" Cindy asked as she leaned over and placed her hand on Jim's forehead. His eyes were once again closed and his head laid back. She looked at Drew. "Did he just say your name?"

"Yea, I think so," Drew answered.

"Jim?" she asked, trying to get Jim's attention once more. Still, there was no response. "He hasn't said a word since he got here," she said to Drew. "Jim, honey?" Cindy lifted Jim's hand and began to lightly tap it.

"Should we get the doctor?" asked Drew.

Cindy pressed a blue button on the wall behind the hospital bed to page the nurse. Within seconds, the nurse came over the intercom in the room.

"May I help you?" the nurse asked.

"I think he said something," Cindy stated.

"I'll send in the doctor," replied the nurse.

Jim raised his head just slightly once again and began to open his eyes. Cindy placed a pillow under his head and continued trying to get his attention. He pulled on his wife's hands as if he wanted her to come closer. Just then, a young doctor came through the door.

"Well, is he comin' to?" the doctor asked in a positive tone.

"I think so," Cindy answered.

The doctor proceeded to listen to Jim's heart and take his blood pressure while asking him a series of questions. While Jim was obviously awake and moving on his own, his answers did not come automatically. Cindy seemed concerned but the doctor reassured her and said that there was nothing to worry about.

"I...need to speak to...Drew," Jim uttered, pointing to where Drew was standing.

"Okay, you can speak to whoever you want big guy," responded the doctor. "But, the police are going to want to hear from you as soon as they get back, alright?"

"After...I talk to Andrew," Jim said.

Drew and Cindy both found this peculiar but did not argue. Whatever the reason was, they were both confident that it was good enough. The doctor's primary concern was that perhaps he had hit his head or something and was not exactly clear on what was going on or what he really needed to do. Still, he had no problem allowing Drew to sit and talk with Jim while they were waiting for the police to arrive. There certainly could not be any harm done. Jim pulled on Cindy's hands once again, as if he wanted her to come closer to him. She leaned over for Jim to whisper something into her ears.

"Oh," she said. "Okay, honey." Cindy kissed her husband on the cheek and stood back up. "He wants to be alone with Drew for a few minutes." Jim had also asked her to promise not to let the police in until he and Drew were finished, but she did not want to say anything unless it was necessary.

"Okay," the doctor said as he finished writing notes into Jim's chart. "I guess we can do that."

The doctor held the door open for Cindy as they walked out into the hall, leaving the door open behind them.

"Shut the door, Drew," Jim said, pointing at the open door.

Drew was not sure what to expect. He nervously closed the door and then sat back down in the chair next to Jim's bed. Even in his condition, Jim never seemed so serious before as far as Drew could remember. He had a look on his face that made Drew think maybe what he was going to tell him was something bad. If this were the case, however, then he could not understand why he had even asked Cindy to leave the room. Jim held out his hand for Drew to take.

"Is…" Drew had a lump in his throat as he grabbed Jim's hand. "Is everything okay, Jim?" Jim sat up as much as he could in the bed, which the doctor had inclined a bit while examining him.

"There's something I need to tell you son," Jim said. Jim had always called Drew son, even before the death of Drew's father. "Something…your Daddy wanted me to tell you when the time was right."

"Um…okay." This was the best response Drew could come up with at this point. It was still too early in the conversation for him to know how to react. Judging by Jim's expression and the way he was acting, however, whatever he had to say was a big deal.

"You're not…" Jim coughed, and then continued. "You're not exactly…" He stopped as if he was not quite sure how to word what he was trying to say.

"It's okay Jim," Drew reassured him. "Whatever it is, I can handle it."

Jim sat there, staring at the door in front of him. "I knew this day would come, and I've prepared for it for many years. But…" He stopped once again, still staring forward. Finally, he tightened his grip on Drew's hand and turned to face him. "You're not exactly who you think you are Drew."

IV

Thirty five miles east of Adjacent Cove was a small community of about eleven and a half thousand residents. Campbell was located just inside the eastern boundaries of Trenton County and had just recently found its name on most state maps. Five years ago, the state of Texas had decided to build its new state of the art penitentiary just outside its city limits. Construction had begun four years ago, and prisoners were transferred in almost immediately after its opening two years later. At first, the residents of Campbell had welcomed the idea because of the attention that it would bring the town; however, recent security issues were now causing them to question their original thoughts.

Many state officials believed that the construction of Ware State Penitentiary had been rushed and that the proper authorities had allowed it to open its doors and cells much too quickly when construction was completed. The influx of crime and prisoners in recent years had unfortunately made the construction of the new prison system, as well as one other in north Texas, one of urgency, and state leaders felt that the speed of the operation had been as controlled as possible. Supporters argued that either way, what was done was done, and that all they could do at that point was to make the necessary corrections and move forward. This view, although true, was found to be insensitive to many.

The family of a local victim to a robbery and homicide, carried out by an escaped convict from Ware, was currently suing the state alleging that proper and thorough inspections had not been carried out before the prison opened. This was one of three incidents involving the escape of one or more inmates in just two years. All of the escaped prisoners were captured immediately except the before mentioned, who was killed in a shootout with the police ten days after his escape and three days after he killed a man for the contents of his wallet. In recent days, it was announced that the state would designate a minimum of ten million dollars to the upgrade of security at the facility, in addition to the three million that had already been spent in the previous year.

Despite its problems, Ware successfully housed over a thousand inmates, ninety seven of whom were on Death Row. Since Ware did not have a death chamber, inmates sentenced to death were sent to Ware and would remain there until a few days before the scheduled date of their execution. The entire facility covered over four hundred acres and contained a number of buildings serving different purposes. In addition, more than four hundred guards, cooks, grounds crew, and others, many from surrounding communities including Campbell, were employed at the prison. Security, which had been drastically stepped up since the prison's opening, was tight to say the least, and according to the warden, was now virtually impassable.

Of all of the system's many extensions, one in particular had already gained the darkest of reputations among both inmates and those on the outside that had either experienced it first hand or had heard about it from prior victims. The solitary confinement section had gone from being officially called the "Hole" by employees to being rightfully nicknamed the "Devil's Hole" by prisoners in just over two years. Criminals who violated the prison's strictest of policies would be sentenced to time in solitary confinement for anywhere from four days to several weeks depending on their offense. The prisoner holding the current record for time spent in a solitary confinement cell at Ware was a death row inmate who served four months for assaulting and seriously injuring a guard with a shank made out of a toothbrush. Rumor was that the experience had caused the inmate to go insane, although this was never confirmed.

The Devil's Hole was a new concept that borrowed certain aspects from prisons of old. The governor of Texas had re-created the guidelines regarding the construction of a solitary confinement facility during the planning stages of the Ware State Penitentiary in an effort to cut down on prison violence. The newly approved tactics were strongly opposed prior to their approval by those sympathetic to the civil rights of inmates. Still, other states were beginning to follow suit due to recent increases in crime and the overpopulation of prisons. So far, only one solitary confinement facility like the one at Ware existed in the state of Texas, but plans were already rolling to install similar ones in many of the other prisons.

At Ware, solitary confinement was housed one hundred and fifty feet below the ground. In order to access the fifty cells in the Devil's Hole, one had to use stairs that began in the basement of the main facility. The wide, circular staircase was cold and dark, with the only light coming from a few dim lamps a few feet apart along the cement walls. Guards were required to carry flashlights as they escorted prisoners up and down the stairs for safety. Upon reaching the bottom, a line of two inch thick steel doors lined either side of the long, thirty foot wide hallway. Each door was inset about a foot into the wall and was equipped with a lens for one way viewing into the room and a rectangular hole about a foot wide and four inches tall with a medal flap that opened and closed in the middle for serving meals and for handcuff placement or removal.

The room itself was six feet wide, six feet deep, and eight feet tall. The walls were made of an impenetrable mixture of concrete and steel and were three feet thick on all sides and painted jet black. The only light that ever entered the cell came through the rectangular opening in the door, which could only be opened from the outside. The toilet was a hole six inches wide in the back right hand corner of the room that led to an underground sewer system that was flushed hourly by large pipes of fresh water coming from the prison's water supply. One roll of toilet paper was given to each prisoner when they arrived and then every four days that they remained. A three inch round plastic pipe extended from the ceiling at each corner of the back wall, providing oxygen and fresh air to the cell. Prisoners entered with nothing but the prison issued jumpers they wore.

The Devil's Hole was guarded by six men positioned at various spots along the hall, two outside the door at the bottom of the stairs, and two outside the door at the top of the stairs. Ventilation systems covered by large fans at each end of the hallway provided guards with plenty of fresh air. The cool temperatures of the underground, which remained constant throughout every season of the year, provided a comfortable environment for the most part. Of all the prisoners sentenced to time in solitary confinement, just three had been placed there more than once. Of those three, one was visiting for his fifth time.

The sound of chains dragging the floor filled the entire place as the door at the top of the stairs opened, and a large man in his late thirties followed by two guards began their decent into the cold and dark hole. The man stood well over six and a half feet tall as he ducked his head through the door. His hands and feet were bound by cuffs connected to a series of chains that limited his walking to short steps and kept his hands together at his lower torso. His head hung over the front of his orange jumpsuit, his face just barely hidden by his dark hair. His thin, orange shoes complimented his attire, courtesy of the Ware State Penitentiary.

Overcoming the difficult walk down the stairs, while bound tightly at the ankles by heavy chains, might have been a challenge for the man except he had done it several times before. The guards walked closely behind with one hand on their holstered weapon and the other on the man's back. The man said nothing and gave the guards no trouble as he slowly descended the concrete stairs. Upon reaching the bottom, the man stopped suddenly and slightly lifted his head, revealing a smile under the man's freshly shaven face. One guard poked him in the back with his fist and ordered him to move forward. The man looked back at the guard and grinned.

"Forward it is," the man said to the guard, who was slowly pulling his pistol from its holster. The man turned back and began to walk again. The guard, still disturbed by the deceiving smile that the man had just given him, returned his gun and took a deep breath.

The second cell on the left, named Hole three was already opened in anticipation of the man's return. The man walked towards the cell and examined the open door and the outer walls of the cell.

"Get in, Walker," one of the guards said with force. By this time, three other guards already stationed in the hole had joined the others.

The man turned around and lifted his head. "I told you to call me by my first name," he said. "Walker is just a tag, a tag that connects me to the man I'm told is my father, the man that killed my mother and sister and nearly killed me. I won't accept that man's name. Do you hear me?" His voice began to get louder and included a strange growl that grabbed everyone's attention. "Do you hear me you little…" The man's face was scrunched in anger, and his eyes seemed to glow a bright green in the barely lit environment.

The man's anger ended in the middle of his sentence, just as quickly as it had begun. The guards stood ready with their hands on their weapons and their clubs drawn. The man turned back towards the cell and hung his head once again. He slowly made his way into the dark room with the guards following closely behind. He turned and raised his arms to allow a guard to remove his chains. Under his thick bangs, he simply smiled with his eyes closed. One of the guards slowly approached, followed by another for backup. He removed a set of keys from his side and removed the cuffs and chains from his wrists and feet. The guards then quickly back-stepped out of the cell and closed the large steel door.

The room became pitch dark. It was as if he no longer existed…as if he had been buried, soon to be forgotten. Not a single sensation to accompany any of the five senses. The room was overcome by a darkness not known to the average person. Not even the greatest of eyes could adjust to its blanketing affect. The man's green eyes pierced through the room as he opened them. He began to laugh in an inhuman manner. His evil stare into the imminent shadows of the room, accompanied by a horrifying cackle that seemed to echo off the walls, and his mysterious disposition, created an environment suited solely for the most evil of inhabitants.

James Walker had grown up in the Adjacent Cove area and attended its schools until the tenth grade, when he finally dropped out of school at the age of eighteen. He lived with his foster parents, who had adopted him at age eleven, for another four years or so and then moved in with a friend in a small apartment on the eastern side of Adjacent Cove. That was the neighborhood known for drugs and violence. It was there that James got his first gun and began to learn the rules of the streets. He never used drugs and just used alcohol a few times when he was young. "Drugs are the enemy of the mind." This was James' motto concerning the matter.

James was always serious. He always knew that he was destined to something big, and although he had never achieved much and basically had to steal to live, he was never impatient in his waiting for the right opportunity. His friends used to laugh at him when he talked about these types of things, but the laughing only lasted until James broke a chair over their head, or shoved a knife through their hand. Friends came and left, but none ever crossed James more than once. He was a big guy with a tall and wide stature. He was never overweight, and made sure of it by working out on a regular basis. An old acquaintance had given James free membership to his small gym on the east side for many years, and James took well advantage of it.

James never slept much and never went to the doctor for anything. In fact, he was never really sick or injured badly enough to seek a physician's help. Even still, he feared that doctors did more damage than good. Anything that had the potential of altering his natural human state, James Walker had nothing to do with.

Over the years, James had been in and out of several jails for a number of offenses, from theft to armed robbery. He had a rap sheet longer than anyone else in the history of the area. He truly felt that this was an accomplishment. He considered himself an enemy of the system. He was against anything that was good, pure, clean, or whole. It was no wonder. His life was filled with brokenness. James had kept so much pain in his heart over the years that it eventually overtook him. Eventually, anything painful would roll off his back like water off a duck's.

When James was a teenager, he began to take an interest in a satanic cult that existed secretly in the streets of eastern Adjacent Cove. The group was called Los Ultimos Dias, or The Last Days. They considered themselves to be Theistic Satanists, meaning that they believed in the spiritual and even physical existence of Satan, or Lucifer. In order to join, each member had to take a blood oath to live for, follow, and carry out the will of Lucifer for the remainder of their lives.

Los Ultimos Dias had been formed only a few years before James moved in to the east side of town by a Spanish man named Richard Rodriguez. Richard originally started by preaching on the streets about their time being the last of days, only he did not call for the salvation of souls, but rather the rising of souls to fight all that is good. Of course, most people simply viewed him as crazy and discarded everything that he said. A few, however, listened. Before too long a group of about twenty-five people began to meet secretly in an abandoned warehouse on the east side under the guidance of Richard, who soon became known as The Beast.

Los Ultimos Dias grew to a strong seventy-two people under Richard Rodriguez's leadership until he was imprisoned for arson a few years after James had joined. Richard's obvious choice for a person to take over while he was gone was James. James had proven his allegiance to the group over and over with various acts of violence and cruelty to the religious society, and had even assisted Richard in burning down a Methodist Church on the northern side of town, for which just Richard was caught and prosecuted. In addition to being large, strong, and overly demanding, James had built up so much hate over the years that he fit into the role like a glove. If anyone in the group had been against James' promotion in the cult, they wouldn't have dared spoken it.

It all began when James was just six years old. One night while he was asleep he was suddenly awakened by his father dragging him by his hair off of his bed and onto the floor. His father drug him into the living room, where his mother was tied to the recliner and his younger sister was tied to a small wooden chair from her room. James struggled and fought but was no match for his very large father. Before he knew it, he was tied to a chair from the kitchen and couldn't move. A handkerchief was shoved into his mouth and tape was tied over the cloth and around his head, just like on his mother and sister.

James' father was furious and not acting like himself. They lived in a small mobile home on a two acre lot about seven miles from Adjacent Cove. His mother and father were always arguing. James' father was a carpenter and stayed busy, but never seemed to bring in enough money. His mother had been forced to get loans from two different banks and both were now refusing to give any more loans because of their inability to make their current payments on time. Money was a problem at the Walker home, but it wasn't the only issue worth arguing over. Mr. and Mrs. Walker would argue over almost anything. If Mr. Walker was late getting home, if Mrs. Walker did not clean everything one day, if another appliance was not working, they bickered and squabbled for hours, growing more intense at the hours passed. Sometimes it turned physical, but neither would ever talk about it to anyone again.

Unable to move or even make a sound, James Walker was quickly frozen in fear. His father stood before him holding his last container of gas in one hand and a box of matches in the other. Mr. Walker's eyes had turned solid black and his face had turned pale and had conformed to an evil and almost unrecognizable state. James trembled at the sight of his father staring so coldly back into his eyes. Mr. Walker then began to pour gasoline on the floor surrounding James. Before he could pour the gas on James as he had to his sister and mother, the can ran dry. Mr. Walker threw the can to the floor and made his way to the door.

James watched in fear and utter confusion as his father walked out the door, indifferent to the screams of his family. Almost immediately after Mr. Walker disappeared into the night, a lit match flew back through the doorway and into the gasoline soaked living room. The flames spread and grew in a matter of seconds, enveloping everything in the room. Over the crackling fire and the screams of his mother and sister, James heard what sounded like a gunshot outside. The flames seemed to dance in between James and his mother and sister as he watched them struggle and cry.

James' mother began to pray in her screams. In terrible pain and imminent death, she cried out to God for deliverance. All James could do was watch. Tears filled his eyes and rolled down his face as he altered between fighting to get free and watching his mother and sister suffer. After a few moments of this terror, the screaming finally stopped and James, who was surrounding by a wall of flames, dropped his head and passed out.

In the end, a neighbor had seen the commotion and called 911. A sheriff's deputy arrived first, only to witness Mr. Walker taking his own life with a .38 caliber pistol that he had purchased just two days before. The mobile home was already completely engulfed in flames and was beginning to collapse when the fire department arrived. James and the chair he was sitting in fell through the floor before the flames could reach him. After the flames were extinguished, he was found lying on his side and unconscious underneath the charred remains of the mobile home, still tied to the chair. He was unharmed.

Suddenly a dim light broke into the darkness of James' cell as a guard opened the feeding slot to check on the prisoner. James was still sitting on the floor in the back of the cell with his knees raised and his head lowered. He hadn't moved or spoken since he arrived.

After a few minutes, the slot on James' door opened, letting the light in.

"You have a visitor...," the guard said. "...already. It's Father Newbright from the Catholic church.

"Oh, great," James said under his breath.

Father Newbright had come to see James many times in prison, from the time he was a teenager to now. James was sort of an ongoing project for the priest and had been for many years. James did not dislike him, but he was not altogether fond of the visits either. Still, Father Newbright had done many favors for him, including the influencing of judges to give him lighter sentences.

"James?" Father Newbright asked, peeking into the slot on the door. "You there?"

"Hello Father," James responded. "What good news do you bring this time?"

"Good news?" the Father responded. "Well I suppose I'm bringing you the same good news I always do."

"Oh boy," replied James, sarcastically. "So I can still have that eternal life then huh?"

"Yes, James, you can," said Father Newbright.

Father Newbright had been the priest of St. John's Catholic Church for as long as anyone could remember. St. John's was the community's only Catholic church, but it wasn't always that way. Another, smaller and older church had also existed in the town until the mid eighties, when the long time priest of the parish passed away and people simply stopped going. All of the church's parishioners joined St. John's church after that. Father Newbright is more comfortable calling it a "merger" between the churches.

In addition to being the priest, Father Newbright had always been very involved in the community. It was said that on his first day at the church, he went to the local children's club and simply asked what he could do. The hours that he put in to volunteer work made some wonder how he was still able to be a priest. His response was that God "lengthened" his days for him to give him enough time for everything.

"So how ya' doin' buddy?" Father Newbright asked.

"So I'm your buddy now?" asked James. "When did that happen?"

"Okay, then how are you James?" the Father asked.

"How do you think I am?" James replied. "They got me locked up in this God forsaken dump of a rat hole and you wanna' know how I am?"

"Now look," Father Newbright said sternly. "I waited four hours to talk to you because when I got here I was informed that you were being transferred to the hole. Four hours James. So if you are just going to be like that then let me know and I will leave because I'm not waiting another second for you to come to your senses."

The room was quiet for a moment before either man spoke.

"Have you thought any more about our last conversation?" Father Newbright asked.

"You mean, our last conversation, and the one before that, and the one before that, and the one before that?" James asked.

"Yea, I guess you could say that."

"Yes I have," said James. "I think about it all the time. In fact, not a day goes by when I don't think about it."

"And?" the Father asked.

"And what? What else can I say that I haven't already said before?"

"Well let's see," said Father Newbright. "You could say that you want to know more, or that you are starting to believe everything I've told you, or…"

"It's not a matter of belief," James interrupted. "I do believe everything you've told me Father Newbright. I just don't accept it. There's a difference. You've presented me with your side and I simply prefer to stay on the side that I'm on."

"But why?" asked the Father. "Why would you give up silver and gold to get rocks and dirt? Why would you give up diamonds for coal? Why would you choose an eternity in hell over an eternity in Heaven? This doesn't make sense to me."

"It doesn't have to make sense to you Father. It's just the way that it is."

"Why did you get sent to the hole?" the priest asked.

"Ah, it was nothing," James responded. "Just another fight over bread."

"Sir," said one of the guards at the bottom of the concrete steps. "You have a phone call. You can get it upstairs."

"A phone call?" the priest asked. "That's peculiar. Why would anyone call me here? I'll be right back James."

The slot closed and several moments passed before it opened again. The priest was still gone, but the guards were routinely checking on the prisoners as they did every hour.

"You still breathin' in there big man?" The guard asked.

James raised his head and smiled. His green eyes and devious grin raised the already heightened alertness of the guard, who stared back at the prisoner. He began to close the slot, until suddenly, he was pushed against the door with enough force to take his breath away. The other guards ran to his assistance but were blown back with one forceful wind that threw them against the walls like rag dolls. James looked up as the guard was thrown away from his door and the door blew open with an incredible force. A black figure entered the cell and stood over James, who was looking up at him.

"It's about time," James said as he stood to his feet.

V

"I'm, I mean..." Drew wasn't sure how to respond. What he had heard Jim say could mean one of several different things.

"Listen Andrew," Jim said as his grip on Drew's hand tightened. "You understand that there's a war going on, a war that we can't see or experience in any way because we are men. We've talked about this many times."

"Yes sir," Drew responded, unsure of where Jim was going. "I know all about spiritual warfare, Jim. You picked up where my Dad left off, remember?"

"Yes, Drew, spiritual warfare." Jim leaned back on the hospital bed. "All we can do is pray and do our parts in this world. That is our part in all of it. For us, it is not a physical fight. In the grand scheme of things, we are limited by our mortality..." Jim suddenly went silent. He wasn't telling Drew anything he hadn't before, but this time was different. This time Drew could see a sparkle in his eyes that had never been there before.

"Are you okay Jim?" Drew was beginning to wonder if Jim had been more badly injured than they had previously thought. Maybe he had bumped his head or something.

"You," Jim continued. "You are different than the rest of us, Drew."

"Different?" Drew asked.

"You have a bigger part than the rest of us Andrew. You can see things, do things, things that the rest of us have never dreamed of. You, Andrew...," Jim grasped Drew's hand once again and lifted himself up once again, staring directly into Drew's eyes. "You are not limited by mortality."

"I don't...," Drew could see that Jim was nothing but serious. It was all he could do to keep from taking Jim too seriously. He was certainly just badly injured, but something was telling Drew that he was telling the truth. It was the same instinct that had been driving him through this entire ordeal. "But..." he said quietly with a half smirk on his face.

"Andrew," Jim interrupted. "Your father wanted so badly to tell you this himself. You don't know how it pains me that he is not here." He lowered his head and began to cry. "I prepared you the best that I could my boy. I did my best."

"It's okay," Drew responded, placing his other hand on Jim's shoulder. "I know Jim. It's okay that it's you, really. You've been like a father to me, Jim, and I know my Dad smiles on you from Heaven." Drew was beginning to understand that Jim was telling him the truth.

Jim raised his head and looked at Drew once again with tears in his eyes. His lower lip quivered as he began to speak once again. The words were at the tip of his tongue, but he struggled to release them.

"Jim," Drew said with his hand still on Jim's shoulder. "It's okay, really. Please."

"You're an angel, Andrew," Jim said.

Drew stared back at Jim as he tried to soak in what Jim had just said. "Okay," he began then paused. Drew began to laugh lightly and patted Jim's shoulder. "Well, I try to take the best care of you that I can, my old friend. You have…"

"No, Andrew," Jim interrupted. "You are an angel." The room was dead silent for a moment. "Listen to me. You are half man, half angel."

He was serious. All Drew could do was to sit in shock, without the words to reply. Jim layed back down, as if relieved that he was able to finally get it out. After a moment, Drew stood from his seat, walked to the door, and peered out the window. So many things in his life had seemed odd to him, especially recently. There were the nightmares, the strange instinct that seemed to speak to him as if it was coming from another person, the strange occurrences. Even without any more details from Jim, strangely, things were just beginning to make a bit of sense.

"Well then, how…" Drew turned to Jim, who seemed to suddenly be sleeping. "Jim?" Drew quickly returned to Jim's bed and tried to wake him, only to find that he had somehow slipped back into unconsciousness.

"What happened to you on Three Fork?" Drew asked quietly as he sat back into the chair next to Jim's bed.

"I'm sorry, you can't go in there," Cindy said as two policemen in plain clothes, Detectives Davidson and Richards, approached and grabbed the door handle to Jim's room. "Not yet, please. My husband is speaking to someone very important to him."

"I don't understand ma'am," Detective Davidson stated. "We need to get a statement from him."

"I know," Cindy answered. "Please, just give him a bit more time, it's important to him."

Detective Richards smiled. "We can do that. But we can't wait too long."

"Thank you," Cindy replied.

"Are you his wife?" Davidson asked.

"Yes, sir," she answered. "And the boy in there is Drew, or Andrew, Engel. He is the son of an old friend that passed away several years ago. My husband has been the father figure in his life since."

"The Sheriff's department is going to be here soon," Richards said. "I'm actually surprised they're not here already."

"Why are they coming, too?" Cindy asked.

"Well, technically the incident occurred in their jurisdiction," Richards answered. "The chief wants us here also though because it involved one of our school district's buses."

"It's just the way things go sometimes in small towns," stated Davidson. "No need to worry. As long as your husband tells them the same thing he tells us, we won't have any problems, and nobody will get their toes stepped on, ya' know?"

"So," Cindy asked, a bit reluctantly. "Do you guys have any idea as to what happened out there?"

"Honestly, Mrs. Davis," Richards began as he leaned in to Cindy. "My partner here and I think some nut job tried to catch the bus on fire with a blow torch, but then somebody came along and put the fire out before it could get to the flammables."

"Really?" Cindy replied with her hands on her face. "Why would someone want to do that to my Jim? He's the kindest man in this town and everybody loves him."

"Some people just target anyone who gets in their path," replied Richards.

"But this is just our theory…for now," Davidson added. "I think the sheriff's department is officially going to call it an accident due to a malfunction on the bus. And I think the chief's not gonna' argue."

"Oh my," Cindy said. "I just don't understand."

"Well don't worry ma'am, you don't need to just yet," Richards said. "That's why we need to get in there and talk to your husband, you understand?"

Suddenly the door flung open and Drew slowly walked out into the hallway with a dazed expression on his face. The detectives seemed greatly concerned as Drew walked past everyone and down the hall.

"Andrew!" Cindy called out.

Drew turned and looked back at them. Cindy had already turned and gone into the room. "He's out again, I don't understand why," Drew said to the detectives and doctor, who had just now joined the group. "I don't…" Drew turned and continued down the hallway slowly. He needed a breath of fresh air. The doctor walked quickly back into the room with Jim's chart in hand, followed by the two Adjacent Cove detectives.

"Jim?...JIM!" Cindy's voice could be heard from down the hall, followed by the calming voice of the doctor. Although the doctor had reassured her, she began to cry. Everyone was now turning their attention to Drew, who had made his way into the emergency room lobby.

Drew stared into the empty lobby for a moment and then turned to the woman at the front desk. "Where's that man?" he asked.

"Uh, I'm not sure what man you're talking about," the nurse replied.

Drew turned his head back to the lobby and pointed at the seat where the strange looking man was sitting when he first came into the hospital. "Right there, he was sitting right there. He was wearing a long coat and had long hair."

"Well sweetie," the nurse replied, a bit confused. "I've been here all morning and I haven't seen a man like that."

"Yea," Drew replied as he turned back to the nurse. "Remember, he was sitting right there when I came in. He was looking at me all funny. Remember, 'cause you had to get my attention and…"

"Sir," the nurse interrupted. "I remember when you came in and there was nobody in the lobby. Do you understand? There was no one there, but you. I can rewind the security video if you like."

"No," Drew responded in a puzzled state. "No, it's…it's okay."

"Mr. Engel?" Detective Richards approached Drew rather quickly. "Are you Mr. Engel, sir? The doctor needs you. It's about Jim Davis."

Drew turned to the detective quietly and gaped. "I…" he muttered softly.

"Sir, are you okay?" Richards asked. "You're pale…and trembling."

Drew stood there for a moment before coming to his senses. He could hear the detective talking to him, but it sounded muffled and distant. He began to feel dizzy as his eyesight began to blur. "I…" he said once again.

"Mr. Engel?" Richards asked in a louder tone. "Do I need to get a doctor for you?"

Suddenly Drew was able to somehow quickly recover and gather himself. The detective's words became clear, and he finally realized what was going on. He placed his hands on his head as he started back into the emergency room through the open door, the detective following behind. He was still a bit pale, but alert and calm. "The doctor needs me?"

"Yea," Richards answered. "Mr. Davis is unconscious again and we're just trying to figure out what happened. You gonna' be okay fella'?"

"Yea, yea, I'll be fine. He fell out again right before I left the room." Drew opened the door and entered Jim's room, where the doctor, Cindy, and another Adjacent Cove police detective stood. They all immediately turned their attention to Drew, who walked over to the bed and grabbed Jim's hand.

"What happened?" the young doctor asked.

"Uh, he just stopped talking and laid back down," Jim answered, running his fingers through his own hair. "I thought he went to sleep or something."

"Did he say something or did you say something that was really upsetting?" Cindy asked.

"No, no," Drew answered. "There was nothing upsetting, it was just really intense."

"What was it that he said that was really intense?" the doctor asked.

"Ah," Drew looked down to his feet for a moment.

"Well?" asked Detective Davidson.

Drew wasn't sure what to say. He couldn't tell them exactly what he and Jim had talked about. They would think that Jim was just babbling or something from an injury or because he had been so stressed out by the whole ordeal. The entire room was now fixated upon Drew and waiting for a response, but Drew remained quiet.

"Look, Mr. Engel," Richards broke the silence. "It's very important that we find out what went on out there before this thing gets passed off as just another accident. Do you understand?" Drew nodded his head to some extent. "And the doctor here needs to know what happened while you were in here so that he can help Mr. Davis. Do you understand that?" It was obvious that the detective was growing impatient.

"I know," Drew responded. "And I already told you what happened. He just stopped talking and laid back down. How was I to know that he was going to be knocked out again?"

"Oh, sweetie," Cindy said, with tears still in her eyes. She walked around the bed to Drew and put her arm around him. "Nobody's blaming you for anything, Andrew. I know that you would never do anything to hurt Jim."

"No, I wouldn't," Drew responded as a tear rolled down his cheek. "He's the only father I have left Cindy. I love him with all my heart."

Cindy cried as she placed her other arm around Drew and hugged him tightly. "I know, sweetie," she said as she laid her head on his shoulder. "I know."

The doctor walked over to the two, who were still hugging, and placed his hand on Cindy's back. He looked at Drew and said, "Don't worry, I believe ya'. I get the feelin' that whatever you two were talking about was private, yea?" Drew nodded his head in agreement. The doctor stood and began to walk out of the room. "Mr. Davis is okay. His stats are all normal. I think you might just put these detectives' minds to rest if you told them that you weren't talking about what happened this morning. Maybe you were talking about somethin' else." He winked at Drew and left the room.

"Well?" Richards asked. "Please understand that we're here to help Mr. Davis."

"I know," Drew said as he rose from his seat. "I really do know that, and I promise to tell you everything if he talks to me about what happened next time and you're not in here."

"You promise?" Davidson asked.

"Yes, of course." Drew answered. There was a presence about Drew at this moment that seemed to bring an enormous peace to everyone in the room. Both detectives knew without a doubt that Drew would not keep anything important to their assignment from them. Cindy smiled as she rose to go and use the phone again. The detectives had already cleared the room and decided to go back to the sight to try again to find any witnesses.

"Wait," Drew said, looking down at his phone, which he had just pulled from his pocket. It was working again. The battery was completely charged. Puzzled,

Drew looked back towards Cindy, who was already on the other side of the room looking back at him.

"Um," he continued. "Here, my phone seems to be working now." He handed his cell phone to Cindy, who thanked him and began to dial. She needed to update their daughter and only child Alyssa again, who was living up north where she had attended college just a few years back. Alyssa had also been one of Drew's closest friends for as long as he could remember. "Please tell her I said hello," he said.

"Who," Cindy asked.

"Alyssa," Drew responded.

"How'd you know I was going to call her?" inquired Cindy, who hadn't even started dialing.

"I don't know," he answered. Drew turned his head away and smiled. "I guess I just have good instinct."

"I guess you do," Cindy answered.

"Would you let me know if he wakes again? I'm going to go sit in the lobby for a while."

"Of course, I will."

"We have lots to talk about," Drew said as he rose and walked towards the door. He looked back at Cindy with a face that radiated with confidence. It was one that Cindy hadn't seen since before Andrew's father died, when he was a young teen.

"You okay, big guy?" Cindy asked.

"I'm ready," Drew stopped for a moment and stared at Jim. Cindy had stopped dialing for a moment to focus her attention on Drew and was now closing the flip phone. "I think I'm ready anyway, gotta' start somewhere, right?" he said with poise before he finally turned and walked out the door.

VI

Andrew sat in the empty lobby of the Trenton County Hospital emergency room, confused, but somehow not lost. He sat upright with his arms on either armrest of the chair and looked straight forward at nothing in particular. He wasn't sure what to do with what little information that Jim had given him, and, therefore, had decided to wait for Jim to wake again before making any careless assumptions. This was, hands down, the strangest and most revealing day so far that he had ever experienced. For years, Drew had felt weak and almost disabled by the horrible death of his father when he was young. That was a life changing event, to say the least, and the one that was now starting to bring familiar feelings to Drew that he hadn't felt since it happened.

Drew thought about many things as he sat, but mostly his father. While he was a young teen, Drew's faith life had been much different before his father David's death than it was now. He never completely lost his faith in God, and in fact, was never even angry at God for what had happened. One thing that his father always taught him was that God had a will for everyone's life, and if you give yours to him, your life will go according to that will. While he could not understand why his father had to be taken from this earth, especially at that time, he knew that God had a perfect will for each of his children.

At first, Drew had continued to attend church every Sunday and Wednesday. He missed his father terribly, but each Christmas, each birthday, each graduation, and every other event that his father could not attend eventually took an enormous toll on him. When he returned from college, he attended from time to time, but not regularly. He and his mother, along with Jim and his wife, still attended the First Baptist Church where David preached for a few years before passing away. This made going back to church a painful memory for Drew. He had visited a few other churches in the area, but this just made him feel worse, like he was betraying his father's memory.

Despite not going to church on a regular basis, Drew still felt a deep connection with Jesus Christ. He knew that God wanted him to attend church regularly for a number of reasons, but he just hadn't found the strength. It was only natural for Drew to question God's decision to allow his father's death to be taken from time to time, but he never let it damage his faith. He still wanted God to be number one in his life, and had no plans of changing this. Still, he knew that he needed to get back into church. He had to do it for the teachings and the fellowship. Most of all, he needed to do this for God. Until then, he spent many hours of quiet time in his room by the bed and was continually reading God's word, especially on Sundays.

Jim was instrumental in helping to keep Drew's faith, at the least, where it was. They had spoken about spiritual warfare quite often in their many discussions. Drew always asked a lot of answers and somehow Jim always knew how to answer them. It was as if he'd studied the subject quite extensively. One year, the church held a week-long study on spiritual warfare and for some reason, Jim had been adamant about Drew being there.

At this point, Drew still did not know enough about what was going on and was anxious to find out more. Nothing he had ever heard or read spoke about anything like this before. Maybe he was a first. To just about anyone else, what Jim had told him would have sounded quite ridiculous. He could've easily dismissed it as babble, caused by an injury or Jim's traumatic experience that morning. Drew's instinct, however, was telling him differently, and it was a very strong instinct, unlike anything he had ever experienced before. He longed to hear more, but all he could do at this point was to wait and be patient.

Drew, like Jim, also wished that his father had been there to tell him this. After so many years, Drew had become to know Jim like a father, and although nobody could have ever replaced his father, he was glad it was Jim. The past was the past, and there was frankly nothing he could do about that. Nonetheless, Drew knew that his father was watching. He knew that whatever was going on, it meant enough to his father to trust his best friend to pass the news along at the right time. The right time, however, was another question. Why now and not years ago? This was just one of the many questions he would have for Jim.

Of course, the most important thing on Drew's mind at this point was Jim's health. No matter how crazy what Jim had told him might have sounded, Drew knew that he was speaking the truth, and it wasn't a result of injury or shock. It was Drew's instinct, the same that seemed to be growing as the day progressed. He had always felt that he had a keen instinct, but this did not seem to be human-like. His instincts were even beginning to tell him things about the strange man that he had seen on Three Fork Road and in the hospital lobby. He already knew that there was something wrong about him, but now he was sensing darkness about him, one that even worried him a bit.

Drew bowed his head to pray for guidance. He prayed that God would heal Jim from whatever ailment he was suffering, and that the doctors would be able to figure out exactly what was going on. The tests had all come back negative so far, but obviously, something was going on. It was strange no doubt, especially considering Jim's overall toughness and track record. Drew also prayed that God would give Jim the ability to tell Andrew everything that he needed to. He remembered Jim saying that this was something his father wanted him to know. He wondered why he hadn't already told him. After all, Drew was already twenty-seven years old. Whatever the reason, Jim had good intentions, and his father knew what he was doing when he had first given Jim the instructions.

"Amen," he said as he lifted his head and wiped away a small tear that had escaped his eye. "Come on, Jim. All I can do here is wait. He took a deep breath and ran his fingers through his hair. "But I'll wait as long as it takes."

Two hours passed, and Drew remained seated in the lobby. He hadn't moved much, except to scratch his head a couple of times. Time passed irregularly, however. The two hours seemed like just a few minutes for him.

"Mr. Engel?" the woman behind the desk asked. Drew had not even noticed that there was a different person there now.

"Yes," he answered quietly. "Yes, that's me."

"You're wanted in room seven," the lady said.

"Oh…thank you," Drew said as he quickly picked himself up. "Do me a favor," he said to the lady as he passed. "Let me know if you see a tall man with long hair and a long black jacket come in here while I'm gone."

"Certainly," she answered. "Family member?" she asked.

"Not that I know of. I would rather him not be around Mr. Davis, is all," Drew responded sternly.

"Are you a family member?" the nurse asked.

"Close enough," answered Drew.

"Gotcha'," the nurse said with a wink and a smile. The door next to the desk opened and Drew headed down the hall and back into Jim's room.

"Everything okay?" Drew asked as he peeked through the door. Cindy was now sitting where Drew once did, looking down at her husband's face. A nurse was on the other side drawing blood.

"Yea, yea everything's fine, sweetie," Cindy said as she motioned Drew to come in. "They're gonna' move him up to a private room upstairs. We're just waitin' for one to become available. Shouldn't be long." Cindy began to stroke Jim's face gently with her fingers. "He's still out, Drew. I just don't understand." She began to cry. Drew walked over and placed his arm around her. "The doctor says that he's okay. He just…he won't come out of this and I don't understand. He's a strong man Drew. You know that."

"Yes, I know, Cindy," Drew responded. "But you know what? He is gonna' come out of it. I promise you. He's gonna' be just fine. You'll see. You know that I won't let anything happen to him."

"Oh Andrew," Cindy said as she reached back to place her arm on his. "Thank you. That's what I needed to hear." Andrew laid his head on Cindy's shoulder for a moment, then stood and walked to the other side of the bed where another chair sat next to a side table. "I just need to go get some fresh air, but I did not want to leave him alone, you know?"

"Go ahead," Drew responded. "It will do you some good. I'll stay, don't worry." Cindy rose and grabbed her jacket from the hook on the back of the door. She looked back at Jim and blew him a kiss. "Does my phone have any juice left? Call Alyssa if it does. She's good at making anyone feel better, you know."

"I know," Cindy answered. "Actually, she's on her way here right now. Her flight arrives later tonight. I just don't know if I can leave to go pick her up."

"So I'll pick her up," Drew said. "Just give me the information, and I'll pick her up and bring her straight here."

"No, Andrew, you're so sweet, but I can't ask that of you. Not now."

"You're not asking Cindy, I'm offering, and I'm gonna' do it okay? And besides, it's not for several hours. It's still early. I'll be able to be here all day, except when I go pick Alyssa up from the airport."

"Thank you, sweetie. Thank you so much."

"It's my pleasure, now go get some air before you shrivel up or something." The two laughed as Cindy walked out the door, occasionally taking another look back at her husband, who lied so peacefully, yet so helplessly, on his hospital bed.

On the bedside tray next to Drew lied the possessions that Jim had on him when he was brought in. There was an old pocket knife that he had carried for years, his brown leather wallet, a few various coins, and a familiar, solid silver pocket watch with an empty wooden cross engraved on the front of it. Underneath the cross was a banner that stretched across the length of the watch with the words "He's Alive" engraved in the middle.

Drew picked up the watch and held it in his head. Flipping it open, he noticed an engraving on the inside cover. "To a friend like no other, Yours, Bro. David Engel." Tears began to fill Drew's eyes as he quickly closed the lid.

"Your Daddy gave me that watch," Jim said. "Just a couple of days after he was diagnosed."

"Jim?" Andrew responded with surprise. "You're awake!"

Jim reached out and Drew placed the pocket watch into his hand. "At that time, I did not even know…you know," Jim continued. "He gave it to me out of nowhere, for no reason at all, except to show his friendship. We were having coffee at the donut shop. That's when he told me about the dream he had before you were born."

Andrew listened intently. This was something that Jim had never shared with him during their many talks about his father.

"You know, son," Jim continued. "Technically, you shouldn't have been able to be born. Your mother and father tried and tried to have a child but the doctor finally told them that it wasn't going to be possible because of multiple complications."

"No, I guess I didn't know that."

"But they had you didn't they?" asked Jim.

"Yea, they did," Drew answered, absorbed in attention. "But I never knew that."

"Well, there's a reason for it son, I promise," Jim continued. Your father had a dream, you see." Jim coughed. "But it wasn't just a dream. It was…it was too vivid to just be a dream. Those are your Daddy's very words." Jim paused for a moment.

"What dream?" Drew asked in anticipation.

"The angel Gabriel came to see him." Andrew leaned in as Jim continued. "He told your father not to stop trying, because your wife was going to give birth. He told him not to listen to the doctors because they were going to have a child, a son."

Andrew leaned back in his chair and stared down at his hands. "So, I wasn't supposed to be born?"

"No Andrew, no, I didn't say that. You were very much supposed to be born. But that's not all. Gabriel told your Daddy that you were going to be special, that you would one day fight the powers and principalities of darkness as both man and angel. He said that you were going to be an angel reborn on this earth as a human."

"Reborn?" Drew asked, looking up at Jim. "I don't understand."

Jim coughed some more, then repositioned himself on the bed. Drew adjusted the covers so that he could recover his mentor and dear friend. He sat up as much as he could without readjusting the bed anymore.

"Yea, Andrew, I know. It's difficult to take in, and it's a lot to understand. But the best you can do right now, son, is trust in God."

"So, am I to understand that I'm an angel Jim? Do you know how crazy that sounds?" Drew was obviously confused. "I'm supposed to fight evil as a man and as an angel? How…I mean, what does that mean?"

"That means that God has chosen you, Andrew," Jim responded softly. "It means that you have to trust in Him to equip you properly. You are going to lead us out of the darkness. You are going to be a shepherd, a watchman, a protector. What I'm telling you does seem crazy, I know that, but don't you think the people thought Jesus was crazy when he turned water into wine? They can either believe or not. You can either believe or not." Jim raised his trembling arm and pointed to Drew's heart. "It's all right here, son. Forget about what your head is telling you and listen to your heart."

"Wow," Drew responded. "It's a lot to take in, you know?"

"Well," answered Jim, placing his hand on Drew's shoulder. "Now that you know, I have the utmost of confidence that you will learn what this means in the very near future."

"Well, what else did Gabriel say?"

"That was it. That's all he told him. And you know what?"

"What?"

"Your Daddy has never been steered wrong by our Father in Heaven. Remember, it was a miracle that allowed you to be born. And now things are happening and…"

"Yea," Drew interrupted. "I know, strange things are happening." He almost hesitated to ask, but needed to know. "What happened this morning?"

Jim took a deep breath and lied back into his bed. He looked over at Drew, who was anxiously awaiting his response. "I guess you really do need to know."

"Please," Drew asked.

"I had just gone down Three Forks Road for my first pickup, but the kids weren't there, so I turned around. It was still dark, but suddenly I saw this child, no more than eight or nine years old standin' right in the middle of the road. I'd never seen him before. He was wearing black pants and black shoes and had a pale face and jet black hair. You know how I love kids, Drew, all of them. But this child..." Jim paused for a moment, starting into space. Drew put his hand on Jim's arm.

"It's okay," Drew reassured him. "I know you do."

"He was just a kid." Tears began to fill Jim's eyes. Drew could tell that he was having great difficulty speaking. His eyes rolled back into the back of his head for a moment until Andrew shook him by his arm.

"I know this is hard," Drew said. "But I feel like I need to know this."

"You do, son, you do," Jim answered as he came to.

"Please, I know it's hard."

"This kid," Jim continued. "His eyes were solid black, Andrew. There wasn't even any white in his eyes. And his face...his face was pale. It was white as snow." Jim began to sweat as he continued. "I stopped and just honked a couple of times. Sometimes I get new kids on my route and all, but this was no normal kid, Drew. He wasn't normal at all." Jim gripped the stopwatch in his hand so tightly that it was leaving marks on his palm.

"Please go on," Drew said.

"I, I started to get out of the bus, you know, to see if the kid was in trouble or something, but..." he paused once again. "But I couldn't get the door open. Then, all of the sudden, the child started to, well...shriek. It wasn't just a scream, it was a shriek. I covered my ears but it didn't help much. I honestly thought my eardrums might burst. Then...then the bus just shut off. The bus is just a couple years old, there's no reason why it should've shut off. The kid just kept shrieking and wouldn't stop. I started banging on the horn, but I couldn't hear it over the child's screaming." He stopped and turned to Drew, who was fixed on what Jim was saying. Drew wasn't sure what to say, but he knew that Jim was not lying or even stretching the truth.

"The bus just started going backwards," Jim said after taking a deep breath and a drink of water from the cup on the food service tray. "It was still in gear and dragging backwards. I couldn't stop it, I even started the bus back up and started trying to drive forward and around the boy, but it just drug backwards." Jim stopped once more, seemingly finding it difficult to continue.

"And the fire," Drew asked. "What about the fire?"

"Well, after a few moments, he stopped shrieking. I thought it was over, and he'd go away, but then he opened his mouth." Jim seemed more reluctant now than before he began. As bad as Drew wanted and even needed Jim to continue, he was more concerned about the health of his old friend, who was obviously more than stressed out by having to relive what he had experienced.

"Why don't you just rest a minute okay, Jim?" he said. "You don't have to be in a hurry."

"I do have to be in a hurry, son," Jim responded. "They're trying to keep me from telling you this. They don't want you to know because of what God has made you."

"That's why you went out earlier," asked Drew.

"Yes, but I'm going to tell you this," Jim said with determination. "That boy…he seemed so young and helpless at first you know? Then he starts screaming, and then he opened his mouth, and fire came out."

Drew was startled. "Fire?"

"Fire, Andrew. He breathed fire like a dragon and it was so hot. I had the bus started, but I couldn't see because of the flames. I thought for sure the bus was going to go up into flames at any moment. There was so much fire that just kept coming and coming. I grabbed the extinguisher, but before I could even use it, I was out." He paused once more.

"That's when you passed out?" Drew asked.

"That's when I blacked out," Jim said, his face now covered in perspiration and trembling. "I just…I just went blank. When I woke up, the bus was in a ditch and I was being put into an ambulance."

Drew was speechless. If it had been just about anyone else, he would've dismissed it as crazy talk. Things like this just never happened in real life. Combined with the ever present feeling in Drew's gut that something strange was going on in Adjacent Cove, Jim's revelation of what had happened to him was troublesome, to say the least. What sort of evil could have done this to a man like Jim? Jim had no enemies. He had never had a single problem on the bus. Drew knew that if he told this same story to the officials, they would think that he was out of his mind, but how could he keep that from happening? The police were going to want a statement from him either way, and Jim was not going to lie to them.

Jim sunk his head into the pillow and closed his eyes. "Whatever that was, Drew, it was evil beyond anything I'd ever seen before."

"So what do we do?" Andrew asked with his head down. "We've gotta' find it and stop it right?"

"You'll find out soon," Jim answered, his eyes still closed and near sleeping. "I promise you Andrew, you'll find out very soon. Don't forget, we're on God's time."

VII

As the day progressed, a thick layer of dark and menacing clouds began to move in from the south. By late afternoon, all of Trenton County was darkened. The thick clouds brought with them strong winds and rolling thunder that shook the ground, however, there was no rain, no lightning, not even a change in temperature. In addition, not a single weatherman on any of the local news channels coming out of Austin made mention of the eccentric patch of clouds in their afternoon reports. Neither local nor national weather radars recognized their existence. Calls poured into radio and television stations from all over the county but no one could explain the unusual conditions.

Meanwhile, in the thick woods just east of the city of Campbell, two men came upon a small cabin that had been built from the trees surrounding it. The cabin was dark and seemed empty, although a pillar of smoke rose from the chimney and disappeared into the dark clouds above. The men approached the cabin with caution, trying to see into the darkness through the dirty and cracked windows.

Back at Ware State Penitentiary, alarms screamed into the night, accompanied by an array of search lights that circled both the premises and the surrounding area. An APB had already been put out on James Walker and the dark, unknown suspect that had broken him out. They had walked right out of the Devil's Hole and the building that contained it, through the courtyard, and out the front gates of the facility. Upon seeing the men run through the courtyard, snipers repeatedly struck both of them with rubber bullets, but with no effect. All guards were then ordered to fire live ammunition upon will at both men, an order never even considered before this day in the history of Ware State Penitentiary. The front gates had been blown open by a force that could only be described by guards later as an explosion "with light, but no fire". As the prisoner and his aide were hurrying through the gates, bullets from a variation of pistols and rifles burned through the air towards them. Not a single one, however, had seemed to reach their target, as the two disappeared into the nearby woods without a trace.

James reached over the edge of the small awning covering the entranceway and grabbed a key to the front door. The cabin had no electricity and no running water in order to assist in keeping its existence hidden from the public. It sat about two miles into the wooded area on a piece of land owned by one of the members of Los Ultimos Dias. Another member of the group was a carpenter and others had worked various construction jobs in the past, so building the cabin had not been too difficult a task for the team. A small, freshwater stream ran through the 150 acre piece of land just a few feet from the cabin, providing James with whatever water he would need while living there. For over three years now, this cabin had served as the perfect hide-out for James and a central nerve for his growing group of followers.

Alerted by the smoke coming from his chimney, James turned the key and opened the front door cautiously. Behind him stood his indistinct accomplice, who up to this point had not uttered a word. Whoever had somehow broken into the cabin was certainly not welcome at this point. It was forbidden for anyone to stay at the cabin while James was away. He feared that it would be an unnecessary risk that might draw attention to its location. In recent years, James had become overly paranoid, and for good reason.

By this time, James had only been caught and convicted for a small fraction of the crimes he had actually committed. Detectives were always on his case about claims of robbery, destruction of property, assault, and a number of other offenses. Not even a handful of citizens, all fairly new to the area, had been brave enough to stand up against James in court, only to regret it later. The rest took his advice and kept their mouths shut out of fear. Other members of Los Ultimos Dias had been caught or were suspects of various crimes, but none had a rap sheet like James'. Not even their former leader, Richard "The Beast", who was still in prison in another part of the state.

James looked back to make sure that the opaque man that had accompanied him was still there, and then continued into the cabin. The room was as dark as night, despite what light was left outside under the dark clouds. He removed his prison-issued shoes, which had been frayed and ragged by the long run through the woods. Soon, James noticed the outline of a man, sitting in the worn, leather lounge chair in the middle of the room, with his legs crossed. He quickly stepped backwards towards the door and grabbed the double-barreled shotgun leaning against the inside of the door's frame. The shaded man behind him grabbed the shotgun from his hand almost immediately after he picked it up.

"What the heck?" James said as his head swiveled backwards, then forward again.

"You won't be needing that," the man in the chair said.

"Who are you people?" James began, confused. "And what are you doing here?" He turned his head backwards once again, towards the man standing behind him, as he slowly began to back into the front corner of the room. "And why did you come and get me?" He began to feel around the upper corner of the wall for a shelf that had once held a loaded .38 caliber revolver. James had made it a point over the previous few years to keep plenty of loaded weapons in various places in the cabin, in case of an emergency.

"You won't be needing that either," the man in the chair said, as he looked at his long finger nails.

James had made the erroneous assumption that the man who had broken him out of prison was a member of Los Ultimos Dias. In the hurried moments that had proceeded this one, he had never even thought to question the man's means or abilities. He had not even attempted to recognize the individual's identity in any way, a rare mistake on his part.

"Don't worry yourself with who he is," the man in the chair continued. "Let's talk a bit about you."

Unable to find his revolver, James grabbed a book of matches from the shelf and side-stepped to the front door, never taking his attention off of the man in the chair. He turned slightly to strike a match and light an oil lamp that was hanging next to the door frame. The lamp lit most of the room but was not enough to reveal the man's face, which was shadowed under an old, black fedora hat. He wore a black suit with a black shirt and tie and dull, black dress shoes. The sole feature of his face that could be made out was his chin, which was a pale blue color, like his bony hands. His thick fingernails were as white as pearls and came to a point about a half inch from his fingertips. He appeared to be old and withered, although his posture indicated otherwise. His head was down, but his roguish smile penetrated through the shadow over his face.

"Me?" James asked. He was growing intensely frustrated by this point. "You don't know me. You don't belong here, man, and you better jet before it gets ugly in here." He stopped as the man rose from the chair and began to pace through the darker shadows in the back of the room. His stature took James off guard. There was something awkward about the man and the way that he crept around the room with his hands behind his back, something wicked in a sense.

"I know more about you than you might think," the man continued. He placed his hands on the back of the chair for just a moment and lifted his head. His face was still shadowed, but the blackness of his eyes was apparent against his pale skin. "James Edward Walker," he continued, but this time in a low, devilish tone. James was alerted, but not afraid. The man continued to pace back and forth behind the chair as he expressed a sort of amusement towards the situation by laughing evilly.

"Okay," James said. "So what do you know about me, you freak?" He was now beyond frustrated and growing angrier by the second, yet his curiosity kept him from doing anything rash.

"Well," the man continued, laughing to himself. "I've been called worse, but I guess you're right. I am a bit of a freak."

"What do you want from me?" James asked.

"No," the man began. "No James. It's not about what I want. The question is…what exactly do you want? What is it you seek James?" He stopped pacing once again and faced James, who was slowly inching his way into the room, towards the chair. His expression was one of pure iniquity that caused James to freeze in his tracks. "And more importantly, James," he continued. "Where do your loyalties lie?"

"My loyalties?" James inquired with a bit of sarcasm in an attempt to lighten the ambience of the moment. "I am loyal to my people and myself, that's it. Anyone else, including you, means nothing to me."

"Then you do have loyalties. You do understand what it means to be loyal, am I right?"

"What are you talking about, and who is this guy?" asked James, as he pointed towards the man behind him.

"What guy?" the man behind the couch asked. James turned to find that the man that had rescued him from prison was now gone.

"What is this?" James asked, his frustration growing. "What do you want?" he shouted. "I have people who will come after you like a storm."

The man continued laughing, as if mocking James in a way. "You're just an imp right now, but you'll grow out of it. You'll soon learn."

"Learn what?"

"That's it's all a deception," the dark man said.

"What's a deception?"

"Everything!" the man shouted. "Everything you've ever known up to this point."

"I don't understand," James said as he slammed his fist against the wall. "Either tell me what you're talking about in plain English and quit with this act of yours or get out of my place, now! I'm not intimidated by evil! I am evil!"

"Evil?" the man asked cynically. "Evil, my boy, is nothing more than the shadow of itself. What you see before you is deeper than any darkness or shadow you've ever laid eyes on. What you see goes deeper than the very roots of what you know to be evil. Depravity, corruption, indecency, these are words that tell your story until now, but I tell you this." The man leaned forward with his hands on the back of the chair once again and smiled. "You have seen nothing yet."

Sergeant Evan Daniels had been in charge of the hole, officially called Cell Block X, during the bold escape of prisoner James Walker with the assistance of an unknown accomplice. He was stationed just inside the entrance to the building when suddenly the door blew open with such force that it knocked the heavy steel door completely off its hinges and about fifty feet into the courtyard. The blast had knocked Sergeant Daniels out cold for several minutes. When he came to, every guard stationed in the building and the cell block beneath its foundation had been either severely injured or killed during the attack and escape. The only other guards harmed during the incident were the five stationed at the front gates. In all, Sergeant Daniels lost six men. Five others in his unit, including one woman, were badly injured and taken to the hospital. At the front gates, three out of the five guards were killed and the two who survived were being taken to ICU by helicopter. In the courtyard, another three men were injured trying to stop the two men.

"Here, drink this," the warden of Ware State Penitentiary, Michael Phillips, said as he approached Sergeant Daniels, who was sitting in a chair outside the warden's office with his face buried in his hands. Daniels looked up and saw that the warden was holding out a coffee mug with a warm drink in it.

"It'll help your nerves," the warden continued. Daniels took the mug and the warden sat down next to him.

"I don't know," Daniels began, his voice shaking. "I can't even figure out where to begin. I have no idea what happened Mike."

Sergeant Daniels and Michael Phillips had grown up in the same neighborhood in Austin together. Phillips was a few years older than Daniels, but had looked after him and taken him under his wing in many ways. Not long after Phillips entered the police academy, Daniels followed in his footsteps. Both had served on the Austin police force for a few years before being promoted and assigned to their positions at Ware. Daniels was the man that Warden Phillips trusted more than anyone else; therefore, he was assigned to the most difficult task within the prison system, taking charge of Cell Block X.

"I know Evan," Phillips replied. "I've never in my life seen anything like this."

"I shouldn't have had Leslie come down there," Daniels sobbed as he tried to speak. "She didn't belong down there, Mike."

"Leslie is going to be okay, Evan," Phillips said as he placed his hand on Daniels' shoulder. "I've checked in on all of them, and she's going to be okay."

"What about everyone else?" Daniels asked.

"Most everyone that survived is going to be okay, but we just have to take it one step at a time."

"I just can't wrap my head around this," Daniels began to cry.

"Listen," Phillips stated. "This was not your fault. Do you understand me, Evan? It was not your fault. We're going to find those monsters." Phillips clinched his fist in anger. "We're going to hunt them down and…and crush them. Do you understand?"

Daniels was silent for a moment as he dried his eyes and took a sip of his drink. "How did they do it" he began. "What was that explosive device? I've never seen anything like it. This is number four for us, Mike. Number four in two years!"

"I know. It's bad, but all we can do is take it one step at a time. I don't think any amount of added security would've kept those two in here. We don't know how they did it, but we're going to find out. The surveillance team is getting the tapes ready for me now, but listen to me." Phillips paused for a moment as if debating on whether or not to continue.

"What?" Daniels asked.

"It's no big deal, okay?" Phillips responded. "But the FBI is on its way as we speak."

"Aw crap," Daniels interrupted with disgust.

"I know, but it's okay. It's just standard procedure, you know that."

"I know, I know. I just don't feel like dealing with anyone like that right now."

"Well, ya' know what?" Phillips said as he stood from his chair. "You don't have to, kid. I want you to go home."

"Go home?" Daniels asked, puzzled by his remark.

"Go home to Rachel and the boys," Phillips responded. Daniels had been married to his wife, Rachel, for nearly seventeen years and they had three boys together, all still in elementary school. "I'll take care of everything here. You can come back tomorrow and deal with it, okay? Please, I'm asking you. No, I'm ordering you. You need to clear your head and get some rest."

"They're gonna' want to talk to me," Sergeant Daniels said quietly as he looked toward the floor.

"Yes, they are," Daniels said as he placed his hand on Daniels' shoulder once again. "But they're gonna' have to wait, do you hear me?"

"Yes, I hear you. Thank you Mike, really. I'm just, just so angry."

"I know," Phillips interrupted. "Go home."

The scene at Trenton County Hospital turned from calm to chaotic in a matter of minutes. Ambulances were rolling in with survivors of the incident, one after the other, from various departments and locations. Doctors, surgeons, and nurses were being called in from all over the county and beyond to help tend to the patients. Jim had already been moved to a room in the upper floor of the hospital to stay the night for observation. Drew was leaving to go visit with his mother; then he would be headed to the airport in Austin to pick up Jim and Cindy's daughter, Alyssa, from the airport. As he pulled out of the parking lot, several ambulances were pulling in to the emergency room entrance. Ambulances carrying prison guards with less urgent injuries were redirected to smaller hospitals in nearby towns while others had been transported by helicopter to Travis Memorial in Austin.

Drew stopped, and for a moment thought about going back into the hospital to see what was going on. He opened the door and stepped outside of his truck to try and get a better look. In the distance, he could hear a helicopter approaching, then watched as it passed over his head and into the horizon towards Austin.

"The clouds," he said to himself. "What in the world is going on here?"

VIII

It was still rather early in the evening, even though the darkness of the clouds above made it seem much later. They seemed lower now than they had upon arrival, and were growing thicker by the minute. By this time, a series of weather balloons had been launched in the area in an attempt to determine what type of disturbance was causing the strange pattern and what could be expected in the hours to come. Despite their obvious existence, radars were still unable to track or even detect the clouds, leaving weather experts puzzled. While some residents pondered over the ominous clouds that seemed to be covering just the immediate area, others had refocused their attention towards another breaking story, the prison break at Ware State Penitentiary.

Hundreds of reporters, photographers, and other interested parties stood outside the gates at the main entrance of Ware State Penitentiary awaiting the press conference that was to begin at any moment. The mood was solemn as the public quietly anticipated the latest available news regarding the escape of one of the area's most disreputable citizens. Warden Michael Phillips emerged through the steel door next to the large gates, followed by officials from both the FBI and the Trenton County Sherriff's Department. His face painted the picture of a man with a heavy heart, distraught by the events that had taken place at his prison earlier that day. He wasn't sure what kind of response or questioning to expect from members of the press, but that was the least of his worries at the moment.

Warden Phillips stepped under the large tent that had been assembled for the press in case of rain and then up to the podium in front of a seated audience. Cameras flashed repeatedly as hundreds of photographs were taken of the Warden before he began to speak. Television news cameras and their operators littered the areas behind and outside of the sitting area, some accompanied by a sound technician with a handheld or boom microphone. Uncharacteristic of the moments leading up to an opening press conference such as this one, there was dead silence as Warden Phillips began to speak.

"There is nothing I can say to you right now…" the warden began, fighting through a river of emotion. "…that would accurately describe to you the pain of the loss felt by myself and the entire staff at Ware State Penitentiary." He reached for a white handkerchief that was stuffed into his back pocket and removed his glasses for a moment to wipe his eyes and face.

"Nobody expects this sort of thing to happen. It just happens. The nature of our business involves such risks, but you never expect something like this to happen to you, at your post, on your watch. I still haven't figured out exactly what I am going to say to the families of the brave officers who lost their lives here today. I don't even know what to say to those who were injured, some of whom are fighting for their lives as we speak." The warden stopped for a moment and put his head down, shaking his head as he tried to continue. Trenton County Sherriff Tom Anderson, a thirty year veteran and a good friend of Warden Phillips', leaned forward and asked if the warden was okay to continue. Phillips waived him off as he took a drink from his water bottle and gathered his composure.

"As most of you know," he continued. "This is the fourth escape by a convict being held at Ware State Penitentiary in only two years. In coalition with the FBI and local law enforcement agencies, we will do everything in our power to capture these criminals and get them off the streets as quickly and as precisely as possible. I'm sure I don't need to say that it is our full intention to bring the escapee and his accomplice in alive. They will have their day in court, where they will both account for their crimes and face the justice they deserve." The warden paused to take a deep breath and another drink of water.

"The details of the escape are still under investigation at this time. Security tapes are being inspected for anything unusual or out of the ordinary that might have occurred in the last couple of days. During the escape, some of our surveillance cameras were intentionally damaged before anything of substance could be captured; however, I have been told that we do have at least some good footage taken by cameras in the courtyard, so, we'll see what we can find there."

The warden took a piece of paper from his shirt pocket and unfolded it. His hands trembled from the onslaught of negative emotions that had come over him in such a short amount of time. He placed the piece of paper on the podium and removed his glasses once again to clean them.

An FBI agent standing behind Phillips leaned forward and whispered something into the warden's ear. Phillips covered the microphone with his hand as he listened. He then nodded his head and turned his attention once more to the piece of paper in front of him.

"At this point, these are the facts. At approximately two o'clock this afternoon, a man wearing all black clothing, including a black overcoat and hat, and being described as 'dark and shadowy', entered the basement of Cell Block X, also called 'The Hole' or 'The Devil's Hole' by prisoners. We're not sure how he got there as of yet. In fact, nobody has reported seeing him enter at any point so how he got into the facility to begin with is still unclear. The suspect then used some sort of explosion to blast the door to the prisoner's cell open. This same sort of blast was also used to leave Cell Block X and enter the courtyard. The two men then proceeded through the courtyard, where they were met by a few guards, all of whom were knocked unconscious by a combination of punches thrown by the man in dark clothing and another explosive device.

"Upon reaching the front gates," Warden Phillips said as he pointed towards the large gates at the entranceway next to them. "When they got to the gates they had already been fired upon several times by snipers at various guard posts along the tops of the walls surrounding the facility. These were rubber bullets designed to stop a person without fatal results. By this time, a code red had been sent out by the guards at the front gate who had witnessed the two men attack the officers in the court yard.

"When I was called, I personally gave the order to use live ammunition if necessary before heading that way myself. All available officers were called to assist; however, by the time anyone arrived on the scene, the two men had made it to the other side of the gates at the expense of every single officer in their way. There is no evidence as of yet that any kind of blast was used to get past those guards and outside. I do know that several rounds of live ammunition were fired upon the two men as they fled, but there doesn't seem to be any indication that anyone at was able to hit their target."

Warden Phillips paused for a moment as he folded up the sheet of paper and placed it back in his shirt pocket. Press members were eager to ask questions, but hesitant to interrupt if the warden was not finished speaking yet. After a few moments of silence, a newspaper reporter from a neighboring county raised his hand.

"Unfortunately, right now..." Phillips started, ignoring the raised hand. "...I'm not ready to give you any definite numbers as far as casualties go, and really all that we know right now is what I just told you."

"This is what we know about the suspects at this point," he continued. "James Edward Walker is a white male, thirty-seven years of age, and as far as we know has no alias. He stands six feet eight inches tall and weighs approximately 280 pounds. He has dark brown hair, green eyes and light skin. He could still be wearing his orange prison coveralls with light brown shoes. The back of the uniform will have the letters 'WSP' in black and the front will have Mr. Walker's prisoner number, '264656' just above the shirt pocket, also in black.

"It is my understanding that James Walker is the leader of a secret cult that meets in the area called 'Los Ultimos Dias'. This group has been described as satanic and very dangerous, and according to informants, nearly two hundred members are currently enrolled in the group. If anyone has any further information on Los Ultimos Dias or any of its members, we would appreciate your anonymous tip.

"Mr. Walker's accomplice is unknown at this point, although we do have a few leads. At this time, we are assuming that we are dealing with another male, over seven feet tall, wearing all black clothing, including a black overcoat and some sort of hat. That is all we have, as far as a description goes, at this point. Both suspects are considered armed and extremely dangerous. If you see either suspect, please do not attempt to subdue them in any way. As I've already mentioned, these men are considered extremely dangerous and probably armed. Pictures of both are being circulated as we speak.

"As far as we know so far, these were the only two individuals involved, but we haven't ruled anything out at this point. We will be updating the press with as much information as we can throughout the evening and until this matter is resolved. It appears as though this is going to be a rather challenging investigation; however, we will catch the monsters who did this. I assure you, we will catch them, and they will get what's coming to them."

Outside the roughly 700 square feet, one bedroom cabin in the middle of the woods, a thin fog began to rise. James Walker stood in his bright orange, prison issued overalls, just a few feet from the opened front door. The mysterious intruder who had welcomed him back to his own hideout just a few moments before paced slowly back and forth in the back of the room as if contemplating his next move. He was covered and surrounded by a dark and unexplainable shadow that just added to his mystique.

"Who was that?" James asked.

"Who was what?" the man replied.

"Quit playing stupid with me old man," replied James in anger. "Who was that man who got me out? And where did he go?"

"Ah, you mean Saithe," the man answered.

James had been expecting somebody to attempt to break him out of prison, he just was never sure who would be doing it or when it would happen. In fact, it seemed to come sooner than he had expected. Just a few days earlier, he had gotten an encoded message in what seemed to the normal eye to be an ordinary, typed letter from a friend. This was the way James and his members had always contacted each other through prison walls. It was a simple, but virtually undetectable technique, known solely to members of Los Ultimos Dias. Just in case something was found, the person sending the letter never used his or her real name. Because of this, James had no way of knowing exactly which member had sent the letter, but the list of possibilities couldn't have been too long.

"Who is he and where is he?" James demanded.

"He is here, but he is not your concern at the moment, James."

"Tell him to come out where I can see him."

"He's already in here. Whether you can see him or not is not really my problem, is it?"

"What?" James asked as he strained his sight in an attempt to make out the man's face through the thickness of the shadows that concealed it. "You don't even make any sense. How did you find this place?"

"There will be time for questions," the man answered from the shadows behind the leather chair in the middle of the room.

James was growing increasingly angry, especially by the man's apparent attempt to avoid his questions. Until this moment, he had been certain that even among a membership nearing two hundred, no one except select members of Los Ultimos Dias had known of the existence of this place. Even some who did were unaware of its actual whereabouts. Now, a man stood before him who not just did not belong in the cabin but who also, up to this point, was completely unfamiliar. Although James found himself somewhat intimidated by the situation, a feeling he hadn't experienced in this way since boyhood, he refused to show it.

"You remind me of your father you know," the man said after a slight chuckle.

"My father?" James was beginning to reach his breaking point. He already knew that at some point he would either have to attack the man or run out the door and into the woods, but the man was beginning to make his decision on which to do rather easy. "What do you know about my father, old man?"

"Your father was once a man," the old man continued. "Just like you."

"He was nothing like me!" James interrupted.

"Oh, he was very much like you," said the man. "Until he began to slip."

James' desire to grab and strangle the man was growing by the second. The stranger had obviously crossed the line, but for some reason, James couldn't help but hold back, at least for the moment. It might have been the talk about his father, something James himself hadn't talked more than a couple sentences about in years.

"He met a woman," the man stated, still pacing but now looking back at James as well. "Had a couple kids, tried to settle down. That was a big mistake."

"Why would that be such a mistake?" James asked, still angry.

"Because James. There's no place for all that happy family crap in a black heart. There's no room for all the 'love everyone' and 'be like Christ' nonsense, especially when it's with a Christian woman who's trying to make Christian kids. Come on James, you know all this right?" The man seemed to be taking delight in his words.

James stood quietly for a moment as billows of anger rose throughout every vein of his soul, causing him to tremble ferociously. His white knuckled fists clinched tightly against the palms of his rugged, thick-skinned hands. This was the first time in several years that anyone had dared to cross him, but the first time since he was a child that anyone had spoken of his family and what happened to them. It wasn't that James thought the man was wrong, just extremely disrespectful.

"Tell me who you are!" James demanded angrily. "Now!"

The man stopped and lifted his finger towards James as a reflection of light moved over the dark green center of his narrowing eyes. "You are in no place to demand anything of me!" he responded with a fiery, booming tone that echoed into the thick woods surrounding the cabin.

"You don't know who you're talking to old man!" James shouted.

Suddenly, as the man lowered his arm, the oil lamp hanging next to the front door next to James violently ruptured and burst into flames, sending small pieces of glass into the air and splattering inflamed oil to the wall and a large portion of the floor. The flames quickly began to spread into each other as the cabin began to tremble. In a matter of seconds, the cabin was shaking violently as various shelves and tables tumbled to the floor. The sounds of breaking glass and falling objects could be heard coming from every room in the house. The fire from the destroyed oil lamp was rising and now covered the only doorway into and out of the cabin.

Although startled by the outburst and the chaos ensuing around him, James kept his ground and did the best that he could to seem unyielding. Not even the rapidly spreading fire at his feet and on the wall behind him had caused him to move from his original position. It was as if he was taunting the man, silently telling him to "bring it on." The dark man gazed past James' wide-opened eyes and into his clouded soul, taking careful measure of every moment of his reaction. As billows of smoke filled the room, the two men continued to unwaveringly size each other up.

The dark man began to laugh cruelly while James watched him from across the room, sweating profusely and breathing heavily. The fire between the men was now rising toward the ceiling, licking the rafters above. The two continued to stare at each other, even through the wall of flames and thickening smoke. James widened his stance as his window of opportunity to either escape or attack the man began to close.

"I will kill you!" James yelled above the rumbling and crackling around them. He placed one foot in front of the other and readied himself for whatever was coming next.

"Kill me?" the man responded, still smiling.

All of the rage that had been ensuing over the past few moments seemed to be taking over James' mind and body, suddenly manifesting itself in the form of a vicious lunge in the direction of his dark adversary. With his hands outstretched in front of him, he was just about to grasp the old man's neck when he was abruptly stopped in his tracks, as if somebody had stepped right in front of him. He quickly found himself being held back by some other being, someone or something that had not been there before, and even now was invisible to the human eye. James struggled aggressively, but to no avail. Whatever was holding him back was either extremely strong or not alone. Regardless, James was not going to allow anybody to ignore his belligerent defiance. Not even the highly uncanny events unfurling around him were enough to quiet his fury.

"I am going to kill you." James stated under his heavy, arduous breathing. Exhaustion and heat, combined with the unwavering force being applied both ways, finally forced him to his knees amidst the irrepressible fire. "I am going to kill you old man," he continued with resolve, trying to catch his breath.

"You are going to what?" the old man asked behind a grimace covered smile.

With his arms still being held and his head down, James lifted his eyes towards the man with hate in his eyes. "I am going to kill you," he stated once more

"Kill me?" the man said, laughing. "Why James, you know you can't do that."

"I can, and will," James said, fatigued but unwilling to concede.

"You can't kill me," said the dark man as he lifted his hat off of his head. "You see, I'm already dead. You, however, already know that...don't you James?"

James looked upon the man's pale and withered face then immediately froze in horror. His face turned from red to white as arms dropped limp to the floor.

"After all," the man resumed. "You were there, son."

IX

Drew bit his lip as he watched the television set at his mother's house with close attention. The press conference at Ware State Penitentiary had just ended and pictures of James Walker were being shown about every five minutes. Calls poured into radio, television, and police stations from people with tips regarding Walker and his accomplice. Drew gripped the arm of the couch as he watched.

"What is it, son?" Drew's mother, Barbara asked from the recliner next to the couch. At first Drew didn't respond. "Drew? What's wrong?"

"It's all just so crazy," Drew said. There was another moment of silence.

"All of this weird stuff," he continued. "First Jim gets literally attacked by some weirdo then this weird old man follows me to the hospital, then Jim tells me all this stuff about me and Dad, then there's this escape at the prison. Not to mention the crazy dark clouds overhead. I just feel like it's all connected somehow or something. But I mean, what in the world's going on here?"

"Jim told you didn't he?" Barbara inquired.

"How did you know?" Drew asked.

"How would I not know?" she answered. "You're my son."

"I just don't know what to think. This is all crazy. How could it all be true?"

"Listen to me Drew. When your father first told me about his dream, the day after he had it, my initial reaction was, 'Okay, he's gone crazy.' I thought that surely it was just a strange dream, that's all. But your father, well, he convinced me otherwise. Now when I look back on it I feel guilty."

"Guilty? Why?"

"Because," Drew's mother responded as she started to sob. "I thought he was crazy, even if it was for just a short time. He didn't know that, but he didn't deserve it from me. He was a good man, the most Godly I've ever known."

"You shouldn't feel guilty," Drew assured his mother. "It was a perfectly natural reaction."

The room fell quiet once again as the weather portion of the news was starting. The strange clouds were being called "an act of mother nature," something we've never seen but that we shouldn't be alarmed about. So far, the data that weather teams had gathered showed nothing abnormal about the clouds. It was, however, determined that the dense and dark clouds were slowly dropping. Since they arrived, they have already dropped a little over three inches.

"It's real, Andrew," Barbara stated as she looked up at her son. "It's all real. I know it's hard to believe, but you'll see, I promise."

"Why can't I at least have some sort of guide book or something?" Drew asked.

"Oh, but you do son," interrupted Barbara. "Your guide book is the Bible."

"This kind of stuff isn't in the Bible though. I've studied the Bible my whole life. How can the Bible be my guide if there's nothing there about this?"

"Andrew, look at me," his mother said firmly. "God speaks to his people in many ways, and the Bible is a really big one. If it doesn't apply to you, then it doesn't apply to any of us. That would mean that it only applies to the people who lived during Biblical times. The Bible speaks to each one of us, individually. When you're reading the scripture, you have to apply it to your own life, and your own circumstances. You have to let it take shape in your life and conform to your heart. When you do that, you'll see that the entire Bible applies to you, just as it does to me, and as it did to your father."

"I guess if it was all out in front of me," Drew stated. "You know, if it was just right here in black and white for me to see."

"Where would your faith be if it were all out in front of you, Andrew?" his mother responded. "What kind of relationship would you have with God if faith was not at the center of it? Faith is what connects you to your Father in Heaven. Your faith is what will guide you. What if He just popped up like a genie every time you called on Him? Your relationship with God is made stronger through faith, son. It is necessary."

Barbara cautiously lifted herself from her chair so as not to bother her knee and hopped on one leg over to the couch next to Drew. She knew that Drew's time had come, for him to fulfill God's will for his life. She pulled a small object wrapped in tissue paper from her pocket.

"A couple months before your father died…" she said. "…he gave me this and asked that I give it to you whenever I felt the time was right." Barbara removed the tissue paper carefully and pulled out a small, dark green, metal compass. "This was your grandfather's," Barbara explained as she handed the compass to her son.

Drew's grandfather, on his father's side, was a war veteran who had lived to be nearly eighty. He passed away when Drew was seven years old. Although he never got the chance to know him personally, he had been told stories about his grandfather all his life. Even after Drew's father passed away, Barbara carried on many times about her husband's father and how he was a brave war hero. Miles Andrew Engel III had served in the United States Army Air Force as a pilot of the deadly P-51 Mustang. He retired a highly decorated officer shortly after World War II had ended.

"He gave it to your Dad when he was just a kid," she continued as Drew examined the used and worn compass. "Grandpa Engel told David that he used it to find his way many times during the war, and that if he ever got lost, he should use it to find his way home."

Drew turned the compass over to find words inscribed into the metal on the bottom. Underneath the words was an important Christian symbol, the fish, simply drawn with two curved lines. The three words above the fish were difficult to make out because of the scratches and chipped paint. In addition, there wasn't enough light in the room and Drew's eyes would not focus well enough for him to see what it said. It didn't look like a name, and it certainly wasn't somebody's initials.

"I can't make it out," Drew said to his mother.

"You will son," she responded. "Don't worry, you will. The three words inscribed on that compass will be the only three words you ever need to know."

Drew stood from the couch and walked over to his mother to give her a hug. He always considered his mother a "guiding light" in his life. She never steered him wrong and never let him down. Drew knew that no matter what was going on, he could turn to his mother. Not only did she help Drew find peace during this visit, but she also confirmed everything that Jim had told him.

"I gotta' get to the airport," Drew said as he leaned over and gave his mother a hug.

"I'll leave the light on," Barbara responded. "If you need me."

Adjacent Cove was quiet and dark. Ware State Penitentiary was close enough to the town to cause most people to stay at home behind their locked doors and alarms. Those who did get out did so cautiously. Drew sat at a stop sign in the middle of one of Adjacent Cove's undeveloped neighborhoods. There was nobody around. The streets were dark and eerie.. Many of the street lights were out for some reason and the one above Drew's black SUV flickered as if it was trying to go out too.

Drew sat in his truck with both hands on the steering wheel and fell into deep thought. He deliberated everything that had happened and everything that he had been told. He looked down at the compass in the seat next to him and reached out to grab it. Holding it tightly with both hands Drew bowed his head and began to pray.

"God, I need direction," he began. "You are so incredible and powerful and mighty and I want nothing less than to serve You in any and every way that I can. You've given me so much, some of which I've taken for granted. I don't know where to go from here, Lord. I don't know what…"

Suddenly two giant claws slammed into Drew's windshield, shattering it from side to side. The back claws pierced the hood of the truck with tremendous force as the front claws tore through the windshield and through the dashboard. Drew pocketed his compass as he removed his seatbelt then quickly jumped through the space in between the front seats into the floor board in the back. A loud screech coming from the creature caused one of Drew's ears to start bleeding. Without even realizing it, his forehead was cut open and bleeding down his face from one of the enormous claws that penetrated the windshield directly in front of him.

Although he hadn't seen the entire creature yet, Drew knew without a doubt that this was something other worldly. There was nothing on earth that could do what this thing was doing to Drew's truck. Next he had to try to figure out what it was after. Most likely, it was after him. After everything he had experienced and heard throughout the day, it was highly probable that Drew was going to have no choice but to defend himself. His hands began to shake as he reached for one of the door handles in the back.

The large creature shrieked once more as it began to lift the truck from the ground. It was time for Drew to act quickly and in a manner that would keep him alive. He pushed the door open and pulled himself out before finally falling around ten feet to the ground. Somehow, he had landed on his feet and now stood before his attacker. He felt nothing but poise, no fear, no anxiety, just self-confidence and strength. What he would see next would change him forever.

Drew took a few steps back as he watched the enormous, black creature rip his truck in two with its massive eagle-like talons. The creature then noticed that Drew had gotten out and threw the disassembled vehicle into the empty lot next to them. It then landed about twenty yards from where Drew was standing and let out another horrifying shriek.

The black beast had large, leathery wings with a wing span of at least fifty feet. At the end of its wings were three bony fingers and a thumb, all with razor sharp, pointed nails at the ends. The powerful claws, two in the front and one in the back were like a bird's, black in color and rather large in proportion. Its body and bat-like head were hairless and its mouth was full of white, pointed teeth and drool. The creature stared down at Drew with its blood-red eyes and snarled as it began to growl and hiss atrociously. Acidic drool fell from its mouth and ate into the pavement.

After a momentary shock, Drew closed his eyes and fell to his knees with his arms reaching toward the sky. The clouds above him began to swirl in a circular motion as the wind began to pick up. All of a sudden a bolt of lightning struck the ground with an awesome force right in front of Drew. The ungodly creature waiting to attack him was knocked backwards several feet by the force of the lightning.

Drew remained on his knees with his hands raised to the sky, and his eyes closed. After a few moments, he lowered his arms and head. His hair color had been changed to solid black. Behind his bangs Drew opened his eyes halfway. The color of his eyes had been changed as well, to a very light, almost translucent blue. They glowed brightly in the darkness of the night.

Drew rose to his feet, never taking his eyes off the creature as it picked itself up. He felt different, stronger, and more aware. He heard his father's voice as if he was right there next to him.

"Your struggle is not against flesh and blood," the voice said. "It is against the rulers, against the powers, against the world forces of this darkness."

The creature stood and covered itself with its wings. Suddenly it began to shrink, all the way down to Drew's size. As it opened its wings, the beast was gone and an angel was in its place.

"It is against the spiritual forces of wickedness in the heavenly places," the voice continued. "Remember that people are not the enemy, whether they are good or bad. Everything that happens on earth is the result of what happens in the spiritual realm. You have a sixth sense, a keen awareness of what is going on in the spiritual dimension. This is who you are, son. You are your Father in Heaven's creation. You are an angel, unlike any other."

The angel stood there, across the street, studying Drew carefully. He wore a long white robe with white clothing underneath and was surrounded by an unnatural glow. His hair was short and snow white. His face was as normal as any human being, except for his eyes, which were blood red, just like the creature. The angel had come as the large beast that tore the truck apart in an attempt to harm Drew. The only thing that he really did accomplish was to help Drew find his true self.

After hearing his father's voice, Drew felt more ready than ever. He raised his hands to the sky once more. As he held his hands as high as he could, two blades began to emerge in each hand. They seemed to come from nowhere. Within seconds, Drew was holding a sword in each hand. The identical swords had black handles and blades that were two and a half feet long by one and a half inches wide. The swords were made to be indestructible.

Drew gripped the swords tightly in his hands and put one foot forward to put himself into a ready position. The sword in his left hand was pointed a bit outward and toward the ground in front of him. His right hand was held high with the sword pointed forward a few inches from his face. Both swords suddenly erupted in blue flames, from the handles to the tips. Drew remained ready for whatever was coming next.

The angel across the street had slowly made his way to Drew and was now standing just a few feet away. It was obvious from the beginning that this was a fallen angel, the kind that Drew was supposed to defeat. This was Drew's first time, but he was not intimidated. He had kept both eyes on the angel the entire time and was scrutinizing him with every step. The angel could have come as that ferocious beast and Drew would still be standing his ground ready to attack if necessary.

The fallen angel took one step closer and spoke.

"My name is Boznik," the angel said. "And you must be 'the chosen one' who's supposed to save your town, and your whole county. Am I right?"

"You messed with the wrong Christian today," Drew responded.

"Is that right?" Boznik stated as he laughed. "You are nothing boy. You should go back home and just leave this kind of stuff to the real angels."

"This is your last warning," Drew sternly declared. "Leave this town, leave this state, and never return."

Boznik let out a vile laugh that echoed into the night. "Seriously kid," he said. "You can't do this, and you know it. You will be on your back looking up at me while I choke the life out of you."

Drew never did like threats, especially if it was a threat to kill. It made him angry, angrier than he already was. Without warning, Drew sprung at his adversary swinging both enflamed swords with control and precision that he never knew he had. Boznik ducked and pulled back to avoid being struck by one of the blades. Drew continued to attack as his opponent continued to shift in exact movements to keep from being hit. All of a sudden one of the tips of the blades landed on Boznik's face, cutting him deeply across his cheek.

Boznik was temporarily stunned as black blood began to run down the side of his face. This gave Drew the opportunity he was looking for. A swift and perfectly executed roundhouse caught Boznik on the jaw, knocking him to the ground. Drew stood over him and crossed his swords under the demon's neck.

"You can't kill me," Boznik said, laughing quietly.

"Who said anything about killing?" Drew asked. "You are headed to the Abyss."

Boznik stopped his laughing and looked up at Drew. One side of his face was covered in black blood and the other was bruising at the jaw. His glow was gone and his demeanor changed.

"How does it feel?" Drew asked.

"How does what feel," the angry demon asked.

"To be lying on your back looking up at me, just before I take the life out of you?" Drew responded.

Boznik hissed and growled at Drew as he struggled to get free. Drew had one foot on Boznik's body and the other on the ground. The swords were still crossed at the fallen angel's neck. Drew quickly pulled the swords apart, completely severing Boznik's head. The demon wailed aloud as his body slowly turned to dust and flew away into the darkness.

Drew stood up, breathing heavily. He could barely believe what just happened. He had never taken a single martial arts class, he had never handled any kind of weapon in his life, excluding a pocket knife here and there. There had never been a time in his life that he felt as strong and confident as he did at that moment. The two swords disappeared into his hands and his eyes stopped glowing. His eye color was still a very light blue and his hair was jet black. He wasn't sure how he would explain that to people, but he did not want to worry about it too much at the moment.

As he began to walk down the street, he reached for his cell phone to call a taxi. He still had to get to the airport, and soon. Directly in front of him was the front half of his destroyed SUV. As he walked by, he noticed his hair and eyes in the reflection off of one of the windows. He stopped and looked at himself in bewilderment. His vision had changed dramatically but he never knew that his eyes had changed in appearance as well. He ran his fingers through his black hair.

"Crazy…" he said to himself before continuing on down the street.

All of the streetlights began to turn back on, making it easier to see where he was going. While digging for his phone, he found the compass that his mother had given him earlier. He pulled it from his pocket and turned it over. The words inscribed on the bottom were as clear as day. He stopped for a moment and sat down on a curb, still looking at the bottom of the compass.

There it was plain and simple, a message of guidance and hope. Underneath the words was the Christian fish. According to his mother, these were the three words that would get him through everything. Drew held the compass tightly to his chest and looked to the sky as he whispered the words to himself.

"Forget Me Not."

X

Drew opened his eyes to complete darkness. He was lying down on a hard, smooth surface that must have been solid black. There was a bit of a fog, making it that much more difficult to see anything around. As he stood up, Drew noticed that he was wearing a robe, though he could not tell what color it was. It was cold and eerie, and the dark was dizzying. Drew held out his arms and stepped forward with caution.

"Hello?" he called out. His voice echoed back to him with no response. As he moved through the darkness, the mist parted and moved around him, making it more difficult to grasp his equilibrium. He continued to walk forward with his arms out, trying desperately to see anything around that would let him know where he was.

"Is anyone there?" he cried. The space beyond his reach remained still and quiet. Drew stopped and took a deep breath as he tried his best to collect himself. Searching for his bearings seemed hopeless, but that didn't stop him from trying. He searched throughout his robe, trying not to be frantic, looking for his compass and cell phone. There was nothing, not even a pocket.

Suddenly, a gust of mist passed swiftly by his side, causing Drew to turn around. He held out his hands, trying to discover what was in his presence. Whatever it was, Drew couldn't decide whether to reach out for it or prepare to defend himself.

"Hello!" he yelled out once more. "Who is there?" Once again, his cries only echoed back to him from deep within the darkness in front of him.

Again, all of a sudden, a breeze blew past Drew, this time in the other direction and on the other side. It was obvious that somebody or something was there, toying with him. He turned around once again, trying to follow the path of the gust. The mist in front of him began to thin out, making it possible for Drew to see just a few inches in front of him. It was still dark, however, making mobility extremely difficult. Drew felt that he had no choice but to brace himself and prepare to leap out at whatever was there with him. His timing would have to be perfect.

With the thinning mist, Drew was able to see further ahead of him, making it possible to see when there was a disturbance coming his way. It wasn't long before his opportunity came. He hurled forward towards the coming gust and quickly found himself in the path of what appeared to be a dragon. His eyes widened and his heart raced as the monster darted towards him with its mouth opening, revealing its large, razor sharp teeth. Drew looked to his hands as his two swords emerged and lit up in blue flames. As he readied to defend himself, suddenly everything went blank.

The dark and misty environment, the evil dragon, the swords, everything disappeared as Drew found himself once again lying down with his eyes closed. This time, he was back on the street where he had been previously. He picked himself up and shook his head. He must have fallen asleep. It was all a dream, a rather intense dream, but nothing new for Drew. He walked over to the edge of the street and sat down, trying to refocus himself on the reality of his situation.

Drew sat on the curb under the streetlight looking down at the pavement in disbelief of what had happened before he apparently fell asleep. It had all happened so fast, giving him no time to prepare. Still, he managed the situation quite well, without having any prior experience in fighting or facing such an opponent, or any opponent for that matter. He pulled his compass from his pocket and looked into the reflection off of the glass covering its needle. His hair and eyes had both turned back to their normal color.

As he stared into the face of the compass, Drew wondered, and even began to worry, about where he was supposed to go and what he was supposed to do next. He turned the compass over, rubbing his fingers over the inscription on the bottom, as he began to pray. All of his life, Drew had been trained to pray anytime he found himself in darkness. Now, he needed God more than ever.

"I won't forget You, Lord," he said aloud as he closed his prayer. "Just please don't forget me either."

Just as his mother had said, Drew could do nothing at this point but remember the inscription. As long as he kept the Holy Spirit in front of him, he could conquer anything. He also remembered what his mother had told him about the Bible. Now more than ever, Drew could see what she was trying to say. There were many verses that he had memorized over the years that now had a very real meaning that tied into his personal purpose.

"I can do all things…" Drew began to quote from the book of Philippians. "…through Him who strengthens me." With his head still bowed, Drew was suddenly startled by a voice coming from across the street.

"Come with me," a man said, standing just a few feet in front of Drew. His face looked familiar and Drew realized that it was the man who had followed him to the hospital earlier that morning and sat in the lobby for a while. This time, however, he wore a long vanilla colored robe with a black sash and brown sandals. He looked like he came straight from a Biblical movie set. The man held out his hand towards Drew as if silently asking him to trust him.

Drew stood to his feet. The man was strange, and certainly out of place, but seemed harmless enough. Still, he was cautious. Judging by the preceding events, Drew was a bit unsure of who to trust at this moment. His senses were strong, but a long way from being completely fine tuned.

"Who are you?" Drew inquired as he slowly made his way towards the man.

"A friend," the man answered. "My name is Alazar. Please, come with me."

As Drew approached the other side of the street, the man stepped onto the sidewalk and began to walk. Drew stood on the street for a moment, contemplating what he should do. His situation called for caution, but at the moment, he felt that it also called for trust. Finally, Drew gave in and began to walk with the man. As the two walked down the fairly lit sidewalk, Alazar remained quiet for a time before beginning to speak.

"You were created for a special purpose Andrew," Alazar began "You are different, as I'm sure you've just discovered."

"You can say that," Drew responded.

"You are an angel," Alazar continued. "Part man, part angel. This gives you an advantage that no other angel has. This is why they wish to destroy you. You will always be an angel, but you will not always be a man. You were actually created long ago. Then you were reborn as a man. You have always existed."

Drew stopped for a moment. "I don't understand," he stated.

"Please," Alazar pleaded. "Keep walking, we don't have much time."

Drew started walking again. "So, can you explain that to me?" he asked.

"It's simple," said Alazar. "You were created with all of the other angels. Your name is Eleazar. A few years ago, God sent you on a special mission, which required that you be reborn as a man. This way you would have an advantage. You are both man and angel. You can exist both in your natural dimension and in the spiritual realm. You will remember who you are in time. This, you will simply have to trust me on."

The two continued to walk down the dreary sidewalk, until the man suddenly stopped and turned towards a line of trees beside them. As Drew followed, Alazar parted the large bushes in the tree line and walked through them. Drew followed him through the thick brush and trees until they came to an opening. Suddenly, they were in a large park with walkways and benches. The paths and benches were lit by small street lamps, providing the exclusive light in the area. A thin haze blanketed the area, compliments of the low, dark clouds overhead. An odd feeling came over Drew as they walked through the quiet and still landscape. Something wasn't right.

"You need to understand," Alazar stated. "Spiritual war is a major conflict. It is the war of all wars. Everything that happens in the spiritual realm manifests itself in the physical world. Everything from individual people to the very culture itself is affected by what happens in the spiritual war. The impact is greater than you can imagine."

Drew listened closely as they walked towards one of the pathways in the park. Alazar crossed over it and continued up a small hill towards another tree line. As they reached the top, they turned to see a boy walking along the pathway towards a bench. He was listening to an mp3 player and bobbing his head to the music. He wore a blue jean jacket over a hooded sweatshirt with the hood covering his head.

"You have a great power Drew," Alazar said. "…as well as a great responsibility. There are people and angels alike that will be relying on you."

The young boy, no older than fifteen, sat on the bench and rocked back and forth as he continued to listen to his music. On the other side of the park, in the trees, Drew could see several pair of yellow eyes moving about in the trees. Whatever they were, he could hear them rustling around, laughing, and hissing. Drew was still giving Alazar his full attention, but was occasionally distracted by the commotion, as well.

"You will know in your heart where you are to go and what you are to do," the man continued. "The Holy Spirit will guide you. But you must remember that man is not your enemy. You will have the ability to distinguish between a man who is possessed and a fallen angel who has materialized as a man, but you must make the right choice."

"What about the monster that tore up my truck?" Drew asked.

"Boznik was sent to destroy you," Alazar answered. "They don't want you to be what you are. They want to take the mortal aspect away from you. But you responded the way that you did because of what you are."

"I just…changed," Drew said.

"You acted as the angel," Alazar responded. "…because you had to."

The boy sitting on the bench began to reach into all of his pockets. He was looking for something, but there was no way to tell what it was. Suddenly, the boy pulled a .38 caliber revolver from his sweatshirt pocket. As he did so, the creatures in the trees began to jump around in the branches. The boy was unaware of what was going on in the trees as he began to load the weapon with bullets that he carried in his jacket pocket.

Alerted by what he was seeing, Drew began to run for the boy until Alazar grabbed his arm and pulled him back. The boy on the bench finished loading the pistol and placed it in his lap. He was alone and unaware of the existence of anyone or anything around him.

"I have to do something," Drew said with haste. "He's gotta' gun."

"He can't see you," Alazar responded, still holding Drew's arm. "Trust me Andrew, I didn't bring you here to watch a disaster."

Drew watched intently as the boy pulled out his ear buds and raised his head to the sky. Tears streamed down the boy's face and his entire body trembled in fear. He lifted the gun to his temple and pulled back the hammer. As he looked to the sky he cried out as loud as he could.

"Jesus," he said, crying and trembling uncontrollably. "…if You're real, now is the time to prove it."

At this the creatures in the tree began to charge forward towards the boy, one by one. The beasts were ghastly, all alike, with large leathery wings. They were solid black with pointed ears, spikes for teeth, and yellow eyes. They snarled through their snub noses and hissed through their teeth as they sprung towards the boy. The boy closed his eyes and shook, with his finger on the trigger and ready to fire.

All of a sudden, a bright blue light dashed through the sky above the trees behind Drew and Alazar. It was headed straight for the demonic creatures gaining on the small boy. One of the beasts reached out for the boy with its fierce claws and just before getting to him the blue light struck the ground in front of them, knocking all of the demons backwards. The boy remained in his position, with the gun to his head, unaware of what was going on around him.

Drew stood motionless as he watched the scene in awe. From the ground in front of the boy emerged an angel clothed in a white robe and yielding an enormous sword that gleamed against the light surrounding him. He had large wings protruding from his back that were covered with snow white feathers. The angel stood in front of the boy with his sword in front of him, ready to protect the boy from the evil creatures. One by one the demons picked themselves up from the ground and attacked with all they had, and one by one the angel drove them back with his mighty sword.

The young boy on the bench finally repositioned the hammer on the pistol and lowered it to his lap. The tears ceased to fall as he continued to look to the sky. The boy then smiled as a gust of hope and peace flowed throughout his entire body. He opened the revolver and dropped the bullets to the ground in front of him.

Meanwhile, the angel protecting the boy stood firmly in front of him with his sword ready. Weary and defeated, some demons flew away and others fled on foot, their wings too damaged to fly. Drew watched closely as the angel turned and looked down at the boy. He sheathed his sword and placed his hand over the young man's head.

"Peace be with you," the angel whispered, before opening his wings and disappearing into the night sky.

The boy rose from his seat and tossed the pistol into a trash can next to the bench. As he walked back down the pathway in the opposite direction, he dried his tears and smiled. Drew, moved by what had just occurred, dropped to the ground on his knees.

Alazar walked closer and placed his hand on Drew's shoulder. "Do you see?" he asked.

"I see," responded Drew.

Drew watched as the last of the demons disappeared into the bushes on the other side of the park. Alazar turned and walked towards the tree line behind them. Drew stood and turned to follow him, occasionally looking back at the park bench. The two men made their way through the thick brush of the tree line and into a thick wooded area. Just a few feet ahead was a clearing with lights, assumed to be some part of Adjacent Cove.

As they moved through the trees, Drew began to pat his pockets in search of his cell phone.

"What's wrong?" Alazar asked.

"My cell phone," Drew responded. "I know I had it earlier." Reaching into one of his back pockets, he retrieved his phone and started pressing buttons. "Ahh," he said. "Battery's dead."

"What do you need it for?" inquired Alazar.

"Oh, just...I need to call someone," Drew answered. "I'm supposed to be at the airport right now."

"But you are at the airport," Alazar said.

"What?" Drew asked.

Suddenly a loud noise coming from behind them alarmed Drew, causing him to duck. A bright light appeared, like a car headlight, but much brighter. Whatever it was, it was flying low and coming fast. Drew crouched nearly all the way to the ground as a 747 jet airliner flew directly over them with its landing gear down. Drew sighed in relief as he picked himself up and tried not to be embarrassed.

"I've uh," Drew began. "I've seen a lot tonight, you know. It's been a bit crazy and all."

"No need to explain Andrew," Alazar responded over a hushed laugh. "Now go."

Just through the clearing was one of Austin International Airport's many runways. Drew was just a jog away from making it to pick up Alyssa. Of course, he still had to figure out how he was going to get her to Adjacent Cove without a vehicle, but at this point he was quite thrilled to have made it this far. He stepped out of the brush and took a deep breath before brushing off his clothes and fixing his hair. Just before walking away, he turned to the man behind him, unsure of what he wanted to say.

"You're going to be fine," Alazar said, before Drew could say anything. "Just trust your gut and forget Him not."

"You never told me your story." Drew stated.

The man walked out of the wooded area and stood directly in front of Drew.

"I am known as Alazar of Bethany," he said. "I was once in total darkness. My arms and legs were bound and I could not move. I was cold and afraid. I thought I'd been lost forever. I thought of my family and friends. I thought of the birds chirping in the trees and the gentle flow of the fresh water spring near my home. I was so afraid. Then, all of a sudden, a light appeared in front of me. It seemed to come from nowhere. I could even see it through the linen that covered my face. Then I heard a familiar voice, the voice of a dear friend of mine. He said three words, and I was free. Free from the darkness, and free from the strips of cloth that were wrapped around me. It was like being freed from a dungeon.

"Please understand Drew, I have come to bring light into your darkness. I have come to free you from your doubts. What I have told you and shown you tonight is absolute. Nothing can take who you are away from you, nothing and no one. You have a gift, and with that gift, a responsibility. You must go forward now and seek God's perfect will for both yourself and your world around you. Your town, your whole county, is in danger. It is in grave danger Drew. You must go forward and deliver your people from the clutches of Lucifer. You cannot let your town fall to him, or he will use it to take control of every town around it, then every county, every state, and so on.

"God has been preparing you for this your entire life Drew," the man continued. "He has been working in His own way, being careful not to make you aware of your destiny too soon. It's a lot to grasp in such a short time, I know this. But you are the only person in the world who is capable. Remember, you were an angel before being reborn as a man. You literally have thousands of years of experience at this kind of thing. For you, in this situation, it will just be a matter of remembering it all, like you did earlier tonight when you faced Boznik. You, Andrew Engel, have been chosen"

The man came closer and looked directly into Drew's eyes as he placed one hand on his shoulder. "You," he stated in a rigid tone. "…have been chosen." He patted Drew's shoulder and then turned and walked back towards the tree line.

"What were the three words?" Drew asked with his arms crossed.

The man stopped just before entering the thick brush and turned back.

"Lazarus, come forth."

XI

Just outside the eastern city limits of Adjacent Cove was a large hill that residents called "L Mountain" because of the particular rock formation on the side that formed a perfect "L". On the other side of the hill laid miles of rocky, tree covered hills and small valleys that stretched deep into the horizon ahead. For the most part, the land was privately owned, and a large portion of that was farmland. It was the Texas Hill Country at its best, laced with everything from dirt roads to paved country roads.

Approximately four miles out, in between two hills laid a small valley, half of which was an indentation that had once been a reservoir. The twenty or so acre valley was owned by local Englishman Thomas Jasper, a wealthy banker who had built quite a reputation for himself since moving to the area from his homeland seventeen years ago. After opening and then selling a successful chain of banks in England, he had decided to try his luck in rural America, where he would feel the most comfortable. So far, his plan was paying off, with over thirty branches having been opened in south Texas to date. His first branch, Trenton State Bank, had been opened just a year after his move to Adjacent Cove and within a year was serving thousands of local citizens in and around the city.

For many years, Mr. Jasper had served on multiple boards and councils, including the school board, and currently held a seat in many of the local social clubs and organizations. His physical stature was nothing impressive, at just five feet eight inches, but his voice in the community, English accent included, had earned him an enormous amount of respect over the years. He was not married and had no children, but was never alone outside of his home. Even on Sundays Thomas was never short of those wanting to sit with him at the First United Methodist Church of Adjacent Cove. Still, as with any public figure, there were those that wondered if Mr. Jasper was only trying to create an image for himself, and wasn't really concerned with the general welfare of those around him. The doubts of these might have been warranted, or might have been the result of pure jealousy, but it was difficult to know with a person that was so good at hiding his personal life.

Mr. Jasper had acquired the piece of land just a few years ago, with plans to refill the reservoir and build a park around it that would welcome the public. Unfortunately, his plans fell through just months after purchasing the land and acquiring the necessary permits to build and eventually publicize his park. According to rumors, he had been audited by the IRS and charged a large amount of money for back taxes. In the end, he still owned the property, but it was largely ignored since its acquisition. After a couple of years, this gave a certain order of locals the opportunity that they had been waiting for to move their operations out of the city in order to preserve their secrecy.

Just outside the valley on Mr. Jasper's land was a small wooded area, ten or so acres squared, that provided the perfect cover for Los Ultimos Dias to meet without drawing attention to themselves or being bothered by nosy citizens. Luckily, most of the forest cover was a part of Mr. Jasper's land. The other, small portion of the woods belonged to a retired farmer who never ventured far enough away from his home to notice anything, especially at night. For a time, Mr. Jasper had been completely unaware of what was going on, but was not against the group's use of his property when eventually approached by James Walker. This time, however, it was not James' usual intimidation methods that had convinced him, it was also the percentage of stolen cash offered him. For a person like Thomas Jasper, money spoke louder than words themselves, especially after apparently losing so much to the government.

Behind the thick trees and brush and hidden quite well by the tree line on Mr. Jasper's land was a large barn made of wood. The barn was new, built in recent years, not unlike any other structure that would be expected to be found there. Of course, it was just another cover to keep outsiders from being suspicious of anything. Inside the barn were several rows of chairs, enough to seat around two hundred people, with standing room for many more. At the end of the barn, in front of the chairs, was a large stage that stretched across the entire width of space with a bulky podium in the middle. The podium had a pentagram carved into it that was colored red. On the wall behind the stage hung an authentic goat's head that had large, curling horns protruding from either side. The floor of the barn was nothing more than small rocks and dirt. Both the outside and inside of the barn were painted black, both to further conceal it in the trees and to provide a dark atmosphere inside. Light was provided by several oil lamps hanging along the walls and behind the stage.

Los Ultimos Dias had been meeting at this location every Saturday night for the past few years. Their leader, James Walker, spoke passionately from the podium about his plans for what he called a "new world order" involving the ousting of Christian influence and ideas and the introduction of Satan's order. They had many rituals and animal sacrifices there which took place outside, just beside the barn in a large clearing in the woods. There was a stone altar in the middle of a large pentagram that had been drawn onto the ground by rocks embedded in the earth. Around and within the pentagram were used candles and small fire pits.

The air seemed unusually thick on this night and was littered with patches of fog, possibly provided by the cloud cover and strange weather pattern that had moved in during the day. The lamps in the barn were already lit and the doors were open, though no one was around. It was as if somebody had recently been there to prepare the place in anticipation of an unscheduled gathering and then left for some reason. The flat, grassy area next to the empty reservoir where the members of Los Ultimos Dias parked their vehicles was especially eerie. The fog seemed to twitch and swirl sporadically from time to time as if something was there moving around. The long path leading up to the tree line where the barn stood, which was basically two lines of flattened grass and dirt created by member's vehicles, disappeared into the darkness just a few feet away. The immediate area seemed to exist in a world of its own, buried in the shadows of the rest of the world.

As expected, a meeting had been specially called to take place shortly. When an impromptu meeting such as this took place, the members would contact each other through a phone tree so that everyone knew about it. It always started with a call to a couple of men from Jarvis Nixon, James' number two man. An assembly such as this would be called if James needed assistance with some sort of illegal activity, what he called an "assignment", or if something had gone wrong with one. But, after watching the news all day, everyone knew what this particular meeting would be about. Most were quite cautious about attending, in fear of being picked up by the sheriff's department or even the FBI. Their membership up to this point had been handled with extreme discretion, with some men even hiding their double lives from their own families.

The calls circulated rather quickly, as usual. The message was the same for everyone, "Poker at three." That meant to meet at the barn at three o'clock in the morning. Only about half of the regular members, totaling somewhere around one hundred and fifty, planned to attend. The others were either too afraid or simply could not get away for one reason or the other. Jarvis and a handful of others would arrive about a half hour early to unlock the barn doors and light all of the lamps, unaware at the moment that someone had already done this well ahead of time.

James woke from unconsciousness unable to open his mouth or eyes. He was hanging upside down with his wrists and ankles bound by thick, steel cuffs. Although he couldn't see, the breeze of the night air made it evident that he was outdoors. The last thing he remembered was staring into the face of the man he had loathed since he was a boy, the man that had killed all of his family save him and then himself. His father had been dead now for more than twenty years, and James was nothing short of perplexed by the sight of him. Before blacking out, he had made one final attempt to attack the man that was supposedly his father, but was stopped short by a blow to the head.

A few yards from the cabin James hung by his feet from one of the thicker branches of an old oak tree in the woods. His neon orange jumpsuit was torn, battered and even bloodied in several places, all obvious signs of his previous struggle. A large chain with cuffs at each end had been thrown over the branch and attached to his ankles, cutting off the blood circulation to his swollen and bruised feet. James' wrists were bound behind his back by another set of cuffs, these connected by two chain links in order to keep them close together. Four pieces of black duct tape around five inches in length formed an "X" over each eye, and his lips were sealed shut by some sort of water resistant adhesive that covered his entire mouth.

James struggled momentarily, just to discover a piercing pain in his nostrils and sides. Two thick and rusty fish hooks usually used for deep sea fishing had been placed deep into his nose and were attached to small chains that were bolted to an exposed tree branch on the ground directly below him. Even larger hooks were run through his sides and fastened around his bottom rib on each side. These hooks were attached to similar chains that were fixed to the large trunk of the tree a couple of feet behind him. James had nowhere to go and no option but to remain as still as possible in order to prevent further agonizing pain and damage to himself. It was painful enough to be hanging still.

After a few moments James could hear something rustling around in the distance. The sound of dead leaves moving around and crackling twigs under heavy footsteps came closer and closer, making him nervous. He wasn't sure whether to be relieved or alert. After what he had experienced earlier, this could be anybody, or anything. As the being came upon him, it stopped directly in front of him, without making a noise. James could not even make out any breathing. He ever so slightly nodded his head in an attempt to make whatever kind of contact he could with whomever was there.

Without warning, the tape over James' eyes was ripped off, piece by piece. At first, all he could see was a blur of darkness. He blinked his eyes repeatedly, trying to clear his vision, as the being then ripped the adhesive from his mouth, taking a layer or two of skin with it. James let out a groan and then stretched out his mouth a bit before closing it. His vision was finally beginning to clear up as he tried to focus in on the large inverted figure in front of him. Even with his eyesight returning to normal, there was not much to make out. Light from the moon was shining on the clouds above, providing a dim, backdrop that made it possible to discern the outline of the person, or being from everything else.

The tall figure began to laugh rather subtly as it squatted down some in order to look James directly in the face. By his stature and laugh, James could only assume that it was a man. He was wearing a black robe with sleeves that covered his entire body and hung over his feet. A hood covered his head and shaded his face. Upon closer inspection, it was apparent that the man actually had no face at all. It was dark grey colored and completely blank. Startled, James began to pull his wrists apart and kick his feet, ignoring the intense pain that it brought.

"Calm down, James," the man said in a hissing voice. "You're not going anywhere."

James stopped and looked at the dark being with disgust. His mouth salivated with anger and hate as his breath grew heavier and more intense. He could feel his heart beating heavily under his chest, as if it was about to jump right out of his body. The muscles in his arms and legs had become so tight that they were jerking occasionally without will. The hooks embedded in his sides and nose were tearing open his skin and doing serious damage to both tissue and bone. The ones in his nose were now even threatening to stab directly into the chambers of his brain if he didn't stop fighting them.

"Come on James, you remember me right?" the creature said, turning his head to the side.

James stopped once again and stared into the blank face of the being in front of him. His breathing calmed a bit as he tried his best to remember if he had ever come across this individual before. For a moment, he seemed familiar, as if he had indeed seen him at some distant point in his life. Despite his best effort to remember, he had no answer.

"It'll come to you," the dark figure said before he stood back up. James had to look down in order to see the man but did the best that he could to keep his eyes on his face at all times.

"Who are you?" James asked, his voice quivering from the pain.

The man turned and walked a few feet away from James, then sat on a stump and faced him once again.

"I don't know who you are," James said with frustration but still in very much pain. "Are you the man that broke me out?"

"No," the man answered. "That was Saithe, and I must say, he did quite well. He managed to kill all those people and pass half the blame on to you. They won't catch him, but you, well, you're human. I'd say you're in quite a jam, not considering your current circumstances, of course."

James was beginning to get dizzy. He was starting to black out again, despite his efforts to stay alert. Blood was now running down his body from both his ankles and his sides and was coming out from under his uniform and streaming down his face. Pain was something that James had a high tolerance for, but he had never experienced it to this magnitude. Even if he had wanted to keep struggling, he could no longer find the strength.

"Stay with me James," the dark creature in front of James' hanging body said.

"Who...," James uttered quietly but with all of the strength he could muster. "Who was that? Was that....my...?"

"Your father?" the man interrupted. "Yes, of course it was James. Who else could it have been?"

"My father is dead," James said.

"No, your father is very much alive," replied the man. "Everyone thought he was dead. That was the point."

"I saw his body," James stated. "He…he shot himself"

"You saw *a* body," the man answered.

"No…" argued James.

"Yes James," said the man as he stood up and walked towards James once again. "If you saw him dead, then how is he alive? You just saw him with your own eyes. It was all part of the plan."

"No," James stated once again, closing his eyes.

"You weren't supposed to live…" the creature continued with his voice seething evilly as he spoke. "…but yet here you are, in the same worthless and forsaken place, spreading a little hell of your own. You were supposed to burn with the other two wastes of human flesh."

The man squatted and looked James directly in the face as if taunting him as he spoke. "That's right James Walker. You are nothing, do you understand? You serve no other purpose than to take up space. All of your work, all of your so called assignments, everything you've done has brought you no closer to anything but your grave. Your worship of the prince of darkness himself has been nothing short of ignored. You are no better than the rest of the filth that went up in flames that night."

Beyond the ability to struggle or even argue to any degree, James' intense anger could solely be expressed by tears. He closed his eyes tightly and tried to somehow tune the man out, but his physical pain, now joined by intense emotional pain, was too much to allow his mind to wander. Although he didn't fully believe what the man was saying, just the thought of it was enough to upset him to this degree. Still, James was a fighter, and he had always been one. Although his options were extremely limited, he did what he could to turn the direction of his thoughts towards surviving.

"Someone…" James managed to get out using every bit of strength he had in him. "Someone will be coming for me, very soon."

The dark creature, still pacing with his arms behind his back, turned and looked back at James. He laughed under his breath as he slowly turned and squatted down where he stood with his hands on his knees.

"You mean…one of your so-called followers?" he asked sarcastically as he laughed a little louder. "One of the empty souls from your little tree house club of half wits, wanna-be's, and wishful thinkers? Are one of those guys going to come for you James?"

James looked back at the man, his anger intensifying with every word that came from his mouth. There were very few members of Los Ultimos Dias that knew of this location, but they were the most loyal and included James' right hand man, Jarvis Nixon. James knew that they would have seen the news and could only assume that he had retreated to the cabin. It was the only safe place that he had, and had served him well many times in the past. Additionally, this was what the cabin was built for to begin with. All of the men would have known to hold off for a bit so as not to alert and lead any officials to the location, but at the very least, Jarvis would be coming before too long to bring food and check in.

"Unfortunately my ambitious friend," the man continued after he stood and continued pacing. "You called one of your early morning get-togethers when you first arrived here, so all your little soldiers are going there to meet you."

"I didn't call anything," James responded, still trying to keep from blacking out.

"Oh, but you did," the man stated. "And just so you know, it looks as though they're going to be tied up for a while, so I wouldn't expect to see any of them soon."

A burst of anger was just enough to provide James with the strength to struggle once more. He twisted and pulled at every device holding him down as hard as he could. Thick streams of blood poured down his legs and now his arms and out of his sides. His once orange jumpsuit was becoming more and more drenched in blood so thick that it appeared black in places. After a half a minute or so, he lost consciousness for the second time as his body went completely limp, finally giving into both a loss of blood and the intense pain.

"Sleep, you louse," the dark creature said as he walked away. "You just might need it."

XII

Time passed and the men gathering at the barn on Mr. Jasper's land were beginning to wonder where there leader was. Jarvis Nixon, James' second hand man, was seated on the stage behind the pulpit, where he always sat during gatherings in order to keep an eye on the congregation and doors. He looked at his watch repeatedly as half an hour pasted, then an hour. Jarvis, along with the rest of the hundred and fifty or so men in attendance would have to be on careful alert during this meeting. James had been in trouble before, but he had never been the subject of a state wide manhunt of this magnitude.

Jarvis kept a steady eye on the closed doors of the barn. Everything inside of him told him to cancel the meeting and send everyone home. At the same time, he didn't want to let his leader and friend down. Finally, after waiting just over an hour, the doors at the back of the barn opened. Everyone held their breath as they waited to see who was on the other side. What they saw was unexpected, to say the least.

The atmosphere outside the barn was dark and ghostly. A thick fog added to the visual deterrence and rolled into the interior of the barn as a large, dark figure emerged, pacing rather quickly down the aisle in the middle of the chairs towards the front. He was strikingly large, standing at least seven feet tall and wearing a solid black robe with sleeves and a hood over his head. The man was looking to the floor with his hands joined as he walked closer to the stage. Following behind him was Thomas Walker, James' supposed dead father, wearing a black, sort of ceremonial robe made of a silk-like fabric with decorative embroideries in red going down the sides and around the cuffs. A small pentagram was stitched on his chest, also in red. He too wore a hood over his head that was red on the inside and black on the outside. At the time, of course, nobody in the audience recognized this man as James' father nor would they have any reason to assume such. They all simply looked on in wonder as the two walked up the aisle and onto the stage.

Saithe was a warrior demon who was normally assigned as a bodyguard to other highly ranked demons on special missions, but several years ago was given a new post at the side of Thomas Walker, a demon possessed human given charge of sparking the well planned *Impetus Malignus*, or "Revolution of Evil". Saithe, like the rest of the demonic army, could only take human form by possession of a human being, therefore had found the largest and most intimidating person he could find to take over. It was a skill that took years of work on the demon's part. They had to possess a soul that was not already in possession of Christ, and then they had to work on that soul until they broke it to the point of complete submission. At that point, the demon would be given total control of the human's body and function. Over time, the human's physical appearance would even be affected by the possession. At times, it was as if the body was dying as the soul went into submission of the possessing demon.

Thomas Walker was a good example of a once perfectly healthy and strong man, in complete control of himself, until he allowed his soul to be taken over by one of the most evil and depraved demons of them all, a general in Satan's Army of Darkness. His skin was pale and his veins were blue. He had bony fingers that were tipped with straight and pointed nails that appeared razor sharp. Although he had always boasted a full head of hair, Thomas' head was now covered by transparent strands of silver hair that were layed back over his head and disappeared into the hood behind it. The man's lips and tongue were as black as the entire inside of his mouth and his teeth were marble colored and sharp, like the end of a sharpened pencil. Probably the most evil part of his entire feature was his eyes. They were black with a green tint that came and went, revealing cat like eyes that stared sharply ahead and seemed to peer straight into the souls of anyone who dared to face him. Mr. Walker was always a large man but now seemed shriveled a bit by age. Still, his pose was unmistakably firm and his stature demanded the attention of those in his presence.

The man once known as Thomas Walker began to speak immediately upon reaching the podium. Saithe stood beside him, his black eyes and pale skin barely visible in the shadows of his hood. Some of the men stood in their places, while others remained seated, though lightly.

"I am Bethliel," the old man said in a raspy voice with a hissing undertone. "Those who serve me will serve Satan himself."

"What is this?" Jarvis asked after stepping out of the shadows of the very large Saithe. "Who are you and where's James?" He was only the first of those ready to speak up, but would certainly be the last.

Saithe looked to his commander, who simply nodded in return, then thrust out his arm towards Jarvis, who was standing next to him. His fist emerged from beneath his robe just before striking Jarvis directly in the middle of his chest, sending him flying backwards several feet before slamming into the wall of the barn behind them. One of the oil lamps that had been placed on either side of the goat's head exploded upon Jarvis' impact, causing everyone in the room except the two at the front to duck in their places. Jarvis laid on the floor unconscious from the blow and bleeding from his collision with the wall.

Those who were standing now sat in their seats along with the others. An air of nervousness and uncertainty quickly came upon the congregation at the sight of the demon's power causing those who had wanted to speak to keep their mouths shut for the time being. On the stage, the two demon-possessed men stood quietly as the fire from the erupted oil lamp calmed. The fire had filled the ceiling with a thick black smoke that mixed with the fog and hovered over the interior, adding to the darkness of the environment.

"Serve me, and you will find all the glory that you desire," Bethliel continued. Though his voice was grating, it seemed to echo throughout the room. The men looked on, unsure how to react. Some were beginning to rise in their seats, as if ready to become subject to the dark figure, while others clung low to their seats prudently. The very air of horror was strong and the thick smog in the ceiling began to swirl around the room like a funnel cloud.

"Serve me…," Bethliel stated as the greenish tint in his eyes suddenly became more visible underneath his hood. "…and you will be kings."

Bethliel was a general in Satan's Empirical Forces of Darkness. For centuries, he had served as the chief enforcer and commander of the armies over the Middle East, causing the archangel Michael many problems. Many years ago, however, he was given a new assignment by Satan himself. A teenager in the southern part of America had sworn a vengeance against society, having been placed in a juvenile delinquency facility for a crime he didn't commit. Bethliel was to possess this young man and wear him down over the years. His mission so far had been a great success, having even driven the grown man to kill his family and fake his own death. This then gave him the years that he needed to completely take control of Thomas Walker and plan his next move, the spawning of Impetus Malignus.

Bethliel looked over the group of men seated in the seats in front of him as if looking directly into the very being of each individual there. One of his greatest attributes was the ability to see into a man's soul and determine everything from his motives to his personal desires. The men's nerves began to get the best of them as the environment seemed to darken by the second. There was not the slightest movement, not a single whisper, as the man at the podium began to speak one final time.

"Become my loyal subject…," he said in a devilish tone. "…and you will become greater than humanity itself."

James opened his eyes to find himself lying on a pile of leaves. His vision was blurred and he could barely move any part of his body. He had lost a lot of blood, causing him to become weak beyond the ability to even lift his head. Suddenly a white figure approached from the darkness and knelt down beside him. He could feel a hand on the back of his head and water and his lips.

"Drink," the figure said, holding a small, pottery cup to his mouth. "You need water."

James felt refreshed by the cold water as he took it in. Although it pained him, he dragged his hand across his stomach and to his side. The hooks were gone and his wounds had been stitched and cleaned. Unable to lift his hand back to his chest, he simply dropped it beside him, until the figure in white gently grabbed his wrist and placed his hand back where it was.

"What…" James whispered before trying to clear his throat.

"Don't speak," the man in white said. "You need to preserve your strength." The man placed the cup at James' mouth once again. "Here, drink," he said.

James took another couple of sips from the cup, this time feeling a sensation of comfort and relief from his horrible pain as the liquid passed down his throat and into his body. He turned his head as much as he could to see the man stand and walk away into the darkness. James lifted his trembling hand and held it out but was unable to say anything else as he swiftly drifted back to sleep.

What seemed like just moments later, James awoke once again, this time with better eyesight and seemingly more strength. The man in white was sitting on a downed tree at his side, watching him closely. He had snow white hair and wore a long white robe with silver lining. His face was soft and his blue eyes were both welcoming and calming. He was encircled by a supernatural glow that lit up their immediate surroundings and his presence was accompanied by the occasional sound of rolling thunder in the clouds above them. There was no doubt that this man was not your average good Samaritan or passer-by, he had to be from somewhere otherworldly, somewhere like Heaven.

Despite his care, James was skeptical. His past had taught him to be so in any situation. In any case, the man was taking care of him; so, for now, he would at the very least, welcome his attention. The man stood and walked to the other side of James, where he crouched down and placed his hand on James' forehead.

"I am Gabriel," he said in a soft voice. "You don't have any reason to fear me."

James lifted his head slightly and looked down at his battered body. He was wearing clean, vanilla white pants with no shoes or shirt. His face was swollen and bruised, especially on and around his nose and over his left eye. Some wounds were stitched and others were covered with white cloth bandages that were taped to his skin. All of the blood had been cleaned, but there wasn't a single square inch of his body that wasn't damaged in some way. James laid back down, discouraged by his wounds, but biting his lip in anger at the same time.

"You are angry," Gabriel said as he stood and began to walk back around to the other side. "That is obvious, and rightful I should say."

James placed his elbows on the ground and mustered all of the strength that he could to lift himself up. The pain in his sides and legs was intense, but he was determined to fight through it. In his mind, there was no time. He had to get himself up and find a way to seek out and face his father once more.

"No, no," Gabriel said as he quickly knelt down and forced James back to the ground. "You have to rest."

"I…" James uttered with his lips quivering. "I have to go," he said in obvious pain.

"Where will you go, James?" Gabriel asked. "You have been betrayed and framed. You are being hunted for murders committed by Saithe. As we speak, your group of followers is being corrupted and subverted. Those who were most loyal to you are soon going to be loyal to Bethliel."

"Bethliel?" James inquired.

"Bethliel is the demon that has taken complete control of your father," Gabriel answered as he stood and sat on the tree once again. "You have to understand, James, your father is nothing but a memory at this point. He is not the man that he once was. When he was young, he effectively gave himself to Bethliel's power and control, and there is nothing left of Thomas Walker as you once knew him."

James seethed in anger. He had never been an emotional person, reserving any and every feeling as best he could. "Emotion is weakness," was the message to his cohorts any time the subject was brought up. Now he was finding it impossible to hold them in. Though the sentiments were unfamiliar, they were as real as his own flesh and blood. He did not seem to care that his father was now fully possessed by a demon. To him, he was still his father, and he was still the one that had betrayed him not once, but now twice.

"God sent me to save you, James," Gabriel continued. "You were left for dead, but God chose to show you mercy and give you a chance to redeem yourself."

"I have nothing to redeem," James stated firmly beneath his anger. "I have only to avenge."

"To avenge?" Gabriel asked. "You were hung in the woods by shackles and hooks and guarded by Kriti, a demon not easy to drive away. If you seek vengeance, you will only find yourself in a similar position. Bethliel meant to kill you when you were a boy, but the man inside of him overruled. This time he meant to kill you and ordered it done. He meant to kill you slowly, so that you would suffer, for living. He wanted you to suffer for making him weak enough to let you live when you were a child." Gabriel leaned in towards James and looked him directly in the eyes. "You are powerless against him. Don't you see that?"

"I...," James began, his voice trembling in fury, and both emotional and physical pain. "I have to face him. One way or the other, I have to find a way."

"Then you are lost," Gabriel replied. "You will face him, but you will not receive your vengeance."

James was quiet for a moment in thought. He clinched his fists in anger and began to pound them against the ground. His eyes closed as a single tear fell from each and ran down the sides of his face.

"You will not succeed, James," repeated Gabriel. "I tell you this with the utmost of regard, do you understand?"

James seemed to ignore Gabriel and concentrate particularly on his own thought. It wasn't even in him to appreciate being delivered from death. Only hate filled his heart, a heart that had been blackened by his experiences as a child, namely the death of his family and what he thought was the death of his father as well. Redemption was nothing but a cry for help to James, and a way to gain acceptance in the society that he so hated. It was something he felt that he would never fall back to, most certainly not at this juncture.

"Redeem yourself, James...," Gabriel pleaded. "...and find peace, comfort and joy."

"No," James stated firmly and in a louder voice. "I want my vengeance. I want...my vengeance!"

Gabriel shook his head in disappointment then stood from the tree. "Then, I'm afraid...," he said to James. "I can be of no further assistance." At this, Gabriel turned and walked away, leaving James once again in the darkness.

"I want my vengeance!" James yelled as Gabriel disappeared into the woods. "Do you hear me!" he yelled with all of his anger and might. "I want my vengeance!"

XIII

"What's with the cab, dude?" Alyssa inquired. It was late, even by the standards of a younger generation, and Drew had just picked Alyssa up from the international airport in Austin. He had hoped with minimal expectations that the question would not surface, at least not for a while.

"Just wanted to welcome you home in style," Drew jokingly responded with a smirk on his face. "Besides, this was the only guy that would drive this far."

Keeping something, anything, from Alyssa was never a small task for Drew, who rarely kept anything from her to begin with. They were very close friends growing up, partly because their parents were always getting together at each other's houses on the weekends. The two families had even gone on vacation a couple times to Disney World and the Ozarks. With both children being an only child and Alyssa being just a year younger than Drew, they were all each other had to play with during these times. As they grew older, playing turned to going out on the town with mutual friends and things of this nature.

"What happened to your truck?" Alyssa asked.

Alyssa was short and thin with straight brown hair that hung to her shoulders and big brown eyes. She was an attractive girl, very smart, with a laid back and down to earth sort of attitude. Everyone got along with Alyssa, especially Drew, and was even voted "Best Personality" in high school. She had been quite popular in high school although she avoided most extra-curricular activities such as cheerleading and sports.

"A bug hit the windshield," Drew responded, carefully. It was the best he could do on short notice.

"A bug?" Alyssa inquired with a smirk on her face.

"Isn't this the long way?" Drew asked the cab. He was trying to change the subject, but curious nonetheless.

The cab driver did not respond or even so much as move a muscle in response. He had exited on Highway 37, a few miles before the usual exit to go to Adjacent Cove. This was the back way, rarely used unless there was bad traffic or an accident on the highway. The highway weaved through the hill country for several miles before finally entering town on the east side of Adjacent Cove.

"Sir," Drew said. "You exited too early. This is the long way."

Once again, the cab driver showed no sign that he had even heard what Drew was saying. Normally, Drew might not have been too concerned. After all, this was one of the ways one could go to get to Adjacent Cove. This night, however, was different. There was a thick fog and the night was darker than normal, and Drew was already still on alert because of what had transpired throughout the day and evening.

"Hey mister!" Drew said in a loud voice. Still receiving no response he leaned back in his seat and sighed.

"It's alright," Alyssa said, trying to calm Drew down. "I'm sure he knows the way."

"Well, he said he did," Drew responded. "Something just doesn't feel right. I know he can hear me."

"Did I tell you I'm thinking about moving home?" Alyssa stated, trying to change the subject by changing Drew's focus.

"Really?"

"Yep," she said. "Michigan is okay, but it's nothing like home."

Just a few years ago, Alyssa had received her Master's degree in education from Michigan State University. The only reason had decided to stay was because she was offered an administrative position at a school district in a small town west of Lansing. At first, she didn't want to take the job because she had wanted to come home upon graduating, but changed her mind when finding that the job market at home was a lot more difficult to penetrate at the time. This way, she figured, she could get some quality work experience to help her advance in her field and give her more and better opportunities back home when the time was right.

"I was going to be coming home sometime this week anyway so I can start looking around here for a job with one of the school districts," she continued. "I've been saving some vacation time."

"Wow that's great!" Drew responded. "I thought you'd be up there forever." His attention was no fully focused on Alyssa.

Throughout high school and beyond, Drew had found himself falling for his close friend more and more, but never had the courage to act on it. He had figured that his status as a good friend would keep her from feeling the same way about him. In fact, his very personal reason for not marrying yet was because he had not found a woman quite like her. After college Drew hoped and prayed that Alyssa would find her way back home, and was devastated to discover that she was going to stay. Now, he was more than interested in the possibility of her moving back.

"So what do you make of this whole thing with Dad?" Alyssa asked. "From your perspective."

"Well," he began to answer, but his voice was suddenly drowned out by the sound of the cab driver honking the horn repeatedly. They had driven into a clearing in the fog as Drew looked up to see a small boy standing in the middle of the road just a few yards ahead of them. The boy was wearing black clothing, almost like a school uniform from the 1800's. He had short black hair and his eyes were black as night against his pale face. He opened his mouth and just as the cab driver began to swerve to keep from hitting him, flames shot from his mouth towards Drew's side of the cab. The fire shot through the front seat of the car and engulfed the driver as he did his best to avoid them.

With the driver now drenched in fire and no longer holding the wheel, the car turned over on its side and began to flip violently over and over. The screams of the cab driver could be heard the entire time that the car was turning out of control off the road and into a pasture. It finally came to rest upright next to a large, circular bale of hay that quickly caught fire as well.

Drew's first concern was Alyssa, who was unconscious but appeared unharmed. Drew himself was unharmed as well and fully alert. The cab driver, however, was still on fire but scorched beyond recognition. There was nothing he could have done or could do for him at this point. He reached over and put his arms under Alyssa and at the same time kicked the door on his side completely off its hinges.

After removing Alyssa, who was still unconscious, from the car he began to run as fast as he could back towards the road. His feet began to lift off of the ground and before he knew it he found himself gliding through the air a few feet from the ground, over the road and towards a line of trees on the other side. The cab suddenly exploded violently, sending balls of flames and debris flying through the air. Just as Drew's feet returned to the ground a flaming tire from the cab struck him in the back and bounced off as if it was hitting a firm wall. Drew barely even reacted as his attention remained focused on getting Alyssa to safety.

As debris and ashes settled around them, Drew ensured that Alyssa was safe and settled then stood to his feet to survey the damage. The sole thing remaining of the cab was two axles and a pile of twisted metal. The road and surrounding grass and bushes were littered by parts of the cab and ashes, some still on fire and others simmering. The child that had caused the damage was nowhere to be found. Drew looked one more time at Alyssa then began to slowly walk towards the road. He was still in disbelief that he had actually flown over the damage previously and was trying to figure out just how he did it. At the time, his focus was on getting Alyssa to safety, and he would do whatever it took to do just that, even if it meant leaving the ground momentarily.

Drew's cell phone had been sitting on the seat next to him, and was certainly lost. Alyssa's was in her purse, also lost in the explosion. His strategy would be to wait and hope that somebody saw the explosion from the distance or that somebody would be passing by soon. Unfortunately, the only people that usually drove on this road were those that lived somewhere along it, and they were all most likely in bed at this hour.

Suddenly Drew felt somebody tapping on his shoulder lightly. He turned quickly to find nobody there. Again, he felt a tap on his shoulder, and again he turned to find nobody there. He reached over his shoulder hoping to catch whoever or whatever is was to find that there were two swords strapped to his back in an 'x'. He reached over both shoulders and pulled the blades out and immediately they were lined with blue flames that glowed in the night. They were the same blades that he had used earlier in the day to ward off an assassin trying to take his life. He pulled one of the blades closer to his face and saw in the reflection that his hair had once again turned black.

He was an angel, and if ever he had any doubts, this event once again reinforced the fact. Alyssa began to stir behind him and he quickly sheathed his blades and turned to him. She turned over in the soft grass and pushed herself up a bit.

"What…" she said, quietly.

"Shhh," Drew said softly as he placed his hand on her shoulder. "Just rest."

Alyssa lied back down on her hand and closed her eyes. She apparently had not noticed anything different about Drew and he was not going to point anything out at the moment.

The wooded area just a few feet away from them was dark an eerie. The fog that had cleared in the area was now beginning to close in on them. This, combined with the smoke from the several fires, was making it difficult to see even a few feet away. Without warning, it became evident that they were not alone. From deep in the woods came the sound of something or someone hitting sticks against the trees. Drew rose and placed one hand over his shoulder and grabbed the handle of one of his swords. The knocking sound gradually became louder as more and more of the sounds joined in.

"Who's there?" Drew called into the darkness. There was no answer, just knocking, which was now becoming almost deafening. His primary concern was still Alyssa. She was helpless and most likely had received a head injury in the crash. Drew wanted to step into the woods and try to find the source of the sounds, but his instinct told him to grab Alyssa and make for the road.

The knocking sound continued, and was now joined by hissing and laughter, coming from higher up in the trees. There was a sense of evil in the dark and murky woods like Drew had never felt before. Still, he wasn't afraid. Getting Alyssa to safety, however, was priority one.

Drew picked Alyssa up carefully and slowly backed up towards the road. Upon reaching the highway, he turned and began to walk down the middle of the road, using the yellow stripes as his guide. The further he walked, the faster he went. As he began to run, his feet once again left the ground and he soared quickly through the fog just a few feet from the ground. It felt natural, as if this was something he was used to doing. He lifted his head, and without effort, rose further and further into the air.

The woods, the sounds, the damage, everything had long disappeared into the fog behind him as Drew, carrying Alyssa, flew towards Adjacent Cove, to safety. It was strangely familiar to him, so much so that it took little thought or concentration. His focus was sharp and his determination and heartfelt care for his friend was all the drive he needed for the moment. The evil and malicious beings in the woods were behind him, but only for the moment.

XIV

The sun was barely coming over the horizon, thinning the fog blanketing Adjacent Cove and nearly all of Trenton County. Still, an eeriness stood over the entire landscape, as if time in this one part of the country had stood still, beckoning the presence of darkness against the fight of the sun's powerful rays. Most of Trenton County, including Adjacent Cove, was in a chain of valleys, so locals were certainly no strangers to the occasional fog. This one, however, was completely undetectable and especially malicious.

As he exited the Trenton County Hospital's emergency bay, Drew placed his hand over his face as if he hadn't seen the sun, or at least what you could see of the sun, in years. It had been a long night and he was ready to go home to his apartment for a shower. Alyssa had been seen and treated for a mild concussion and her father Jim was to be released home within the next couple of hours. With everyone taken care of for the time being, this was his opportunity to do just that. He felt revived, in some way, partly because he had gotten a short nap in the emergency room and partly because he felt like he was truly discovering himself for the first time. All of his questions about life, and in particular his life, were finally being answered. No doubt it was happening fast, but at least it was happening.

Drew sat down on the curb, awaiting the arrival of the local taxi to come and take him home. There was a lot to sort out, and a lot to learn, and Drew had no idea where or even how to begin. All he knew was that at this point, his trust and faith in God would be absolutely crucial. After all, it was God who made Drew what he was. It was God who had him carry out this mission of becoming human to begin with. Foremost, it was God who loved him and would see him through it if he allowed.

Running his fingers through his thick hair, Drew was suddenly surprised and taken back by the sudden passing of a sheriff's car. The vehicle nearly ran over his toes, as if he wasn't even there. Just a few feet away from Drew, the car came to a sudden stop and two deputies, one badly hurt and being helped by the other, and the sheriff of Trenton County. Drew rose to his feet to see if he could assist and quickly grabbed the deputy's other arm. Sheriff Sandoval walked in front as a nurse with a stretcher came to meet them. As they began to carry the injured deputy away, the sheriff grabbed Drew by the arm and pulled him to the side.

"You okay Andrew?" he asked. Drew noticed a sense of both exhaustion and terror in the man's eyes that was shared by his deputies.

Sheriff Pete Sandoval had been the sheriff of Trenton County for many years. He was also a member of and taught Sunday school at the First Baptist Church in

Adjacent Cove, where Drew and his mother still attended faithfully. So many people had been good to them both over the years and the Sheriff and his wife were no exception. Many times Mrs. Sandoval and had visited over the years. Their two sons and two daughters had all grown up around the same time as Drew, with the exception of one son that was much older.

"I'm okay Sheriff Sandoval," Drew responded with a bit of haste. "Why?"

"I found your truck earlier this morning," Sheriff Sandoval responded.

"Oh," Drew said, almost with a bit of relief, considering all that was going on. "Yea, I know. I'm gonna' get someone out there to get it I promise."

The Sheriff seemed a bit confused. Nevertheless, if the world was going to know what he was, he didn't want it to be in this manner. Drew tried his best to come up with a reasonable explanation for the mess that was once his truck, as well as why he left it there.

"Why would you need to do that?" Sheriff Sandoval asked.

The Sheriff's confusion was now shared.

"Well, I know I shouldn't have left it there, but..." Drew continued, unsure of what Sheriff Sandoval was getting at.

"Drew," the Sheriff continued. "I found it down on Park Street with the keys in it and the ignition turned on. Even the headlights were on."

Drew responded with a bewildered gaze.

"It was at a stop sign," said the Sheriff, as if trying to jog Drew's memory. "Was it stolen?"

"Oh," Drew responded, as if he had some idea what was going on despite the fact that he was completely clueless. "Yea, okay, where is it now?" he asked.

"Drew," Sheriff Sandoval stated as he closed in a bit. "Are you sure everything's okay? 'Cause if you're in some kind of trouble I want you to tell me."

"No, no. Thanks. I just got a bit sidetracked is all." Drew cringed inside at his explanation. It was the best he could do on the spot.

Sheriff Sandoval stood quietly for a moment, giving Drew every opportunity to give a better explanation, but one never came to mind. If it weren't for the nurse trying to drag him away, he probably would not have left that spot until he was satisfied. To Drew's relief, however, he had to attend to his injured deputy.

"It's at the station," said the Sheriff. "Get the keys from Mrs. Betty, and Drew," he said as he walked away. "Be careful out there son. Things are kinda' nuts right now.

"Yes sir, will do," Drew said. His concerns now even more enlightened, he walked back outside to a waiting taxi so that he could go and pick up his apparently fine truck. It certainly wouldn't be the strangest thing he'd seen in the last several hours.

Adjacent Cove woke up to both a criminal and financial crisis the likes of which nobody in the area had ever witnessed nor heard of in all their lives. Within the city limits were four major banking branches and one operated out of the front of a major grocery store. The four banks in a building their own were the First State Bank of Trenton County, the Jamestown Bank, Southern

Financial, and the McCombs National Bank. Sometime during the night, all of these had been broken into and robbed. This had law enforcement officials from all over the county swarming in to assist. The robberies hadn't so much as set off an alarm until early in the morning and three of the four security guards were reported missing. The fourth, a young man working part time and going to the community college, could only remember going blank and then waking up surrounded my police.

In each case, a large, gaping hole was found on the side of the building that housed the vault. Whoever had done this was able to successfully tear through concrete and steel several inches thick in order to access the safe. The first report had actually come in before the alarms went off, all of which had been set somehow by the burglars to go off at five o'clock precisely that morning. Suzy Johnson, an elderly native, had noticed a hole in the side of the bank across the street from her house while on her way to a prayer meeting at church. This made her, for the moment, the sole thing even close to being a witness.

At every bank that had been broken into, the scenario was the same. The culprits had gone into the safe, robbed all of the safety deposit boxes, but then burned all of the cash using gasoline. Every bit of cash locked away in every safe had been reduced to ashes. In addition, a three foot long wooden cross was hung upside down either from an open safety deposit box or from the wall. Police were baffled. They hadn't been on the scene for very long but hope of finding some sort of lead was dwindling with time. Security tapes had been erased, fingerprints removed, officials could not even figure out how they managed to destroy such a large section of the wall out, especially without arousing an alarm or another person in the area.

If the ensuing law enforcement nightmare in town wasn't enough, reports were now filtering in that the Trenton County Sheriff's Department had responded to several calls over night regarding a group of men in black clothes roaming around in the hill country. Two of the men had been violently attacked and supposedly one of them was even killed. Up to this point, however, nobody knew who else was involved. All they knew was that they were attacked by men in the dark. Drew's experience with the taxi cab was also beginning to surface, though nobody knew who the passengers were as of yet.

"I don't even know how to describe this," Detective Stulken stated to one of the uniform police officers, staring at the large hole in the side of the Jamestown Bank.

Detective Mark Stulken had been with the Adjacent Cove police department since he first graduated from a police academy out of state twenty seven years ago. Just a couple of years ago, he had been promoted to a detective after passing all the required exams with flying colors. It had become an acquired interest after years on the job and so far, this was his biggest test by far.

"I've never seen anything like it," the detective said.

"Tell me about it," Officer Spencer, standing beside the detective commented. "In all my years of law enforcement I've never seen anything like this."

Detective Stulken carefully climbed over the rubble on the ground by the hole in the wall and stepped over into the vault. Officer Spencer followed. The two had gone to school together in Adjacent Cove and were good friends. Officer Spencer had considered becoming a detective at one point but changed his mind when a detective in a nearby town was shot and killed while accidentally stumbling upon a meth lab in someone's home.

"Why would they burn the money and take the stuff in the deposit boxes?" asked Officer Spencer. "That just doesn't make any sense."

The detective leaned in for a closer look at the upside down cross hanging by a thin rope from an opened safety deposit box. He noticed that a small section of the crudely made cross had been burnt or the wood used to make it had been in some sort of fire. He assumed by the smell of the spot that the burn had happened recently. He began to move the cross around with his pen so that he could get a closer look when Detective Stulken' daughter, Julia, who worked for the local newspaper, began to climb into the vault through the hole.

"Stay back sweetie!" the detective stated, holding his hand up. "I don't want you to accidentally contaminate something."

"Dad, have you heard?" his daughter asked.

"Probably but tell me anyway," Stulken replied, exhausted from bad news.

"There was a big fire last night," Julia began. "Out on Thomas Jasper's place."

Detective Stulken sighed. Suddenly the bus fire from the previous day was taking a back seat to the disorder turmoil of the new day.

"They're saying people died in a barn fire," Julia continued. "Like, several people."

"Thomas Jasper…" Officer Spencer said to himself. "Isn't that the fella' that wanted to build the city park out there?"

"What is going on in this place?" said Detective Stulken in obvious disgust. "Hey Charlie…" he yelled to his partner outside the bank.

Charlie Winters had just transferred from west Texas where she served as a police officer for thirteen years before aspiring to become a detective. She was still new but had taken to the job quite well in her first few months. She was an eager and aggressive detective, always coming in early and working late. This approach was fine with and even encouraged by Detective Stulken, who was getting up there in age. The one set back to Detective Winters' energy had been the simple fact that very little happened in Adjacent Cove that required their attention. Still, she was ready to go at any moments' notice for whatever was sent her way.

"What's up?" Detective Winters stated, peaking her head through the hole.

"You got anything on this barn?" he asked.

"We've got a couple uniforms out there," she responded. "Sheriff's department has their hands full."

"What's it look like?" Stulken asked.

"Right now, it's not clear. They're calling for back up. Want me to run over there?"

"Yea, go check it out," answered Detective Stulken. "I'll catch a right with Spencer."

"On it," Winters responded as she walked away.

"Oh, and Charlie," Stulken yelled out.

"Yep," she said, poking her head back through the hole.

"Be careful, for God's sake. Seems the whole city's goin' nuts."

"You think it's all connected?" Officer Spencer asked Detective Stulken, who was back to examining the upside down wooden cross. "Yesterday was bad enough with the prison break, and the bus fire in the morning. But now all this and this barn and the taxi cab that just explodes for no reason and people walking around in black robes in the middle of the night."

Stulken sighed and took a step back for a moment. "I don't know," he said, taking off his hat to wipe his brow. "But I'm starting to think that somehow it is."

"But who could be doing something on this scale?" the officer inquired, not looking for any particular answer. "And if they're not after cash money, then what are they after?"

Detective Stulken pulled a chair from the table in the middle of the vault and sat down. "Chaos," he stated, staring at the inverted cross. "Chaos From control."

XV

James scurried through the woods as quickly as he could in hopes that a clearing would help him to gather his bearing and get on track. He had been running through the thick trees of the wooded area all night and had become disoriented not long before the sun rose. The cabin had been completely destroyed by fire while he was unconscious along with every means of protection and communication that was available. Luckily, some of his clothing, save for a decent pair of shoes, and a few other small items had been scattered about in the woods around it before the fire. After a night of frantic running through the unforgiving vines and branches of the woods, however, his blue jeans and black t-shirt were now torn and battered and his feet, with nothing on them, were cut and bleeding.

With no clearing in sight, James stopped for a moment and rested against a tree. Several years back, he and other members of Los Ultimos Dias had cleared a path from the cabin to the closest major road, just a couple of miles away. Most likely, the path had become grown over a bit since then, but its existence would have still been noticeable. By now, James had been running for well over six hours although to him, it had seemed like mere minutes. Knowing full well that he could not be on the same path that he had created prior, all he could do was to stop, sit down, and do the best he could to gather his bearings. Using the sun would be impossible, because of the thick fog. He would have to find another way.

After a few moments of catching his breath, James stood to his feet and began to walk. There were many wooded areas in this part of Texas, but this one couldn't be more than a few miles squared, he figured. The night time and fog had most likely caused his disorientation and his anger and anticipation had probably fueled it. The best thing to do now would be to walk in the straightest line that he could until he reached an opening and hopefully, a sign of life.

Several feet away, James finally happened upon a clearing in woods, but not the kind he had hoped for. It was a small clearing, only a few yards in diameter, in which there were no trees or bushes, just grass. What was odd, however, was its shape. It was a perfect circle, as if somebody, or something, had made it that way intentionally. Against his better judgment, James stopped once more to try and gather his bearings. Even without trees, the sky was of no help because of the dense fog covering the entire area. All he could do at this point was to guess at which direction to go. After a few moments of trying to look as deep as he could into the tree line all around the circle, he started towards the clearest part that he could find.

Just before re-entering the woods, James heard the sound of thunder directly behind him, nearly knocking him to the ground. He turned quickly to find the circular clearing suddenly free from fog, revealing a bright blue sky. The sun, however, was blocked by an object that was slowly descending, apparently towards the clearing. Within seconds, the object, which now appeared to be a person clothed in a robe, was gravitating just a few feet from the ground in front of James. It was definitely a person, shadowed for the time being by the great light surrounding it. James was knocked backwards to the ground by a gust of wind that radiated from the being with great force as its sandal covered feet settled onto the ground. James picked himself up almost as quickly as he had fallen and took a couple of steps towards the man, who, at the moment, was standing quietly in the middle of the clearing.

"I've already told you," James said to the figure. "I don't want any part of you. Just leave me alone!" James was growing angry before the man had even opened his mouth.

Suddenly the light that the figure had been giving up diminished slowly, revealing a man in a black robe with a hood over his head. The man stood about nine feet tall and had stone grey skin and blood red eyes. The whites of his eyes were also red, but more translucent than the corneas. His hair was orange and black, like fire. At first, he stood quietly with his hands joined in front of him underneath the sleeves of his robe.

"Who are you?" James inquired. "What is this about?"

The man smirked and began to laugh under his breath, opening his mouth to reveal his ivory colored teeth with razor sharp bicuspids that resembled those of a traditional vampire. His glare alone was enough to strike fear into the most audacious of men, including James.

"I thought you'd never make it James," the man said in a low, almost growling tone.

"What are you talking about?" asked James, standing firm. "Make it to what?"

"You're here aren't you?" the man suggested. "I've been waiting for you."

"Okay," James said. "I'm here, but who are you?"

"I've been called by many names, but that's not important."

"I'm getting sick of this," James stated angrily. "I'm sick of the games and I'm not in the mood to play. How do you know me?"

"Let's just say," the dark figure answered. "I know your father."

"My father is dead," responded James.

"Oh, but he is very much alive," the man affirmed. "Very much alive indeed."

"My father is dead," James maintained. "I saw the man you call my father and that is not him, plain and simple."

The dark man laughed, making James angrier than he already was. Any fears that he had quickly turned to animosity and exasperation as he lunged towards the man, head first. Immediately the man threw his arms forward, throwing fire to the grass in between the two. James stopped abruptly and jumped backwards, unable to handle the heat being generated from the fire. Slowly, the flames began to disintegrate into the soil until they finally dissolved completely.

"I'm not here to fight with you James…," the man declared, "…but let this be your warning. I will end what pathetic life you have left if you come at me again."

James picked himself up off the ground and brushed the grass off of his pants and shirt. He figured, if nothing else, he could at least stand his ground. For a moment he considered turning and running into the woods, but then figured the man would come after him if he did. Besides, he thought to himself, maybe this person could help him destroy the man that used to be his father and take his group back.

"What do you know about Bethliel?" James inquired.

"Bethliel is the fallen angel who has taken possession of your father's body," the man answered. "Unfortunately, your father has taken control of his self once again and is veering away from my plan."

"What plan?" James asked.

"That's not important."

"How is that not important?" James inquired. Despite the warning in flames, he was growing more and more impatient. "I'm sick of hearing 'that's not important'. If it's not important don't talk about it. Otherwise, you're gonna' need to give me details if you want me to sit here and watch your little one man circus."

"I need you to stop your father," the man interrupted, getting right to the point. "He is no longer useful to me. With him at the front of these battle lines, we will lose."

"Who's 'we'?"

"All of us who live in darkness, including you."

"What if I said I want you to help me, not the other way around?" asked James.

"At the moment, this isn't your show James," the man answered. "But it could be. You take out your father and I will give you life like you've never had it. I will show you how to rule in darkness. I will free you from your mortal life. I will break your chains of restrictions, rules, values, and even morals, placed upon you by your human captors. All you have to do is kill your father. Blood may be thicker than water, but evil is thicker than blood. Evil is the only shot you have."

"So if I kill my father, you're going to give me all these things?" James asked. "Why in the world should I believe you? How are you going to help me? Why should I do anything at all for you? I don't even know who you are! How am I supposed to…"

"I will also give you command of a portion of my armies," the man interrupted.

The air outside Drew's apartment was thick with malice and enmity. Darkness fell once again upon the land as if the sun had simply disappeared behind the horizon well ahead of schedule. Drew stood in front of his door, hesitant to open it but knowing full well that he had to. He reached for the door knob to find it blistering hot. The heat left a burn mark on his hand that faded and disappeared within seconds. Once again Drew reached for the door, this time using a handkerchief to turn the knob and open it. Outside fires were burning in every direction. Even the other buildings in his apartment complex were up in flames.

Suddenly a blast coming from outside of Drew's view knocked him back into his apartment and onto the ground. From his right a ball of fire streaked into the scene and struck his truck, which was parked just a few feet away from where Drew had been standing. The truck was obliterated, leaving just the tires to burn where it once stood. Drew picked himself up and walked out of his apartment once again, this time with more caution than before. In the distance he began to make out what sounded like a woman crying out for help. He couldn't see anyone, but there were plenty of obstacles that could have been hiding her as well. The best he could do was to cover his mouth to keep the smoke out of his lungs and start out to find her.

"Hello?" Drew called out into the fiery chaos. On the street a small pick-up truck had been turned over on its side and was providing cover for a woman and her three young children.

"Over here!" the woman cried from behind the truck. "Please! We're over here!"

Drew made his way into the street and to the turned over truck to find a middle aged woman hovered over her three young children in an effort to protect them. Suddenly another ball of flames hurled through the air, this time hitting Drew's apartment and throwing debris everywhere. Drew looked on as everything he owned was either destroyed or up in flames. He turned his attention back to the woman and her children, despite being unaware of where he was going to take them now.

"No, no," the woman said as Drew tried to help her to her feet. "We have to stay here!"

"Ma'am, we need to leave before another one of those fireballs hits this truck," Drew insisted.

"No, we can't leave," she said frantically. "They're coming! They'll see us!"

"Who is coming?" Drew asked.

"We have to hide," the woman added. "We can't let them see us!"

"Who is coming Ma'am? You have to tell me who is coming or I can't help you."

"They'll take my children and either kill me or send me away," said the woman, in tears. "Please don't let them take my children away from me!"

"Ma'am," Drew said with a bit more force as he grabbed the woman by the arm. "Just come with me."

"No!" the woman screamed as she yanked her arm away. "You don't understand, they are coming and they will get us if they see us!"

"Who Ma'am? Who is coming?"

"Are you a Christian?" she asked in a trembling voice.

"Yes, Ma'am, I am," responded Drew.

"Then you're dead too."

Suddenly out of nowhere Drew heard another voice calling to him, this one familiar. Drew raised his head to find himself in his office at work. The principal of the junior high where he worked, Ed Hastleburgh, was trying to wake Drew up from a deep sleep.

"Go home Drew," Mr. Hastleburgh stated. "You've had a rough night.

Drew rose his head and felt around him to make sure everything was real. He had been sweating so much that his arms left marks on the desk in front of him and his hair was dampened. He had encountered the same dream many times before but this time it seemed more real. He could even still smell the ashes as if something was burning right in front of him.

"I'll be okay," he stated to his boss, who was now sitting in the chair across the desk from him.

"No, really Drew, go home," the principal insisted. "It's okay. Everything will be here when you get back. How's Jim?"

"He's okay," Drew responded. "Just a little freaked out is all. He went home earlier this morning though."

"That's good," said Mr. Hastleburgh. "Now it's your turn. Go home and get some rest and then come back tomorrow refreshed."

"Okay," Drew finally agreed. "Thank you."

XVI

"It looks like they just plowed through the wall with some kind of tractor or vehicle, but there are no tire tracks or marks," said Detective Stulken as he looked over the rubble. He and Officer Spencer had now moved on to Southern Financial bank while Stulken's partner, Detective Charlie Ellis, was still at the scene of the fire. "But if it wasn't a vehicle of some kind, then what in the world could have done this Spence?" he added.

"You've got me," Officer Spencer responded. "That's why you're the detective here buddy."

"All four banks had to have been hit at the same time," the detective stated. "Unless they were done really fast, but I don't see how that would be possible."

"I'm thinkin' they were probably trying to make a statement more than anything else," said the officer. "Why else would they leave all the money and only take the contents of the safety deposit boxes?"

The two men continued to sift through the rubble in search of any kind of clue they could find. Meanwhile, a crowd was beginning to form outside. Residents were just beginning to hear of the tragedy and many were headed to their respective banks to try and see what was going on. No press release had been issued by anyone as of yet and the most anyone knew was that the banks were broken in to. Further details would have to wait until Detective Stulken could get a clearer picture of exactly what had happened.

"What's going on," one man asked a uniformed police officer keeping the small gathering of people as far away from the scene as possible. "I'm going in there."

"I promise you we'll let you know something as soon as possible," an officer responded as he held his arm out in front of the man.

"That's my bank, and my money. I want to know what happened now," the man said as he tried to push through the policeman's arm.

"We'll let you know something as soon as we can sir," the officer restated. He now stood in front of the man to keep him from advancing.

"This isn't right," a woman in the crowd stated. "What do I do if I need to get money out of my account?"

"Ma'am, we're doing everything we can," another officer said. "I promise you we'll get you the answers you need soon. We just have to give the detectives time to sort everything out."

Detective Charlie Ellis and reporter for the local newspaper, Julia Stulken, approached the remains of what appeared to be a barn carefully. There were already two squad cars and three policemen on the scene. All that was left of the structure was a few charcoaled beams and ashes. Lines of smoke rose from a few pieces of wood that were still red hot from the fire.

"Has anyone gotten a hold of Jasper?" Detective Ellis asked the officers.

"Yea, Marge took care of it," one of the policemen answered. "I'm assuming he's on his way 'cause I haven't heard back from her." Marge was the receptionist at the police station and had been for many years.

"So what do we got?" the detective asked. Julia stayed back near the car until Ellis could look everything over and determine that the site was safe.

"Looks like it was a barn of some sort," an officer responded. "But there's not any hay or signs of animal life around, just a bunch of metal chairs and some old, busted oil lamps. This place was used for something, I just don't know what."

"There's some kind of altar and a stone formation in the ground back here," an officer yelled to Detective Ellis from behind where the barn once stood. "This is just creepy," he added.

"What happened here?" Detective Ellis asked herself as she pulled out her tape recorder and began to look over the remains. "Have any of you moved anything?" she asked the officers.

"No ma'am," an officer answered. "Everything's where it was when we got here."

"Tuesday, October thirteenth," Ellis said into a small digital recorder as she approached the site. "Eight forty-five am. Structure on Thomas Jasper's place appears to have been destroyed by fire sometime during the night."

"Is it safe?" Julia yelled from behind, still standing at the car.

"Better stay back until I give it a look," Detective Ellis answered.

"Holy…" one of the officers was startled. "You should see this detective."

Detective Ellis quickly made her way to the officer to see what he found and was shocked upon her arrival. This was the first time she had seen anything of the sort and most likely the first time anything like this had happened in the area. She kicked away a portion of a beam and used her pen to sift around in the ashes beneath it.

"There are what appear to be human remains…" she continued speaking into her digital recorder. "…found underneath some rubble by Officer Jack McKnight. No confirmation is necessary, these are definitely human bones." The detective stood up and pulled out her cell phone to call Detective Stulken.

"Want me to call the morgue Charlie?" one officer asked.

"Yes, please," Detective Ellis replied. "And the rest of you keep looking and let me know if you find something."

"Okay, we need to bring Thomas Jasper in as soon as possible," Detective Stulken said into his cell phone. "Just keep me up to date."

"Word on the fire?" Officer Spencer asked.

"Looks like a homicide," Stulken answered as he took off his hat and rubbed his forehead. "What in the world is going on here Spence?"

"Do you think it's one of the missing guards?" Spencer asked.

"At this point," the detective responded. "I would have to say yes although I would hope to say no."

The two men stood scratching their heads for a moment at all the events of the past couple of days. Adjacent Cove was a quiet and peaceful town. The worst crime committed there before the previous day had been arson, committed by James Walker. There were no murders and certainly no burglaries of this magnitude. Criminal activity seemed to be taking over the entire county, leaving law enforcement agencies stunned.

"This is a peaceful city, a peaceful county at that," Detective Stulken stated. "Whatever is happening, I have a feeling it's all connected in some way."

"It must be," stated Spencer. "But how?"

"I don't know, but we've gotta' figure it out. We can't let whatever this is win. We can't let them have control."

"I gotta' get back to my patrol," Officer Spencer said as he reached out to shake his friend's hand. "It's gonna' be alright Mark, just hang in there. If you need me just call."

"Thanks Spence," Stulken said. "If you need me, do the same, and please keep your eyes peeled out there. I don't know what's going on around here but we've gotta' get to the bottom of it, and fast."

Suddenly, from the corner of his eye, Detective Stulken noticed something on the brick faced wall just on the edge of the large hole that had been made. It was something he hadn't noticed at the previous bank. He walked over to investigate closer and found what appeared to be a series of four scratch marks across several of the bricks. He pulled one of the loose bricks off the wall and carried it to a table outside the vault so that he could further examine the scratches.

"I need a magnifying lense," the detective called out to a group of bank employees and police officers standing inside the bank. "Does anyone have a magnifying lense?"

Robert Cook, the bank's manager, hurried over to the detective to see what he had found. Mr. Cook had been the first person to arrive at the bank that morning and had called the police before he even entered. Any time the alarm was disabled, it was protocol for the manager to wait for police before entering the building himself. He was especially distraught over the situation and desperate to discover to the culprits and recover his customer's valuables from the safe deposit boxes.

"Did you find something?" Cook asked.

"I don't know but I need to take a closer look at this," the detective answered. "Let me see your glasses."

"My glasses?"

"Yes," Detective Stulken demanded. "Let me see them."

The room fell quiet as the detective examined the brick using Cook's glasses as a magnifying glass. Everyone in the room was interested, but momentarily turned their attention to a beeping noise coming from inside the safe. It was barely audible but not easily missed amidst the quiet. Stulken stood from his chair, handing the glasses back to Mr. Cook.

"What is that?" a uniformed officer asked.

"I don't know," Stulken answered. "But I want everyone out of the building now, and call the bomb squad."

"The bomb squad?" Cook asked.

"Just to be sure," assured the detective.

"You think there's a bomb in here?" Cook inquired as he began to panic.

"I don't know," Detective Stulken said. "But if there is, you don't want to be in here when it explodes do you?"

"It's just a beeping noise," Mr. Cook argued. "It could be anything."

"Exactly," an officer said from behind, grabbing Cook's arm. "It could be anything, including a bomb, so let's go."

The beeping continued as Detective Stulken headed back towards the safe. Afraid of tripping some sort of trap, he peaked inside and looked around to try to find the source of the sound. The safe was a mess with empty safety deposit boxes littering the ground and table in the middle. Stulken began to carefully sift through the boxes, unable to find anything there. He then slowly made his way to the back of the safe, carefully inspecting every square inch of the vault as he went. The beeping sound was quiet, but loud enough to pinpoint its location in time. Upon reaching the back of the safe, Stulken noticed a wooden box in the corner. It was a crate with rope handles on each side that was typically used by the army to store and transport munitions. Stulken isolated the beeping sound to the box and reached down to open it. Inside was a digital timer connected by a series of wires to four blocks of what appeared to be C4. The timer was at thirty five seconds and steadily dropping.

Detective Stulken stood and ran as fast as he could out of the safe, dropping the brick that was in his hand behind him. All but a couple of criminal forensic team members had been evacuated from the bank, leaving it nearly empty. Stulken ran through the bank and lobby and toward the glass doors in the front of the building as quickly as he could, yelling out to the forensic specialists standing near the heavy steel door to the safe to do the same. His efforts were in vain as the bomb exploded violently behind him, sending him flying through the thick glass of the doors and windows in the entranceway, all of which were shattering simultaneously, and into the street in front of the bank. Chaos ensued as the scene was quickly filled with falling rubble and paper and a dark colored dust that slowly began to settle on everything in sight.

Stulken opened his eyes and looked around, unable to hear the screams of horror and anguish coming from officials and the crowd of onlookers in the street. His ear drums had been blown in the blast and his ears were both bleeding profusely from the damage. He hadn't even noticed that his wrist had been shattered while using it to break his fall. The detective stood to his feet in disbelief as suddenly the ground shook from another explosion somewhere else in town. Another came shortly after. All of the banks in town, save for the branch located within a grocery store, were being demolished by C4, one after the other. Detective Stulken wasn't the only one in disbelief. Some even doubted the reality of the situation, thinking that maybe they were in a dream or something. Adjacent Cove had never seen tragedy of this magnitude and locals were nothing short of stunned by what was going on.

As quickly as he lost himself in the complete anarchy of the situation, Detective Stulken pulled himself together and used his many years of experience to maintain personal order so that he could somehow figure out a way to gain control of the scene before anyone else was injured or killed. Unable to hear anything, he would have to rely on the rest of his senses to guide the way. It was not until he began dusting himself off before he even noticed that he was injured himself.

Without warning, as the detective began to limp his way back towards the bank he was knocked viciously from his feet by a black horse traveling rapidly down the street, towards the center square of downtown that housed the county's courthouse, just two road blocks from where Stulken stood. The horse was dressed with red reigns and a black leather saddle and the man atop was completely concealed by a long black robe with a hood that flew in the breeze as he rode. Even the dark figure's hands were covered by black leather gloves, concealing any possibility of even a hint towards the characteristics of his identity.

"What the...? Stop!" Detective Stulken yelled to the horseman as he rose to his feet once again. There was no answer, not even so much as an acknowledgement in response. Unable to hear anything anyway, Stulken decided to play it safe and stay with the bank. No sooner had he reached the thick of the bank's still settling rubble that the man on the horse ran by once more, this time in the other direction, giving way to the intuition that the dark rider was connected in some way to what was going on.

Stulken ran for the nearest empty squad car and hopped in, doing the best he could to keep his injuries out of his mind. It wasn't long before he was hot on the rider's tail and gaining quickly. The detective grabbed the radio and began trying frantically to raise a law enforcement official in the area that could assist him in the chase.

"This is Detective Stulken requesting immediate backup… in pursuit of…you won't believe it…. a black horse with an unidentified rider, going east on 37…I am currently unable to hear and injured. I repeat, I need immediate backup…in pursuit of a suspect riding horseback along Highway 37, all available units…"

The pain in Stulken's right wrist was becoming excruciating from having to use that arm to navigate the vehicle. He was still a bit dazed and in shock from the explosion and his hearing had gone completely out. Still, he felt the need to aggressively pursue the horse rider and had no intention of stopping. The man stayed in the middle of the road in an attempt to keep the detective from coming up on his side and giving him a clear shot with his weapon, as well as to be able to dictate the pace of the pursuit himself. It was almost as if the man on the horse was trying purposely to lead the detective somewhere, just as he had effectively gained his attention in town. If it was a trap, Stulken knew already that he had been taken, but if it was not, he was determined to find out what was going on and how this man was linked to the bombing.

"Stop!" the detective yelled into the car's bullhorn. "Stop your horse now or I will shoot!" Stulken was yelling at the top of his lungs, though he couldn't hear anything but ringing with his severely damaged ear drums. He reached into his jacket with his good arm and grabbed his Browning automatic .45 caliber pistol and pointed it towards the back end of the horse from the patrol car's shattered window. With just a few feet separating him from the rider, he popped off a shot, only to miss.

As the chase, which was leading east out of the city, ensued, the fog around them began to thicken to the point of dangerously low visibility standards for either person. Within moments, the man and his horse seemingly disappeared into the fog, leaving absolutely no trace as to which direction they had actually gone. With both his hearing and sight now almost completely disabled, the detective came to a stop in the middle of the road to either wait for backup to come and get him or for the man on the horse to resurface. At this point, sitting and waiting was his one option.

The detective's arm was pulsating with pain and his ears were both still bleeding. The best he could do for now would be to bandage himself up a bit while he was waiting to see if anything transpired and then head back to town. He pulled the squad car over to the side of the road and began to search the interior of the car for the standard issue first aid kit that could be found in every police vehicle. Before he could find anything, he noticed something in his rear view mirror. It was a young man standing directly in the middle of the road, wearing a white robe and sandals.

"Sir? Hello? " he turned and called to the man as he stood from the vehicle and shut the door. "Are you okay?"

The man didn't respond. He smiled back at him in a way that sent shivers down the detective's spine.

"What are you doin' out here in the middle of the road?" Stulken asked.

Before Detective Stulken could even reach the back of the vehicle, the man disappeared, as if being swallowed into the mist, and his image was replaced by that of another police car, with its lights flashing. It was traveling at an enormous rate of speed and headed straight for the detective and the car he had driven to this point. Stulken had just enough time to react emotionally before the blazing patrol car slammed into the back of the other, crushing both of them in a mere instant. Despite being knocked to the ground by the force generated by the collision directly in front of him, Detective Stulken received no further injuries than what he already had.

Shortly after bringing himself back to, the detective pulled his cell phone from his pocket and started to dial 911, just to find that his phone had been cracked somewhere in all of the commotion and was no longer working. He made his way as quickly as he could to the squad car that, just moments before, had come barreling into the other car just a couple feet in front of him. To his surprise, the car was empty without another soul in sight. Neither door was open, though almost all of the windows had been shattered, and there was no sign of anyone having ever been in the car from the beginning. What had seemed bad luck at one point had turned impossible and was growing stranger, even sinister with each passing moment of the morning.

The woods behind Detective Stulken were thick and impossible to see into through the heavy fog. In the distance, he began to hear what sounded like a large group of people marching through the trees and shrubs. It seemed a long cry from reality, until he began to hear the sound of horses galloping as well. It was as if an army from centuries ago was fast approaching and getting ready for battle. The detective did the only thing he could do, which was to head back to town on foot, hoping that an officer had responded to his call and was on his or her way. It would be too dangerous to investigate on his own given the apparent size of the mob. For now, all he could hope for was that the same luck that just moments ago had saved him from being hit by a car would be with him as he made his way back to Adjacent Cove.

Almost a mile above Adjacent Cove, in the wide open skies was an Angelic military post, the newest of its kind in North America. Existing only beyond man's three-dimensional world, the post could only be seen through spiritual eyes. It was rather large, about thirty feet squared, but small in comparison to most others. Over the past several years, it had grown substantially as more and more angels were being assigned to the area. There were now two full legions and another being built up, all three of which would then form a plethos, commanded by an archangel.

White banners with a gold lion on its hind legs others with a solid shield in gold adorned the post, as these were the symbols of the two legions present. Directly in the middle was a white tent, big enough to hold the Sunedrion, or higher council, and more. The Sunedrion, one of which existed in each plethos, consisted of nine high-ranking angels including the three legionnaires, three Guardian Commanders, the Stratuema, who was the guardian and assistant to the archangel, the Senior Messenger, and the archangel, who was also the chair of the council. The archangel and stratuema were normally assigned after a plethos was completed, therefore were not present at the time.

"Do you think he's ready?" asked Psifus of the group. Psifus was a guardian commander under the

Tarsious Ω Legion. Tarsious was the name that the plethos would soon take, once the forces were built up to complete it. Psifus, just as the other angels, looked like a normal, ordinary man. He wore white armor with the symbol of his legion, a solid gold shield, on the breast plate. His sword had a pearl handle and was thin but long. He also carried a dagger that was sheathed on his lower right leg.

"I do think he's ready," answered Loque, a guardian angel that was sitting in. "Besides, we don't really have a choice." Loque was enormous in stature and wore silver body armor that matched his long, silver hair. He carried a pair of sai swords on either side of his waste and a long, medieval style sword down his back. He was a ruthless warrior and extremely dependable guardian. He had always been known as a front man that led many troops to fight in any battle at any location.

"What about his legion?" asked Psifus.

"They're ready," said Queli, another guardian angel. "They'll be glad to have him back." Queli was also fierce in battle. His leadership skills were the primary reason he had been asked to serve on the Sunedrion for now. He wore a dark grey colored armor but not as much as most angels. He didn't like how it restrained him in battle. Angels could not die, of course, but just like the fallen angels, they could be injured temporarily.

"We know that they're ready for us," stated Esthre'el, who was the legionnaire over Tarsious Ω Legion. Esthre'el was known quite well by all of the angels. God had chosen him many times to perform very important tasks. He was the angel, in fact, that was given the task of freeing Paul from prison during Biblical times. Just like he did in all of his tasks, Esthre'el accomplished his mission with great precision, despite being outnumbered in the ordeal six to one. He had chosen to perform the task alone so as not to give away his position or intent too soon.

"They've been ready for us for years," he continued. "That's the problem. Bethliel jumped the gun on this one but we couldn't have known that he was going to do it until it was too late."

"Well there's nothing we can do about it now," responded Rav, who was to be the legionnaire of the third legion once it was fully in place. His legion would eventually be represented by a silver eagle and called Tarsious Y Legion. Rav had been working in North America since the formation of the states in the eighteenth century. He was vastly familiar with the landscape, trends, and culture of all fifty states, but even more so in the south. This was the very reason God had chosen him for this task.

"Rafael's going to pay him a visit by what I understand," he continued. "If anything is wrong, he will know."

"And if need be we can give him more angels," said Psifus. "Right?"

"No," Esthre'el answered with certainty. "That's not a part of the plan, it's not the design that Jehovah gave us. He will be okay with his own legion. The rest are to stay at the post and continue to prepare and grow. Once we have a full plethos in place we will start to plan for its immediate future but for now this is how it has to be."

"What's going to happen with the men who are possessed?" Queli asked.

"Unfortunately…," answered Rav. "…they are going to decide their own fates."

"Is there nothing we can do?" Queli asked.

Angels were extremely protective of men, whether good or bad. Their philosophy was that every bad man could turn good, and many did. Every battle plan ever devised was done so with great consideration of the men involved. It was their duty to protect man and they did so as much as they possibly could in every scenario. Just as man was the enemy of demons, demons were the enemy of angels, but it was because of their need to protect man from the fallen angels attacking them.

"Nothing," Esthre'el responded. "They are too far gone for us to have the ability to do anything for them. We have to protect them as best we can but they have to decide if they want that protection or not. It's just not up to us."

XVII

Drew sat on his living room couch with his face buried in his hands when he heard a knock on the door. He had been watching the news for several hours as Adjacent Cove seemed to slip away to chaos and destruction. He knew in his heart that he was going to be the one that would have to initiate some sort of defense on behalf of everyone else in town, he just was not sure how. The images on his television set served as stark reminders of the damage that could be done by Lucifer and the fallen angels, and the worst, Drew feared, was yet to come.

"Who is it?" Drew called from the couch. There was no answer, just another knock. Drew sat quietly, not wanting to answer the door without knowing who it was.

"Who's there?" he inquired once again. Finally, after the third knock on the door, Drew stood up and walked over to his door.

"Don't worry," a voice said to Drew from behind him. "There is nothing to fear."

The voice came from the kitchen in Drew's one bedroom apartment.

"Who's there?" Drew asked as he slowly walked towards the kitchen. He reached behind him and pulled his swords, both of which were immediately immersed in blue flames. Too much had happened over the past couple of days for him to be any less cautious in this situation.

Suddenly, a man manifested from thin air just a few feet from where Drew was standing. The man wore white, loose fitting pants and a white shirt and had a long white robe that was lined in silver and gold. He wore a large sword at his side with a pearl handle and silver sheath. On his sheath was engraved the words "Fidei Defensor", which is Latin for "Defender of the Faith". He was light skinned with short, snow white hair, and had bright hazel colored eyes that reflected light like glass. On his head he wore a crown made of silver vines and leaves. His appearance was intimidating, but brilliant at the same time.

"Don't be afraid," the man said to Drew, who was standing to defend himself if necessary. "I'm not here to hurt you, only to guide you."

"What's your name?" Drew asked. "How do I know you're not one of them?"

"My name is Rafael," replied the angel.

Drew lowered his swords but kept them in his hands for the time being. For some reason, the angel began to look familiar to him, as if he'd seen him before. Never the less, he remained cautious until he could find out more.

"It's been a long time my friend," Rafael said. "I know you don't remember me now, but you will in time."

"How do you know me?" Drew asked.

"You were once my stratuema," he answered. "I am the archangel in command of Tarsious L, the plethos in which you have served since the beginning of time."

"What is a stratuema?"

"You were my guardian and assistant, until you were reassigned to this mission."

"And a plethos?" asked Drew.

"A plethos is a unit of 250,000 warriors in the hierarchy of the Angelic Army. You are still a member of Tarsious L, you're just not my stratuema anymore."

"How'd you get in here?" Drew demanded.

"I'm an angel," Rafael responded. "I don't have limits in the three dimensional world."

Relieved that Rafael was not another demon sent to kill him, Drew sheathed his swords and sat back down on the couch. He grabbed the remote control to turn off the television as Rafael sat in the recliner across the room.

"Something's bothering you?" Rafael asked.

"Yea, you could say that," answered Drew. I have no idea what I'm doing here Rafael. People keep telling me that I'm an angel and all this but I don't remember anything from before I was born as a man."

"You have to trust what you've been told Drew," Rafael stated.

"It's not that I don't believe it to be true, especially not after everything I've seen in the last twenty four hours. I just don't know what to do with it all or where to start."

"That all will come to you," Rafael reassured Drew.

"Okay, that's great, but when?" Drew asked. "This town is falling apart and I know I have to do something about it."

"Let's go for a walk," Rafael answered as he stood.

Drew stood and grabbed his keys off of the counter before they both headed toward the front door.

"You won't need those," Rafael said.

"My keys?" Drew said in response. "I don't want anyone getting in while we're out. This hasn't exactly been my lucky week."

"Trust me," answered Rafael as he gestured for Drew to lead.

Drew reluctantly placed his keys back on the kitchen counter and took the lead. Upon opening the door, a bright light exploded from the doorway, lighting up the entire apartment. Drew covered his eyes and turned to look at Rafael, who was gesturing him to keep going through the door. As he walked into the light, he found himself walking on a surface unlike any he'd experienced before. It was as if he was walking on air. Below him, there was nothing. There was no vapor, no colors of any kind, not even some sort of transparent surface such as glass. All around him, including below him, was light, as if billions of particles of light were consuming the entire atmosphere.

The further away he got from his apartment door, the more at ease Drew felt. He was beginning to experience something he had never experienced before, as far as he could tell, but could not put it into words. From head to toe, a peaceful sensation set in that made him completely forget about anything else. Once his eyes adjusted, he was able to make out large, pearl colored gates in the distance surrounded by walls made from bricks of gold. In front of the gates stood two angels, similar in dress to Rafael, holding white shields with gold trimming and long spears made of silver.

"Is this…" Drew asked. "No, it can't be, how can it be?"

"This is reality Drew," said Rafael. "How can it not be?"

The two continued to walk toward the gates, making every detail of their intricate designs more apparent as they went. Behind the gates were buildings of various types and sizes that were all made of pure gold and lined with silver. The streets of gold were full of people, all of them obviously happy and content. In the distance Drew could hear singing. It sounded like a large choir singing praise songs, old and new, to God.

"This is where we stop," said Rafael.

"I want to go in there," Drew pleaded. "I want to see more of this."

"I know you do," Rafael responded, "But you will have to be patient."

"Why'd you bring me here if I can't go in?" Drew asked.

"This is what we fight for Drew," Rafael said. "This is what God has given to His people and we must protect it. We must defend it, all of it. We even have to protect the idea of it. It's all about God's love, His mercy, and His grace. Do you understand?"

"Yes," Drew responded. "I just don't know what I'm doing. I've never dealt with anything like this."

"Actually, you have. You just don't remember."

"So how do I remember?" Drew asked.

"This is the first step," answered Rafael.

Drew stared at the gates, wanting badly to go closer the more he looked on. There was nothing he had ever wanted more in his life. Just to be outside of the gates brought him an enormous amount of comfort and peace, especially after everything he had been through the past several hours. What drove him the most, however, was knowing that his father was somewhere beyond the gates, most likely oblivious to Drew's Ever since he was fifteen, Drew had wanted just one more minute with his Dad and it killed him that he was this close to having it.

"Why did you bring me here?" Drew asked with his eyes tearing up.

"Because this is where you were created," Rafael answered. "This is your real birth place."

"Come," Rafael said after a moment of silence. "Let's walk."

Drew turned away, but aversely, and walked by Rafael's side back towards the entrance to his apartment. After just a few steps, he turned his head once more toward the gates to find that they were now gone. He wanted to go back, but also knew that there was a reason he couldn't pass through the gates and that staring at them would just make him want to go in even more.

"I don't understand something," Drew said. "What exactly is my purpose? I know that I'm doing all of this for a reason, but I guess I just don't know my place."

"You and I serve an important purpose Drew," Rafael answered. "We were created to assist God's people and fight off evil. You have to understand that we are not Satan's enemy. People are Satan's enemy, and we are here to protect God's people from the Devil and his fallen angels."

"I know that but what is my mission exactly and how am I going to go about accomplishing it?"

"First of all, Drew, by God's strength. Without that, it's hopeless. Second of all, you will follow your instincts and know what to do when the time comes to do it. I don't have all of those answers."

"Well then, what can you tell me?" Drew inquired. "You came to me and you brought me here. Can you tell me anything?"

"Look at it this way," responded Rafael. "When little Susie prays to God for protection, who do you think God sends? When Mr. Johnson is in a life threatening situation and calls out to God, who do you think God sends? When an entire city needs to ward off an attack by the Devil that would launch an enormous, nation-wide, campaign to destroy the world, who did God send? I know that's a lot of pressure Andrew, but trust me, you can do this, and you'll have the help of your angelic comrades the entire way."

"So you'll be helping me?" Drew asked.

"Of course," Rafael answered. "We all have tasks to perform but we are all in this together. Every part of this army helps to keep the other parts going strong. The Empirical Forces of Darkness do not work this way. There is constant and bold dissention within the ranks of Lucifer's army and it is always causing problems. A lot times you will face a demon as he faces you and another demon. They fell for their pride, yet they've learned nothing from it."

"Okay," Drew said. "I have another question. How can I be both man and angel at the same time?"

"How can the entire earth be flooded?" asked Rafael. "How can a person be raised from the dead? How could Jesus feed all those people?"

"I know but, how does it work? Sometimes I have these swords on my back, and sometimes I don't."

"You are an angel when you want to be an angel," Rafael answered. "When you want to be a man, you're a man. But you're always both. So the swords are there when you want them to be. It's as natural as breathing."

Drew reached back and pulled his swords from their sheaths and examined them. In one of the blades he saw his reflection, with black hair and bright, blue eyes. It was as if he was looking through a glass into his own soul as he pondered over his entire life leading up to this moment. It was just days ago when he was going about his business as usual, with nothing particularly strange about it. There was no way that he could have known the battles to come, nor how they would come about. The more he looked at himself in the reflection from his sword, the more he could see the angel that God had created.

"You're gonna' be fine," Rafael said from behind Drew. "If anything can pull this off, it's you my friend."

"I hope you're right," responded Drew.

"Don't worry, I've never been more right about anything. I know you. You are Eleazar."

XVIII

It was barely midday and Adjacent Cove was already bustling with chaos and confusion. What was a peaceful city for the most part just a day ago was now beginning to crumble from the foundation and up. The thick fog blanketing most of the county only added to the growing disorientation. Police were stretched thin, despite every one of them being called to duty. The Sherriff's department and law enforcement agencies from neighboring towns were helping out as well. Residents were frantic as they heard of their respective banks being robbed and destroyed. Emergency switchboards were receiving missing persons reports right and left, so many that the police could not come near investigating all of them. So far, 143 men were missing from the community without a word or even a hint of where they might be.

The prison break from Ware State Penitentiary the day before had not gone over looked. An enormous emphasis had been placed on finding the fugitive and his accomplice as soon as possible. Some had even speculated that perhaps the incidents involving the banks were related in some way to the escapee. James Walker had, after all, been arrested more than once for theft and armed robbery. At this magnitude, however, he would have needed help.

Despite the considerations presented thus far, it was obvious that whoever had robbed the banks were bold, good at what they do, and not alone. In fact, most media outlets had already named the team of thieves "Chaos From Control", or "CFC". The phrase had been first borrowed by a reporter when he heard Detective Stulken say it earlier that day. If indeed CFC was connected to the prison break as well, then authorities were looking at a large scale attack of some kind on the citizens' very way of life. So far, the group had already succeeded in causing wide spread panic across most of the county and all of Adjacent Cove. People were staying home instead of going to work and keeping their children at home in fear that more attacks would happen as random as the first ones on the banks.

So far the sole measure taken by law enforcement to keep the citizens calm was to call a town hall meeting for that night. The chief of police, Robert Davis, would be there to inform the residents of Adjacent Cove of what was going on and what they were currently doing about it. He also hoped that if enough people showed up, he could try to gather as much information as he could that would give them some possible leads. Town hall meetings were usually scheduled well in advance and exclusively advertised in the newspaper, but given the severity of the situation, city government officials were going door to door throughout the day to urge people to come.

On Thomas Jasper's land, the scene was becoming grislier by the minute. Detective Charlie Ellis had now stumbled upon not one, but several charred remains of human bodies in the remains of the barn. The morgue had arrived long ago but was now taking several trips to retrieve the bodies as they were photographed and noted. Two ambulances were also on the scene in the event that someone was found alive. At this point, however, that notion seemed hopeless. Detective Ellis was puzzled, to say the least, this being her first homicide case on this sort of level. She had never seen anything like it before, though it had no effect on her professionalism or ability to handle the situation. Without Detective Stulken on the scene, she was the lead person on the case.

"Where are you Mark?" Ellis said as she slammed her cell phone shut. She had been trying to get a hold of Stulken for a couple of hours now with no luck. She even called some of the town's uniformed police, including Officer Spencer, in attempting to reach him. It wasn't like him to not answer his phone or not call, regardless of the situation. Her concern was quickly turning to worry. Detective Ellis turned to find a uniformed officer standing directly behind her.

"Have you heard from Detective Stulken?" she asked him.

"No, ma'am," the officer answered. He seemed disturbed by something but was having a difficult time getting it out.

"Something bothering you?" the detective asked.

"Well, ma'am," he began with a tremble in his voice.

"Ellis," said the detective.

"Pardon?"

"Detective Ellis," she stated. "Please don't call me ma'am."

"Oh, right," the officer responded. "Detective Ellis, there's something you need to know." He paused for a moment, still trying to find the right words.

"Well, spit it out," Detective Ellis demanded.

"I know what happened here ma'am, I mean, Detective Ellis."

The officer's name was Miles Jackson and he had been a police officer in Adjacent Cove for just over two years. He was young, single, and a big part of the night life in nearby Austin when he wasn't on duty. He had joined Los Ultimos Dias a few months prior after a friend of his had asked him to attend one of their regular meetings. Jackson never had attached himself to any kind of belief system, and in fact had referred to himself as an atheist for most of his life. It was not that he felt strongly against Christianity, he just never found the desire to be a part of any kind of religion. Since joining Los Ultimos Dias, however, he had begun to feel strongly against Christianity and especially organized religion. The previous night he had been on duty when receiving the call about the special meeting and planned on stopping in without anyone knowing until he became tied up dealing with a drunken driver. He did manage to make it, but well after the meeting had started.

"Go on," said the detective, just as her phone rang.

The officer sat down on a charred chair as Detective Ellis answered her phone. It was Detective Stulken, who had been picked up by a sheriff's deputy just outside the city limits. He was headed to the police department now and was asking Ellis to leave the scene to the CSI department and head back to the department herself. His tone left no room for response or questioning, leaving Ellis to believe that he was on to something big. As per her partner's request, Detective Ellis let the appropriate personnel know that she was leaving and headed for her car.

"Detective Ellis," said the officer, standing from the chair.

"Oh yea," she said, motioning for him to come with her. "Come with me and we'll talk."

Despite the happenings of the past several hours, the city and county governments were proceeding with business as usual. Trenton County Courthouse was full of people coming and going to handle their various personal affairs and the courtrooms had full dockets. The civil court room handled all civil matters, including divorce and child custody cases. As with any civil court room in America, it was always full and booked for the entire day. Judge Lars Hatchett had been in his seat for many years and had always been looked upon favorably by the community for his fair and just practices and strong moral code. Though well into his fifties, Judge Hatchett brought a certain energy to his courtroom which was both rare and unique.

On this particular morning, Judge Hatchett had been the one to strongly encourage his and the rest of the courthouse staff to continue with business as usual, despite the obvious distractions. Though there was a short stoppage at the sound of explosions coming from the various banks in town, things were proceeding without much delay. Bailiffs and other security personnel were on high alert in order to keep the staff and citizens as safe and as calm as possible.

Just as Judge Hatchett was opening his next case, the divorce of a young couple with a child, the sounds of screams and commotion could be heard outside the large wooden doors in the back of the room. Suddenly, the doors flew open as several men wearing long black robes with black hoods rushed inside. The men carried guns and blades of various sizes and calibers, except one, who walked into the room last. The man wore a black robe, the same as the others, with a hood covering his head. He was large and intimidating in stature, but there was an evil about him that everyone in the room recognized. The man that was once Thomas Walker walked up the isle in the center of the courtroom with an aroma of pride and confidence in what he was doing. The rest of the unknown assailants circled the entire courtroom with their weapons ready to fire.

The bailiff and judge were the only two left standing in front of the room. Everyone else had been demanded to fall to their knees wherever they stood. The bailiff had drawn his pistol when they first came in but was unsure at this point what he should do. Out of fear, the bailiff fired a shot off at one of the men, missing him by just an inch or two. Immediately, the man responded with a blast from his sawed off shotgun that knocked the bailiff backwards to the floor. As he yelled out in pain, another of the men approached him, pulled an automatic pistol from his side, and shot the bailiff squarely between the eyes. The rest of the courtroom gasped in horror at the sight, most of them trembling in fear by this point. The judge remained at his position, refusing to kneel at the men's demands.

"I am Bethliel," said the former Thomas Walker in a raspy voice. He raised his arm, revealing his pale and bony hands and pointed at the judge. "You will bow before me."

Judge Hatchett stood his ground for just a moment before finally giving in to his fear and falling to his knees at the side of his desk. Bethliel approached him slowly, peering right into the judge's soul with his green, cat like eyes. The judge trembled in fear at the mere sight of Bethliel and his depraved presence. All he could do was lower his head and pray. He prayed silently, so as not to make Bethliel aware of it.

"Praying?" Bethliel whispered in the judge's ear. "Who do you pray to if you don't belong to God?"

Bethliel pulled a long, double edged sword from his side and placed the side of the blade to the judge's neck. Judge Hatchett began to pray and cry aloud. Bethliel lifted the blade and with one swift motion decapitated the judge. He then reached down and grabbed the judge's head and placed it on the desk where Judge Hatchett once ruled.

The crowd once again gasped in horror, some of them crying loudly and others passing out. Those who were Christians prayed steadfastly, trying to ignore what was going on in front of them. The men surrounding the room poked at those who were the loudest, threatening them with their life.

Suddenly, in the ceiling above the courtroom, a dark cloud began to spin at dead center, getting bigger as it went. In only seconds, the entire ceiling was concealed by the dark cloud. Occasionally, a solid black, leathery creature with wings would emerge from the billows, some of them letting out a horrifying shriek before flying back into them. Bethliel stood with his arms raised and his bloody sword high as the cloud grew thicker by the moment. Before too long, the malicious cloud was just inches above the heads of those standing. The dark creatures that emerged now would occasionally swoop down and scratch the people below, leaving deep cuts on wherever they landed.

"Impetus Malignus," Bethliel said as loud as he could, which is roughly translated to "Revolution of Evil". "Impetus Malignus!" he repeated with his arms high. The more he spoke, the louder the commotion in the courtroom was. "Impetus Malignus!" he said once more.

"God, I need you now more than ever before," said Drew with his head down and on his knees in the middle of the living room of his small apartment. The television was on and every station was broadcasting continuous coverage of what had now been deemed the "Crisis in the Hills". It was as if, by surprise, the city of Adjacent Cove and the county seat was falling apart and into the grip of a dark force that had its evil hands in every aspect of the local society. Drew knew that everything he had ever done in his life was coming down to this one moment. The only questions remaining dealt with why he was chosen and how he was supposed to overcome this dark and horrible presence that was eating away at everything he knew and loved.

"I know why I am here God," he continued. "For the first time in my life, I am sure of what it is You want me to do with my life. What I don't understand, however, is why you've chosen me God…and exactly what I am supposed to do." Drew's hands trembled slightly as a tear fell down his cheek and onto the floor. He tried his best to put aside the distractions on the television screen and just talk to God, but was finding this to be more and more difficult as time went by and updates to the stories were broadcast.

"I'm afraid God. This is a lot to throw on a person, so suddenly. I've had no time to prepare for any of this and I don't even know where I am supposed to start. I feel lost, like I know my place but I don't know my way. I am only me. I haven't done much of anything with my life God, I know that. Perhaps I could have been more prepared. Maybe I should have somehow known about this sooner. Did I pass you by God? Did I ignore the wrong person?"

The television was now flashing scenes from an army base nearby, where soldiers were readying themselves and loading up to be transferred to Adjacent Cove. It hadn't been done yet, but the entrance of martial law seemed inevitable at the time. Both the courthouse and city hall had been besieged by several men wearing long, black robes and reportedly, hostages had been taken. The men entering town and causing the widespread panic were armed to the teeth, but they never fired a shot. They all possessed a strange sort of amplified strength and speed, allowing them to carry out their mission with great success. Additionally, each of the three groups were led by an especially dangerous figure that carried no weapons at all yet possessed the ability to throw fire and bolts of lightning from their hands. Not a single shot taken at any of the men by law enforcement had met their intended targets as they continued their rampant march through the inner workings of the city and county.

"I should be out there," Drew continued. "I should be helping those people, but I don't know how. Flying through the air is one thing God but this is another thing entirely. These people need somebody to save them from this darkness that is taking over the town. They need a savior, and that's You, not me. Even as an angel, I am nothing God. I am nothing next to Your awesome strength and power. Please God, tell me what to do and I will do it. Tell me where to go and I will go. Wherever You lead God, wherever you lead I will go."

XIX

"Call the national guard," Detective Stulken said with frantic desperation as he and a few other members of the Adjacent Cove Police Department sought refuge at a nearby coffee shop. Only a handful of men and women managed to escape the horror that had taken place at the police station just moments before. Both the police station and the city hall had fallen victim to the same type of takeover as the court house did. What was baffling was how the still unidentified men in robes were able to do it all with such low numbers and nowhere near the fire power as the police. Still, several people were dead and many more were being held hostage by the assailants at all three locations.

"And for God's sake call Ellis and tell her to come here so she doesn't go back to that hell hole."

"I'm already here," Detective Ellis said as she walked through the door. "I saw you guys running over here. What the heck is going on here?"

"These men, with guns," Detective Stulken responded in despair. "They've taken over everything in the city. They have all the power now. We're gonna' need the military to get involved and quick."

"Those men…" said Officer Miles Jackson, who had come in with Detective Ellis. "…do you have a description?"

"All I know is that they're wearing black robes with hoods," said Stulken. "If we could get a shot of just one of 'em we could probably identify the whole group."

"We would have to somehow get a hold of all the security tapes," Detective Ellis chimed in.

"No," said Officer Jackson. "That's not necessary. I know who they are. They're Los Ultimos Dias."

"Los Ultimos Dias?" asked Stulken. "Didn't that group die off a long time ago?"

"On the contrary, sir" replied Jackson. "They are almost two hundred strong."

"So how do you know that this is them?" asked Ellis.

Officer Jackson paused for a moment and dropped his head. "Because I'm a member," he stated.

"Have a seat," Stulken said.

Both Officer Jackson and Detective Ellis sat at a table across from Detective Stulken. The officer took a deep breath, knowing full well that after disclosing this information, this could be the end of his career as a police officer. Being an officer of the law had been a dream all his life and it would be nothing short of devastating to have to give it up. Detective Stulken pulled a small memo pad and pen from his jacket pocket and a small digital voice recorder from another. He placed the recorder on the table and clicked his pen.

"I'm ready when you are," the detective said.

"Should I start with my name?" asked Jackson.

Detective Stulken thought for a moment about everything going on and decided in his mind that there was no reason as of yet to cause the young officer to lose his job or destroy his reputation. Right now he needed all the help he could get until the military could arrive.

"Let's just call you John for now," said the detective. "Now tell me everything I need to know and don't leave anything out.

"Okay," said Officer Jackson with a sigh. "I am a member of a group, or a secret society called Los Ultimos Dias, which basically means the last days. It's Spanish because they guy who founded the group was Hispanic. I believe he's in jail now. Anyway, I only joined a few months ago but I learned a lot about them while I was there."

Both detectives scribbled frantically as the officer spoke. Jackson paused for a moment from time to time to let them catch up, but understood the urgency of the situation as well.

"They, or I guess we, are what you would call a theistic Satanist group, meaning we believe in Lucifer, follow his cause, and worship him as the leader of the fallen angels. There's almost two hundred members now but there are a few that are deeper into it than most of us. They perform what they call tasks for Satan, but I don't know what they are. I have been trying to stay away from anything illegal, you know, 'cause of my profession and all."

"Where does this group meet?" asked Detective Stulken.

"At the barn that is now a pile of ashes and charred wood," replied Jackson. "That's Thomas Jasper's land. He lets us use it as long as we're discreet about it. He doesn't want to smudge his reputation you know. So we meet twice a month, sometimes more, depending on what's going on."

"What do you mean by 'what's going on'?" Ellis asked.

"Well we determine our need to meet based on the world around us, according to James. He calls the meetings as he sees fit."

"James?" asked Stulken.

"James, yea, he's the leader," replied Jackson. "He's the one that escaped from Ware yesterday. He's a big and ruthlessly violent person. I've seen him beat people during our meetings because he didn't like what they had to say or just didn't like them for whatever reason. We keep going back though, even the guys that get beat up. James is very much like a hypnotist. He's pulled us in and gotten our attention and gained a lot of followers."

"How come we've never heard about what's going on out there," Detective Ellis inquired.

"Because we're good at keeping it a secret, that's a part of our code. We feel protected that way, and nobody breaks the code."

"Your code?" asked Stulken

"We have a code," responded the officer. "When we join we're given this card." Officer Jackson pulled a laminated card from his pocket that contained a list of rules that were called the "Code". The officer began to read them off.

"First, we are to 'Conceal the existence of the group and deny membership whenever necessary'. Los Ultimos Dias has to remain a secret in order to properly operate. Next, we are to 'Serve only Lucifer, the Morning Star and the Prince of Darkness'. Next, we are to 'Know the nine Satanic Statements' that are found in the Satanic Bible. The next code says that 'Man is our opponent, but the Christians are our enemy'. After that it says that we are to 'Give everything we are to Los Ultimos Dias' without fail."

"Okay, so tell me more about these men in robes," Officer Stulken stated. "And what about the barn, do you know what happened there?"

Officer Jackson stopped for a moment and put his card back in his pocket. Tears began to form in his eyes and his hands began to tremble. The detectives could easily tell that something had deeply troubled the officer. It was yet another sign that something terrible had happened at the barn the previous night.

"It's okay," said Detective Ellis as she rubbed the officer's back. "You can tell us. We've gotta' know what happened out there."

"I know," replied the officer as he dried his tears and caught his breath. "It was terrible, the worst, most evil and horrible of an atrocity as I've ever seen. I have never witnessed anything even close to being like it."

Officer Jackson stood from his chair and raised his arms over his head to catch his breath as he walked towards the back of the room. His breathing was heavy as he paced slowly around in a small circle. A bead of sweat fell down the side of his face and dripped off of his chin to the floor.

"Is it hot in here to you guys?" Officer Jackson asked.

"Can someone fix the temperature in here and get us some water?" said Detective Stulken. There were at least three others outside the room listening in and monitoring what was going on through cameras placed in the two corners in the back of the room.

"Why don't you sit down?" asked Detective Ellis.

"Because," stuttered Officer Jackson. "I just need to stand right now."

"Okay, let's pick up where we left off then," said Detective Stulken. "Tell us what you saw when you showed up at the barn."

"My career is gonna' be over," said Officer Jackson.

"As far as I'm concerned,…" replied Stulken. "…nobody else needs to know about your involvement with the cult. To be honest, we need you right now, so quit worrying about that and just come sit down and tell us what happened."

Officer Jackson returned to his seat and sat down just as the door opened and another detective walked in with three bottles of water. The detective placed them on the table and left the room. Jackson used his sleeve to wipe off the sweat as good as he could, but his nerves were making it difficult to stop it.

"I got there late," Officer Jackson began. "When I got there I could hear a bunch of commotion going on inside the barn. Then I heard somebody cry out and it alarmed me, so instead of going in I looked through a crack in one of the walls and tried to see as much as I could.

"There was this man wearing a black robe with a hood over his head, he was pointing at men in the group, who would then get up and go to the back of the room. It was strange though, because every person that he pointed to became like zombies, like they weren't themselves anymore. They just…obeyed. It was like the man had some kind of power over them.

"Then I saw this one guy, his name was Tom, he got up really quickly and darted for the back doors. Just before he got there, another man in a black robe who was huge just flew through the air towards him. When he got to him he sliced Tom's back open with a dagger. When Tom turned around, the man sliced his front open. Tom's guts just came out of him and he fell over and died.

"I didn't know what to do. I wasn't on duty so I didn't have my gun or a radio or anything, and my cell phone battery was dead. It was charged up when I got there, but it just died.

"What happened after that?" Detective Stulken asked.

"Well, right after that both of the men in robes walked off the stage towards the back doors. When they went out of the barn the men standing there followed them and then the doors just shut behind them, on their own. Next thing you know, the whole inside began to go up in flames. I ran to the doors and pulled on them as hard as I could but they wouldn't budge. There were at least thirty or forty men in there and they were all screaming and pounding on the doors and walls. I ran around the barn and looked for another way out but there just wasn't one. There was nothing I could do.

Officer Jackson pounded his hand on the table as tears streamed down his face. It bothered him deeply that he couldn't save those men. He had tried everything he could to free the men.

"There was nothing I could do," Jackson repeated as he cried.

"I know," Detective Ellis said as she placed her hand on Jackson's back. "There was nothing more that you could have done to save them. It wasn't your fault in the first place."

"You said there were thirty or forty men in there?" Detective Stulken asked.

"At least," replied the officer. "I had friends in there."

"Do you know who these people were?" asked Ellis.

"Just look at all the missing person reports filed today," Jackson answered. "That's a start."

Alyssa's room hadn't changed at all since she had moved off to college. The walls were covered with mock art, some of which were framed. She had gained a love for art after visiting the art museum in Austin with her sophomore class. She had even tried her own hand at it a couple of times but was not pleased.

After suffering a mild concussion, Alyssa was now battling a migraine headache, something that inflicted her often. She hadn't left her bed since coming home from the hospital and was completely unaware of what was going on outside her window. She knew that she had been involved in some serious accident but the details were foggy. Alyssa was also aware that she was rescued and taken to the hospital by someone. She hadn't told anyone her fear of being called crazy, but she knew in her heart that the person that had rescued her was an angel. She also had some idea that Drew was somehow involved as well. She remembered waking for just a moment and seeing Drew's face as he carried her carefully away from the car.

Startled by a short gust of wind coming through the room, Alyssa awoke and rose up in her bed to find that the window had been opened, letting the occasional breeze into the room. She didn't find it alarming in any way, just curious. As Alyssa slowly got up to her feet, raising her hand over her eyes to shield them from the light coming through the window, she noticed a card on her bed.

The card was small, measuring about five by seven inches in size. The off white paper was thick and looked almost like papyrus from many years ago. A genuine gold line bordered the card and glimmered in the light. In the middle was hand written the words "Forget Me Not" in cursive with a Christian fish drawn below and to the right. The text and fish were also written in what appeared to be some kind of pure gold ink. The whole card was brilliant in appearance, obviously made with an enormous amount of care.

Alyssa held the card to her chest and smiled. For that moment, her headache went completely away. When they were children, Drew used to climb to Alyssa's window and climb in to wake her up and talk for a while or to get her to go with him for a walk. Because of this, she would leave her window unlocked for him. It became a habit. It was no different now, and she had a pretty good idea of who might have left the card.

XX

The entire city of Adjacent Cove and most of Trenton County had been enveloped in a mysterious thick fog for the second day in a row and it showed no signs of lifting any time soon. In the downtown area, the fog had thickened into a blackness that covered all of downtown and parts of the surrounding neighborhoods and business centers. Schools were letting out early and were near frantic, trying to get every child away and home safely. Business owners and other operations were also closing early and retreating to the safety of their respective homes. Fear had gripped the city tightly as events escalated into scenarios of pure horror. With the police department now in the hands of the newly dubbed Chaos from Control, the law fell squarely in the hands of those police officers that were still out on patrol and the county Sherriff's department.

Just two blocks from the downtown square in an older neighborhood lived the Ryers. Jack Ryer was a music minister in one of the local churches and his wife a stay at home mom. Their two children, Drake and Susanne, both attended Rollins Junior High just down the street. They lived in a modest frame home that they had purchased a few years back and fixed up over the years. Jack was just driving up as his two children came running into the front yard.

"What's going on Dad?" Susanne asked, obviously afraid.

"It's okay kids, just get inside," her father replied.

News about what was truly going on was on every local station and now, a national news station as well. Reporters were spread out all over the area at the banks, at Ware State Penitentiary, and even down town. People were being warned to stay away from the area if possible and to bunker in their homes if not. Jack had thought about piling his family in the van and leaving town but decided it would be safer at this moment to stay in. He kept the television on and had his whole family sit on the floor in front of the couch so that they couldn't be seen through the windows. With no significant weapon in the house, he pulled out the longest kitchen knife he had and slid it under his belt on his side.

"If it was okay you wouldn't have a knife," said Jack's eldest, Drake.

"It's just for good measure," Jack replied. "Right now, I just want us to pray."

Just as the family bowed their heads together, the door busted open with an enormous force and three men came through. All of them were wearing black robes with hoods and were carrying guns. Jack immediately recognized one of the men as a long time friend of his and member of his church.

"Get on the floor," the man yelled. "Heads down and on your knees, now."

"Wade?" Jack asked, perplexed by his presence.

"I said heads down Jack," Wade said as he placed the barrel of his sawed off shotgun inches from Jack's forehead. "Don't make me hurt you."

As Wade guarded the family, the other two men tore through the house, destroying everything in sight. The sound of glass shattering and wood breaking rang throughout the home. All but Jack were in tears and feared for their lives, regardless of their recognition of Wade.

"What are we gonna' do Dad?" Susanne asked. "Why are they doing this?"

"It's okay sweetie," said Dianne, Jack's wife, as she placed her hand around her daughter's head. "Just pray."

"Why are you doing this Wade?" Jack asked as he lifted his head. "We've known each other for years."

"I'm not the person you think I am," Wade answered, this time in a raspy voice. His voice deepened and his eyes turned red and he looked back at Jack and added, "You will fear me now, I am a monster!"

Jack was taken back and lowered his head once again. "Pray, guys," he said. "Just pray."

The family prayed frantically on their knees as the other two men continued their rampage through the home. Wade was alarmed by this and hit Jack on the back of his head with the butt of his shotgun. Jack fell to the floor, nearly unconscious but still able to continue praying for God's protection. This agitated Wade further as he began to force the rest of the family to their faces.

"To whom do you pray?" Wade said with a laugh. "To God? Don't you know that He's too busy for your insignificant requests." Wade cocked his shotgun and pointed it at Drake's head. "What about you boy," he said as he knelt down closer to him.

"Please," Jake said, lifting his bleeding head once more. "This isn't who you are Wade. Please don't point the gun at my son."

"You lower your eyes to me," Wade said. "All of you, stop your worthless cries to God and bow to me."

"We will not bow to Satan," Jack said firmly, with his head down again. "You can do what you want with us but we will not bow to Satan. This house bows to God alone."

This angered Wade greatly as he stood to his feet once again. "I did not tell you to bow to Satan," he said loudly. "I told you to bow to me!" He raised his gun towards the ceiling and began to fire rounds around the room. One shot caused the ceiling fan to fall onto the couch behind the family.

"You will obey me and you will bow!" Wade yelled, his eyes bloodshot and deep. The other two men now joined him, laughing at the shaking family on the floor in front of them. "Bow to me!" Wade continued in an evil voice as the others laughed on and fired their weapons in the air as well.

Just as the ceiling was about to completely give in, the door busted open once again. This time a man stood in a white robe, also with a hood, with his hands joined in front of him. He looked to the floor, casting a shadow over his face, but not concealing the blue glow coming from his eyes. It was Eleazar, and Jack knew immediately that it was an angel and that he and his family was saved.

He placed his arm around his family, as far as it could reach, and held them tight before looking up at Wade once more.

"I think he might have some authority over you," Jack said.

Eleazar entered the room and pulled his two blades from behind him. The blades were illuminated by the blue flames that enveloped them. Eleazar swung the swords in front of him swiftly, causing what looked like a sphere of swinging blades and blue flames. Then suddenly he stopped, slowly bringing one blade to his back and the other around his side and pointing towards the floor in front of him. The three men reloaded their weapons and fired as quickly as they could, but to no avail.

The bullets seemed to pass right through Eleazar as he held his position in front of them. After running out of ammo, one of the men turned to run. Eleazar thrust forward his arm from his back, sending an invisible force towards the man that knocked him several feet forward into the rubble that he had created moments before. Another man threw down his pistol and pulled a stick from his side and jumped forward towards Eleazar, who grabbed the man by his throat in mid air and threw him through the window by the front door. That man stood and limped away as quickly as he could. With one man left, Eleazar raised his blades and readied himself for any attack that Wade might throw at him.

"Who are you?" Eleazar asked.

"My name is Wade," he answered.

"The Lord rebuke you." Eleazar stated.

Wade began to laugh. "You've no idea who you're dealing with Eleazar."

"How do you know my name?" Eleazar demanded.

"Oh, we go way back," answered Wade. "In fact, I have a score to settle with you."

"Well then," Eleazar said. "Settle it."

Wade threw his shotgun down and lunged towards Eleazar violently. He grabbed Eleazar's hands in an effort to use his swords against him, but Eleazar twisted his wrists away quickly and landed a right hook into Wade's head with the butt of his sword. Wade fell to the ground but got up just as quickly. He grabbed a recliner that had been knocked over and shot up and hurled it at Eleazar, who dodged it and started walking towards Wade.

With inhuman strength, Wade grabbed the piano, also destroyed, and hurled it towards Eleazar as well, who just dodged the piece of furniture once more. The family remained in their spot looking on as Wade grabbed chairs and tables and threw them at Eleazar.

"Don't stop praying," Eleazar said to the family as he passed them. "Who are you?" he yelled at Wade, who seemed to be desperately trying to find a way out of the situation.

Wade laughed again and finally stopped. "You really don't remember me do you?"

"No, I don't." replied Eleazar. "If I remembered you I wouldn't be asking who you are."

"Does the name Hadeom ring a bell?" Wade asked.

Eleazar stopped. The name did ring a bell. He suddenly began to remember an angel that was his friend before he defied God and fell with the other angels. Past that he couldn't remember much. Regardless of his memories, Hadeom was fallen, and an enemy of the light.

"The Lord rebuke you." Eleazar said once more.

"Yea, you already said that you idiot," Hadeom responded as he laughed.

"The man you've taken is a good man with a family," Eleazar said. "Let him go."

"You have no power over me!" Hadeom yelled, still in possession of Wade's body.

Eleazar sheathed his swords and lowered his head. He positioned his feet as if he was readying to lunge forward. His arms were outstretched in front of him as he suddenly lunged forward with an enormous force towards the possessed man. He passed right through the man, as if he wasn't even there, and in the process pulled a black beast resembling a giant bat from Wade's body, which fell limp to the floor. Drew pulled one sword from his back and with one swift motion cut the head off of the beast, which then turned to dust and dropped to the floor.

Eleazar turned to the family, who were all looking up at what was going on. Jack, who was still bleeding from his head, rose to his feet and ran to Wade, who lied on the floor of what was once the dining room unconscious.

"Thank you," Jack said to Eleazar.

"Keep praying," he answered as he shook Jack's hand and walked through the kitchen and out the back door.

"We're getting out of here," Jim said to his wife Cindy as they sat in the living room watching the news.

"What do you mean?" Cindy asked. "They're saying to stay put."

"I know…," Jim replied. "…but Drew's out there. We need to be praying for him."

"So we'll pray for him right here," said Cindy.

"No, we need to go to the church and pray with others. The more people banding together to pray the better off he'll be."

"Jim, the church is going to be closed," Cindy stated, not wanting to leave their home. "And besides that, Alyssa is still recovering from her accident. We can't just leave her."

"I'll go," said Alyssa from the staircase. "I'll be fine, I wanna' go and pray for Drew."

"But sweetie you have to rest," Cindy replied. "The doctor said that you need to be in bed. You just had your accident last night."

"I know what the doctor said...," said Alyssa. "...but we have to do our part to help Drew and I'm not going to be left out of it. Don't forget that he saved me. It wouldn't be right to sit here and watch the news all day instead of doing something to help him."

"But we can do it right here," stated Cindy. "I know that Drew needs our prayers but we don't have to go somewhere else to do it."

"Like Dad said...," Alyssa replied. "...the more the better."

"If First isn't open, we'll find a church that is," said Jim. "There must be a group out there somewhere that's praying."

"If you say we're going, then I'm with you," Cindy said. "I guess I'm just afraid of getting out. You two have already been attacked once and I don't want anything else to happen to us."

"Drew needs our prayers," Jim stated. "Drew and whatever other angels are out there. Our prayer will give them strength and by the look of things they're going to need all the strength they can get. If we don't find a group that's already praying, then we'll form one ourselves. Either way, we have to do our part. Drew is family, and it's our duty as family. More importantly, it's our duty as Christians."

"We have to send them in now," stated Psifus. The Sunedrion had convened once more, only this time closer to the earth's surface in better view of the Adjacent Cove's chaotic downtown area. They had already fought off a few demons and were expecting more. This was what the angels commonly referred to as a "hot zone", meaning that the area was badly overrun by demons and demonic activity. Managing a hot zone was particularly difficult and only assigned to high ranking angels. The solution for Adjacent Cove had been in place by God for many years now and was about to be activated, much earlier than anyone could have expected. Whether or not Eleazar was ready for his task was a concern, but was nothing that could be addressed any longer.

"We've gotta' send his legion in now before this becomes out of our reach entirely," Esthre'el stated in support of one of his commanders.

"Can we not give him any more support than his own legion?" asked Siamus, a guardian commander under Rav's command. Siamus had been working under Michael in the middle east for centuries before being reassigned to America. God felt that his hardened battle skills would be a great attribute to the particular task at hand as well as others.

"No, this is the way God wants it," answered Rav. "It's gotta' be Eleazar and his legion and no others."

"God's will is perfect," Esthre'el stated. "And only He knows the outcome of this. All we can do is be patient and know that Jehovah is in control."

"I'll drop an amen on the end of that," said Queli.

"Eleazar is going to be fine," commented Haikus, who was the ranking centurion of a cohort in the Tarsious Y Legion as well as an assistant to one of its messengers. "It'll all come back to him."

"In the meantime…," asked Esthre'el. "…are our troops ready in case God wants us to send them in?"

"They are ready," answered Psifus. "But for some reason I do not see it coming to that. Let us not forget that Eleazar is a special angel. He has an enormous amount of wit about him and he's as tough as they come. I have heard stories of some of the situations he has gotten himself out of and they are pretty amazing."

"How come he is not more than a legionnaire?" asked Rav.

"Once again, it is all God's perfect will," Esthre'el answered. "But by what I understand, he doesn't want to be anything higher than that. He likes to be able to be as close to the battle as possible. That is a lot of what makes him so special. Just wait, you'll see what I'm talking about soon enough. Right now it's time to send in the troops."

XXI

The downtown area, which consisted of about ten city blocks, was now overrun by Chaos From Control. The group of just around a hundred and fifty men had now taken over every center of the city's government and was now looking at taking over the county as well. Some of the men had spread out into the neighborhoods and were wreaking havoc on residential areas and businesses alike. The thick black fog that enveloped the area was completely blocking out the sun and causing night time like conditions for everyone in the area. Reporters camped outside the area with all but one of them not brave enough to enter the chaos. The one that had gotten in was the only reporter allowed by Bethliel and the only person, along with his camera man and an assistant, in the small area safe from being taken as another hostage. Apparently, it was his wish to let the world know and even see what was going on and as he put it, "what was coming their way soon."

"The scene inside Adjacent Cove's centers of government is grim," the reporter said from outside City Hall. "As you can see the visibility is quite limited due to a thick black fog that has fallen upon us here in front of City Hall. Inside the group now dubbed Chaos From Control, or CFC, is planning an even larger attack on all of Trenton County. Many, including Mayor Roger Jenkins, are being held hostage in a room in the back of the building. Word is that hostages are being held at both the court house and the police station as well.

"I'm getting word now as well that many of the police officers and personnel have escaped and are now teaming up with the police officers who were out on duty when the takeover occurred to try and form some sort of plan to take the city back. Unfortunately, it appears that CFC has a pretty firm grasp on the city for now, I'll get more word to you as soon as I know more. No word yet on demands for the release of the hostages.

"This is Rob McKnight for channel five news, with continuing coverage of the crisis unfolding in Adjacent Cove."

Inside City Hall, Bethliel and a handful of high ranking demons gathered in one of the conference rooms to plan out their next move. The room was dark, lit only by the dim light coming through the blinds. There was an eerie fog that only added to the inhabitance of pure evil and depravity that occupied the room. Every character had their own vibe but the level of hate for human beings was mutual. Bethliel sat at the head of the table looking at a map of Trenton County. The downtown area had been highlighted and the three buildings that were taken over had been marked with a red 'X'.

Bethliel, in full possession of the man that was once Thomas Walker, was in charge of the mission to take over Adjacent Cove and then Trenton County. Though he was being hasty, he had been the demon chosen by Lucifer to carry out this task several years ago. Bethliel, a general in the Empirical Forces of Darkness, was in charge of a Legion, which consisted of approximately one hundred thousand demons.

"Where do we stand?" asked Citikaih, an assassin demon. Citikaih mostly resembled a man with an enormous stature. He was similar to Saithe, only he didn't wear a robe or hood. His spine stuck out of his back and continued over his head to just over his eyes. Citikaih was a pale green color and wore a sleeveless shirt over his muscular torso and wore thick, leather pants loaded with all sorts of blades and one sword. He had hands and feet similar to the talons of an eagle and were tipped with extremely sharp nails that could rip through just about anything.

Assassins within the Empirical Forces of Darkness were not ranked and worked under or above no command. These were highly skilled, deadly demons with the ability to take out entire groups of people at a time. Many angels feared them, and men who knew of their existence placed them on a pedestal of sorts in the overall hierarchy of demonic forces. Assassins were handpicked by Lucifer himself. Once picked, one could never go back to the title they once held, but none desired to either. It was a revered position and one not easily attained.

"The humans in our control have established a perimeter a mile wide on every side," said Bethliel, with his eyes as black as night. "They will assemble in their places now."

"And you are sure that they will fight for us?" said Beaux Lux, another assassin demon. Beaux Lux was considered one of Satan's top assassins and had been for hundreds of years. His specialty was seeing to the assassination of world leaders and he had no limits or guidelines to follow. It was kill or fail for him.

There is no doubt that Beaux Lux was one of the most foul of creatures boasted by the Empirical Forces of Darkness. He was like a minotaur, with the head of a bull, but the body of a man. Every part of him was enormous in size. His skin was as red as blood and his eyes were black as night. The horns protruding from his head had been used with a great deal of success as weapons many times throughout the ages. He also wore leather like pants but he carried only one blade, his trusty medieval sword that was over four feet long.

Figuring that they would probably need multiple persons killed throughout and especially throughout this campaign in particular, the demons placed Beaux Lux in charge of all the other assassins in the mission. He was ruthless, to say the least, and very good at finding ways to get around his limitations as a supernatural being to get the job done.

"Don't worry," replied Bethliel. "They're mine now."

"They must die." stated Citikaih. ."They must be put to death like the rest of them."

Bethliel slammed his fist on the table. "Yes," he said. "They are no doubt the enemy, but I need them. When I am through with them they will die."

Mordimec, a divisional commander in the Empirical Forces of Darkness, hissed as he spoke. "That is acceptable, as long as you keep your word."

Mordimec had been fighting Michael in the Middle East for centuries before being called to the mission in America. He was so vile a creature that even those closest to him could not be around him for too long. Like all demons, his mind was set on the destruction of the human race, but for him, it was more personal than for most. He had been the demon sent to see to the destruction of the first churches, started by Paul. Despite his many efforts, his every move was thwarted by both the humans and the angels. After Satan reassigned Mordimec, the task of bringing down the church was given to multiple demons, each having their own sector to work within.

Mordimec was smaller in stature than most of the other demons, but he was extremely strong as a leader and vicious in battle. He had been chosen to be a leader in this particular battle because of these traits. He also resembled a man, only his head was almost like that of a bat and he had wings as well only with fur and feathers that were both a dark gray color. His skin was like that of a human only pale in comparison. The most intimidating feature of Mordimec was his green, cat-like eyes that glowed a bit in dark surroundings, where he was most comfortable.

"They will die," Bethliel replied. He growled and hissed as he spoke, with an unimaginable hate in his heart. For years, Bethliel had been working on and with Thomas Walker and for even more years he had possessed the man. Working with a human in this capacity was never easy for a demon because of his hate for all humans, good or bad. It meant working with him all the time and then having to deal with other humans at times as well. This was his chance to get back at them in a brutal and evil way that would get rid of them for good.

A commander was considered a high ranking officer as well as an honor within the structure of the Empirical Forces of Darkness. Commanders only answered to generals, and generals normally had around six commanders under them, though that number was not uniform or set in stone. Each commander had approximately one hundred thousand demons under their command and was held strictly responsible for the activities of his armies.

"And what of Eleazar?" asked Beaux Lux

"Eleazar is nothing," Bethliel replied. "He is just another angel obeying his master. We'll get him. It's time to assemble the armies," Bethliel stated. "There are only a handful of humans, put them out in front," he said looking in the direction of Mordimec. "Beaux Lux, you will bring down my army from above. They will be waiting for you. Citikaih, I want you to come with me."

Bethliel rose to his feet and turned towards the door. Citikaih followed as ordered. Just before leaving the room, he stated, "It's time to take this town. Impetus Malignus!"

Eleazar walked down the street, splitting the fog as he went. The fog spread to about a thirty foot radius around him, creating a pocket of clear air that went with him as he walked. He knew now, full well, what he was going to have to do in order to carry out God's will for his life, both as a man and as an angel. He would have to fight. He marched on with determination before him, ready to free the city that he had known most of his life from its terrible grip and restore order once again. Still, he felt alone, as if he was the only being in the fight against an army of Satan's worst. In some way, he felt as if there should be more to it on his side.

From behind him Eleazar could hear the sound of marching, as if a very large and organized group was coming up the street after him. He turned to look but the fog was too thick to see through. The marching got louder and louder as the collection of either people or spiritual beings approached. Eleazar drew one of his swords, quick to notice that it did not go up in blue flames as it always had prior. Still, he held it in front of him and stood ready to either welcome, or to fight.

Suddenly, an angel emerged from the fog, wearing a long white robe with a white hood just like Eleazar's. The angel approached and looked up at Drew with eyes as blue as the sea. He was wearing armor like that of an ancient Roman soldier's. It was brilliantly white with gold trimmings and two gold lions in attack position facing each other in the middle. His hair was long and snow white and he carried a helmet, also white with gold trimmings, at his side.

"Eleazar, it is good to finally see you again sir," the angel said.

At that, the fog surrounding the two began to quickly lift, exposing at least another mile or two of road behind them. Along the road was a full army arranged perfectly in groups of seven hundred and fifty angels and one leader for each. In front of the group were three angels carrying large banners. One of them was white and had the same symbol with the lions that was on the angel's breast plate. Another was also white and simply had a golden cross on it. The third contained letters from the ancient Greek alphabet. With the fog lifted around them, the rows of angels filling the street could be seen continuing on for as far as the eye could see.

"What is this?" Eleazar asked.

"Forgive me, sir," the angel said. "I am Atheos, and this is the Tarsious L Legion."

"How many of you are there?"

"Eighty thousand, sir," Atheos answered.

"And what are you here for?" inquired Eleazar.

"We are here at your call sir, to serve you and to protect you." Atheos bowed about halfway to the ground, as did the rest of the angels behind him.

"Please," Eleazar said. "Rise, and tell your Legion that we're going to war."

"It's not my Legion sir," Atheos responded. "It's yours."

In the police station the scene was growing ever more intense as armed men had rounded everyone up and was holding them hostage in an office area on the second floor. Below them more members of Chaos from Control scanned every inch of the building for anyone else that might be hiding somewhere. Two police officers lied near the front door on the marble floor lifeless, both shot execution style in the intruders' attempt to let everyone know that they meant business. Behind them was the main office area, with about twenty or so desks in cubicles and a large front desk at the entrance. At the back of the room was a locked storage closet, inside which was one of the station's three gun cabinets containing assault rifles, hand guns, and various pieces of body armor.

Before the men had the chance to see everything that was going on two men had slipped into the closet and were now hiding out, preparing and waiting for a good time to strike. They had all put on bullet proof vests and were all three carrying both an assault rifle and a forty five caliber automatic pistol stuffed in the back of their pants. Only two of the men were actually police men. The third was a janitor and was already in the closet when the other two found their way in.

"Did you see the guy in the middle?" said Darryl Gant, an off duty officer that had come to the office just to retrieve a couple of things from his locker when the men invaded. "He had red eyes, I swear!"

"Yea, I know," responded Michael Ranton, also a police officer.

"There's something about them," Roger Compass, the janitor, added. "They're just not right."

"The guy that shot Bryan and Davidson, the one with his hood off…" Gant stated. "…I recognize him from somewhere. I just can't put my finger on it."

"Alright men," Ranton began. "If we're gonna' do this, we've gotta' do it all out. Know what I mean? It's shoot to kill. They've already shot two of our guys, good cops too, so we're not playing any games here. This is the real deal."

All three of the men were on edge but knew what had to be done. The two police officers had only seven years of experience combined and the Compass had never shot a gun in his life. The tension in the air was intense, thick enough to cut with a knife, and the men's nerves were on their very edge.

"You okay with this?" Ranton asked Compass, who was drying the sweat from his palms on his pants.

"It's gotta' be done and you can use all the help you can get," Compass answered. "I'll be fine once we get goin'."

"Okay, remember the plan," Gant said. "If we stick to the plan we can pull this off."

"Alright, let's go," Ranton said before turning the door knob and cracking the door as quietly as he could. He peeked out and immediately noticed two robed men pacing about in the lobby. He turned to the other two men in the closet and gave them the signal to move out. The three slipped quietly from the closet and got down on their bellies behind desks. Officer Gant was the better shot from a long distance so he picked up his automatic rifle and carefully aimed it at one of the men.

The shot was loud but put the man down. Gant then quickly aimed at the other man and shot again. This time, he only hit the man's shoulder, giving him time to get at least one shot out of his shotgun towards the desk where Gant was hiding. Ranton then fired off a shot at the wounded man, nearly in succession with Compass. This time, one of the bullets met its mark and the man fell lifeless to the ground.

Suddenly the desk that Gant was hiding behind collapsed like a tin can underneath the feet of an enormous, man-like beast that resembled what most would call a sasquatch. The beast reached down and ripped Gant's rifle from his grip and broke the rifle in two over his knee as he gave out a ferocious roar. The giant stood well over all three men, who had all stood to their feet as the attack began. Its, thick, dark brown hair covered all of its body save for the face, which resembled that of a gorilla's. The horrible creature reached down and grabbed Gant by the neck with one hand and lifted him from the floor.

Officer Ranton and Roger Compass opened fire, sending round after round at the beast, but to no avail.

The animal-like monster threw Gant against a concrete pillar in the middle of the room and then turned its attention to the other two men. With both men still firing their rifles, the beast thrust his fist into the janitor's ribcage, crushing it into his chest cavity. One of Compass's ribs penetrated his heart as he fell to the floor limp from the blow.

Unable to bring the beast down or even slow his progress, Ranton turned and ran towards another pillar and hid on the other side of it, hoping to buy himself a little time. He then dropped his rifle, which was now completely out of ammunition, to the floor, put his hands together, and dropped to his knees.

"Dear God," he began to pray. "I know that I don't come to You as often as I should, and I am so sorry for that, but I'm coming to You now, and I am desperate for help. It's not time for me to go yet God but whatever this thing is, I don't think I can beat it. I need You to intervene, please. I need Your strength and Your power to get out of this. I'm sorry for what I've done wrong God and I'm sorry I haven't allowed myself to be closer to You."

Just as officer Ranton was saying the last words of his prayer, the creature gave out a sudden shriek and held its hands over its ears. A light came into the room that was nothing natural but was as bright as the sun. The beast began to swing its enormous paws through the air all around him, as if he was trying to catch something or swat something away. Ranton watched as the beast then fell to its knees screaming, then disappeared just as quickly as it had arrived.

"I can't believe it," Ranton said to himself as he slowly stood to his feet. His friend and fellow officer was down but still breathing. The janitor Compass, however, was dead. The beast had killed him with one strike to the chest. "I can't…"

232

XXII

The Trenton County Sheriff's Department was located about seven city blocks from the downtown area and was currently on lockdown in an attempt to prevent intruders. The department only employed a handful of deputies but all were present and accounted for, except one who was still out on Jasper's land the last anyone heard. Sheriff Pat Sandoval was preparing for the worst, resorting to his own custom procedures in order to keep his station safe and clear of the criminals raiding down town.

Additionally, the sheriff was working with the deputies present and a couple of city police officers that were also there to put together some sort of plan to take back their city. With the police station under the control of CFC, all of the city's patrol and other officers were answering to Sheriff Sandoval as any procedure that had previously been in place for an event such as this had been thrown out the window long ago with the suddenness of the attack. Chaos had forced what law authority there was into a corner and officials were acting out their duties with the best of their judgment. Officers who were on patrol were doing the best they could to restore order in the rest of the town while doing what they could to answer calls close to the down town area.

So far, only two plans were being considered as they were the only two that would give them any kind of chance to overtake CFC and return control to city officials. The problem was that the raiders had placed themselves in such strategic locations that made it difficult to get much further than the current border of control. Also, many hostages had been taken and there was no word as to where they were being kept or how they were being treated. The biggest issue, however, was the one that nobody would talk about in fear of being ridiculed. At least some of the men in the black robes seemed to possess a supernatural power of some sort, something that couldn't be beaten by normal means. Reports that were coming in from calls to 911 and from the one reporter inside downtown were baffling and horrifying. Everyone knew that it would have to be addressed somehow, but nobody was sure how. There was no procedure for this sort of act in Adjacent Cove.

Still, something had to be done, and soon, before more people died. Nobody was even sure who all was still alive that had been taken hostage, if any of them. One deputy recommended somehow drawing them out into the surrounding neighborhoods for urban guerilla warfare, another suggested using the sewer system to gain access to the inner down town area and catching the enemy by surprise. Still another suggested that they just sit it out and wait for the National Guard. The only problem with that plan was that more people could lose their lives while they were waiting, and it wasn't just down town anymore. Some of the men had begun raiding houses surrounding the area and people were being attacked in their own homes. Sheriff Sandoval stated additionally that he didn't want to give the CFC time to spread their area of control to them, which seemed to be the city's only hope at the moment.

According to the sheriff's long time assistant, a woman nearing retirement that also acted as the office receptionist, the National Guard was on their way. Television and radio reports from the area had already given them the confirmation they needed that the small town of Adjacent Cove was being overrun. What they didn't know was how long it would take for them to assemble and reach them. Even the President of the United States had been informed of the incident. Of course, the first thing on most people's minds was terrorism. Without all of the facts, it was their best guess and would be treated as such until receiving word of otherwise.

Two blocks west of downtown, three of the men in black robes walked in the middle of the road through the thick fog as if hunting for something or someone. Their red tinted eyes passed back and forth looking at every business and house carefully. Most of the people in this area had evacuated out, but some remained, in hiding. The men had already raided two homes and an insurance company office, killing one man and injuring two others. There were no women or children present.

Without warning a red, older model pick-up truck broke the fog and screeched to a halt in front of the men. In the front of the cab were the driver and one other man and in the back were three more men. All of them were armed with shotguns and pistols and one had a tire iron as well. The men stared each other down for a moment before the driver threw the truck in reverse and backed back into the fog behind them rather quickly. The robed men looked at each other with smiles on their faces then continued their pace when all of the sudden the truck reappeared, this time traveling at a high rate of speed. The truck ran into and over one of the men and knocked another to the ground violently before doing a quick u-turn and facing them once again.

The men in the back of the truck and the one passenger in the cab immediately begin to open fire at the man still standing and the man that had just been knocked down. Both men were killed instantly by the barrage of gunfire. The man that had been run over, however, had somehow disappeared during the shootings. The three men in the back of the truck jumped out with a new found confidence and began looking under the truck and around trees by the road. After only moments of searching, the man reappeared suddenly, standing in the middle of the road about thirty yards in front of them. The man showed no signs of injury. He just stood there quietly, as if waiting for the men to approach, which they did.

The robed man and member of the newly dubbed Chaos From Control reached up and lifted the robe from over his head. He looked like any other man except for his pale skin, the blue veins in his temple, and his deep red colored eyes. He simply smiled, maliciously, as the men once again opened fire. The bullets and buck shot tore through the man's robe but didn't seem to even touch the man wearing it. After they had fired all that they could, both the three men on foot and the truck began to slowly back away, flabbergasted by what they were seeing.

The man's tattered robe dropped to the ground in shreds. His jeans and white t-shirt were also full of holes but there was no blood and no apparent injury, not even from being run over just moments before. The man tilted his head slightly and gave out an ear piercing shriek that was as loud as it was evil. The men dropped their weapons and tried to get into the back of the truck, but not before a sudden gust of wind began to lift the truck off the ground. The man's face and body seemed to morph slightly as he shrieked and his mouth grew bigger and bigger. It was as if his skin was melting off of his body as his arms and legs grew in length and shriveled to the bones.

The wind grew in intensity as the truck slowly lifted higher off of the ground. The men inside its cab and back looked on in horror, scared literally stiff, as the man in front of them turned into a creature more horrible than anything they had ever seen. It looked like a giant spider with only four legs and had a human like head with an enormous mouth full of pointed teeth. Its body was a pale blue color and its face almost completely white. The beast's thin and partially lucent layer of skin stretched over its body as if it was too small for it revealing blue veins that were darker at the joints. The creature hissed as it drooled pure acid that ate away at the concrete as it dripped from its mouth.

Within just seconds a ball of fire began to form in front of the beast's mouth, seemingly powered by its breath and growing in intensity and size rather quickly. When the fireball was nearly six feet in diameter, the demon blew it violently, as if sneezing, hurling it towards the truck at high speed. Upon impact, the truck exploded ferociously and went immediately up into flames and incinerated everything, including the five men inside of it. In only seconds there was nothing left but a pile of blackened truck parts and ashes in the middle of the road and blast marks on the concrete and surrounding trees.

Normally, when disaster struck in any way in the area most churches opened their doors to assist in any way that they could. On this day, however, very few were open and only one was holding an organized meeting and service. Most pastors feared that opening the doors would victimize some of their members by getting them out of the safety of their homes.

Harvest Avenue Church, located on the west side of town, was not only open but holding a meeting and service as well. The mid-sized church was packed full of people from its own congregation as well as others. Some that were in attendance were not even church goers. Jim and Cindy Davis and their daughter Alyssa were among those in attendance, along with a few others from First Baptist Church. Alyssa was not well, the result of the concussion she had received the night before in the accident, but was in attendance none the less. The pastor had spread the word throughout town that he would open and offer both a safe haven and a front for Christians to gather and pray about their current situation. Unfortunately, his motives went beyond most people's expectations.

The Apocalypse, as described in the Biblical book of Revelations was a subject rarely tapped by most modern pastors. David Stupp, pastor of Harvest Avenue Church, wasn't most modern pastors. The end times were a subject often explored by the pastor and his congregation both in church and in smaller groups. So far the pastor had predicted the end of days six times and was wrong every time. Still, his congregation remained loyal and for some reason believed that he knew something that they didn't.

Today was no different for the pastor of the non-denominational Harvest Avenue Church. The circumstances surrounding them once again gave him reason to believe that the end was coming, and he was doing what he could to convince the congregation of the same. This time, of course, it hit a lot closer to home, so many were on board. His continuous sermon that had been going on for a couple of hours now was based around two major points. First, the Apocalypse was approaching and God's people needed to be ready and second, now was the time to give back to God monetarily in order to receive the "peace and safety that only God can give". The offering buckets had already been passed three times and were already over half full of change, bills and checks made out to the church.

The Davis', like others, had only recently arrived and were already about to leave when the pastor's tone suddenly changed to a deep, ringing tone that seemed to shake the windows as he spoke. If something wasn't already wrong with the service, this was certainly out of place. One man stood and claimed that the Holy Spirit was speaking through his pastor while others looked on, perplexed and unsure what to believe.

"This is the day," pastor David Stupp stated with his arms in the air. "This is the day that we as Christians stand up and give all that we have and all that we are to God in order to prepare our way to His presence."

The pastor leaned forward on the pulpit and looked down into the audience with dark eyes. There was certainly something strange and twisted about his sudden change of appearance and tone, but nobody could find the courage to get up and leave while he was speaking. The Davis' in particular had decided to wait until he took a break to pray or sing to leave.

"Christ has commanded us to rid ourselves of all our worldly possessions and follow him. If you haven't obeyed this command, you must do it now. The end is here and those who are not following are falling. Give it all to Christ's church and you will receive blessings from our Lord and deliverance from the evil that is upon us!"

Most of those who were already members of Harvest Avenue Church, along with a few from other churches and most of the non-believers in the service, were buying into the pastor's words. All across the sanctuary people were pulling out their wallets and checkbooks to give everything they had to the church. Others were even removing their jewelry and jackets to give. Deacons were walking around with the buckets once more. Those who gave were smiled upon but those who did not received a glare and at times a mumbled word or two from the deacon at their row.

"Get on your knees...," Pastor Stupp demanded. "...and submit to the church of the Lord." Something had taken over the pastor that made him seem bigger, even physically, than he was before. He spoke animatedly and with confidence and certainty. His eyes had turned as black as night and the stage where he preached from had darkened as if the lights above him went out. The Davis' looked for even the smallest opportunity to sneak out without being noticed and called out by anyone, especially the preacher.

The demon's name was Feazor and he held a low rank in the Empirical Forces of Darkness. He was a cowardly demon that had been assigned over a thousand years ago to corrupt the church in every way that he could. Unable to make any kind of difference at most of his posts, he had been bumped around many times until he was finally able to gain some leeway at Harvest Avenue.

"I am Eleazar," he responded. "I am here to free you."

All of the sudden the pastor's eyes returned to their original color, just before he passed out and fell to the floor. Immediately Eleazar grabbed his blades from behind him and ran to the stage. Upon arriving he found Feazor cowering and trying to duck behind the pulpit. He was small in stature and resembled a half man, half goat. He stood upright but on hooves rather than feet and had horns protruding from his head.

"I know you," the pitiful creature stated, shivering under all of the hair covering his body. "You're a Legionnaire."

"So they say," responded Eleazar, who towered over the creature. "Now leave, and don't ever come back to these parts again."

"I'm not leaving," the small beast proclaimed. "This is my post."

"You're leaving if I have to drag you out of here myself," Eleazar responded firmly.

"What's the big deal?" Feazor asked. "You don't even go to church here."

"These are my people," answered Eleazar. "These are children of God and deserve the same, clear guidance as the rest. Your corruption only blinds their eyes from the truth, and I will not have it."

"You know," Feazor stated. "If you make me leave here you're going to have to deal with my commander, and he's not easy to deal with. You may be all big and bad but I promise you, my commander is bigger and badder."

"You can tell your commander that I said to bring it on. I don't have time for this, so leave, now, before I send you away."

"I'm tellin' ya'," Feazor insisted.

"Leave!"

Feazor straightened up and began to walk away. To Eleazar's surprise, however, he suddenly leaped towards Eleazar and grabbed on to his neck while throwing punches with the other hand. Eleazar grabbed him by the body and threw him to the floor in front of the front row of pews in the church. Feazor stood quickly to his feet and leaped towards Eleazar once more. This time, he dug his nails into Eleazar's neck and began scratching at his face. Eleazar threw him to the ground again and this time put his foot on the vile creature before he could get back up again.

"Are you sure you wanna' do it this way?" Eleazar asked.

"You can't make me leave my post!" said the demon. "This is where I was assigned and if I fail again there's no telling what will happen to me."

"That's not my problem," Eleazar stated.

Suddenly the demon freed himself from underneath Eleazar's foot and leaped to the closest wall in the sanctuary. He then crawled up to the ceiling quickly, like a spider. After staying there just long enough to catch his breath, he lunged towards Eleazar once again, who this time had his swords drawn. Eleazar swung his blades at the demon, missing him with the first but hitting him squarely in the chest with the other. Eleazar then turned and swung at the demon once again before he could even attempt to stand up. This time, he cut Feazor's throat wide open. Feazor fell to the ground, then vanished.

Eleazar sheathed his swords and turned to check on the pastor, who was still unconscious on the stage floor. Before leaving, he checked to make sure that the pastor was breathing and that his heart rate was okay. Though empty, a new light seemed to come over the sanctuary. It was a soft glow that wasn't there before. The church had been rid of its corruption and was ready to begin anew.

XXIII

"What are we looking for?" asked Detective Charlie Ellis upon arriving at the site where the barn had burned on Thomas Jasper's land the night before.

"You check the cars, I'm gonna' sift through all of this," Stulken answered.

All of the officers, uniformed or not had left in just the past few minutes to assist in the situation in town. While they were there, they had uncovered several human remains. For now, they were all marked with a red flag sticking out of the ground. Processing and identifying all of them at this point was nearly impossible with everything else going on. After things could be sorted out and the men terrorizing the city could be identified, it would most likely be a process of elimination, given the vehicles on the land and the numerous missing person reports filed.

"Those terrorists came from here, I know it," Stulken added. "I want to know who they are and what they're up to."

"And what about all the dead out here? The morgue was supposed to be here by now."

"The morgue is probably locked down like everyone else," Stulken answered, leaning over to take a closer look at a charred skeleton marked by a red flag. "I need these bodies here for now anyway. Nothing or no one leaves this lot until I get some answers."

"Alright," Ellis replied. "I'll go search the vehicles and see what I can find."

"Nothin' but ashes and charred wood," Detective Stulken said to himself as he sifted through the remains with a stick.

Save for the occasional metal fold out chair, everything was turned to dust and ashes. It was the most complete job done by a fire that the detective had ever seen. Whoever had started the fire must have done so with the intention of destroying everything and everyone involved. Never had the detective seen the remains of a fire of this magnitude and strength.

"Musta' lit up the dang sky," he mumbled to himself.

"Sir," Detective Ellis said as she ran towards Stulken. "I found something." She handed him a battered red notebook that had obviously been used many times. On the front was written "Los Ultimos Dias" over a large, hand drawn anarchy symbol. At the bottom of the cover was the name "Jarvis Nixon". On the inside of the notebook were pages of notes taken at various meetings with the dates and times at the top of the pages. Everything was organized into an outline form and very easy to follow. The notes talked about everything from who was present at the meetings, which was usually quite a long list, to what James Walker spoke about that particular time. There were even various criminal plots outlined that were to be carried out by both members and leaders of the organization.

"Perfect, Charlie," Detective Stulken said. "That was fast."

"Thank you," Ellis responded. "I found it between the seats in the first truck I searched. I have a feeling we're gonna' find a lot of answers in that thing."

"Yep," Stulken replied as he folded the notebook and shoved it in his back pocket.

"Shouldn't we bag that or something?" Detective Ellis asked.

"I don't care about that right now. Go see what else you can dig up."

After searching for a few more minutes, Stulken made out what appeared to be a book, like a personal journal, with a leather cover sticking out from underneath a piece of charred wood. He moved the wood with his stick and reached down and pulled the journal from the ashes. How it could have possibly survived the fire was a mystery. Detective Stulken squatted down and began to go through the pages. He soon discovered that it was indeed a journal, handwritten, most likely by a member of Los Ultimos Dias. The journal was basically a log of everything that the group had been up to for the last two or three years. The detective looked for one of the longer entries and stopped to read it.

"Monday, October thirty first of the year 2009. Today is Halloween, and the group will be busy, as usual. James has split us into six groups and asked each group to perform certain tasks laid out by him and a few others. My group's assignment for the night is split in two. First, we are to deface as many graves as we can at the cemetery behind First United Methodist Church. He wants us to kick over and spray paint head stones and set fire to as much of the grass as possible. Second, he wants us to break as many windows as we can out of the church.

"I have to say, I'm not sure how I feel about our assignment, and I think a couple other men in my group feel the same way. There's just something extremely disrespectful and cold about defacing a cemetery. I know that James wants to send a clear message to the community that evil is here and at work, but I'm not sure why we have to destroy a cemetery in order to get this message across. Breaking windows out of a church, that's easy. Destroying graves, however, is not just messing with the living, it's messing with the dead as well."

Detective Stulken pulled his glasses from his coat pocket so that he could see better. He flipped through the pages some more, looking for another entry of interest to read. Before too long, he came to another.

"Friday, February eleventh of the year 2008. Tonight we held a ritual sacrifice behind the barn amongst the tall, dark trees. James killed a rather large cow and then drank its blood. Others in the group went forward and drank from the cup as well. There was so much blood and it was everywhere. Some of the men seemed energized in some strange way by it, James especially. It was like the blood gave them some sort of evil power. Of course, James stated many times that the ultimate sacrifice will be that of a human. I don't know when or if that day is coming but I know that there are those that want it to. I'm not quite sure how I feel about it yet. I guess it would depend on the person.

"You're not going to find much of anything here," a voice stated from behind Detective Stulken. He slowly reached for the pistol on his side and pulled it from its holster.

"You're not going to need that either," the voice said. "I pose no threat to you."

Stulken turned to see James Walker standing before him. He was wearing white clothes with no shoes. He was battered badly but his cuts were stitched and his other abrasions cared for. The detective raised his gun, but had a feeling that he was not in any danger. Walker reached out his hand to shake the detective's.

"I'm James Walker," he said. "You've heard of me by now I'm sure."

"Yes I have," said the detective with both hands on his gun and unwilling to shake James' hand. "I'm afraid you are under arrest. I need you to turn around and place your hands in the air."

James turned and did what Stulken said "Now place them on the back of your head," the detective said.

"I can help you," James stated as Stulken searched him. "I don't know what you know, but I know everything."

Detective Stulken didn't respond. He grabbed James' hands and handcuffed him then led him to the car and put him in the back seat. Just then Detective Ellis noticed what was going on and made her way to the car as quick as she could.

"Is this…," Ellis said, out of breath from running. "Are you James Walker?" she said, leaning down to look at him.

"Yes, that's him," said Detective Stulken. "We've got him."

"I know that you have to arrest me and I am prepared to face my charges, whatever they might be, but

I can help you. I can help you understand what's going on. I know that you came out here to find evidence that would lead you to the truth about what is happening to Adjacent Cove, and you found me."

"And what about what happened at Ware?" Detective Stulken asked. "How can I trust you after what transpired there?"

"Look at the tapes detective," Walker replied.

"I've seen the tapes," stated Stulken.

"Then you know that I didn't hurt anyone. I was taken out of there by a stranger to me. I had a plan to escape, yes, but nobody was going to get hurt with my plan. This guy, or whatever he is, is the one that hurt all those people. I defended myself once but that's it, I didn't hurt anyone."

"Okay, we get it," Ellis interrupted. "If, and I do mean if, we decide to trust you, what kind of information do you have?"

"I have all of it," James answered. "Everything you need to know ma'am. Look, I came here for a reason. I wanted to get caught. If there were no lawmen here I was going to go straight to the police station."

"Yea, good luck with that," Detective Stulken stated. "The police station is no longer under our control."

"You don't understand what's going on here, neither of you do," James said. I do. I spoke to the devil himself out there in the woods. Look at my scars, those are from demons and my father, who is supposed to be dead but is demon possessed. My father is heading this whole thing up and I know what they're trying to do. I heard them talking while I was hanging upside down from a tree by hooks. I know it all sounds crazy but I'm not lying to you, you have to believe me."

Detectives Stulken and Ellis looked at each other over the top of the car and shrugged their shoulders. Neither of them knew what to make of what he was saying. With all the events that had taken place, however, they almost didn't have anything to lose by believing him and hearing everything he had to say. If nothing else, they could check in to his claims and leave the supernatural part of it out.

"Satan himself offered me armies if I gave him my soul," said James.

"And what did you say?" asked Detective Ellis.

"I turned it down," Walker answered.

"Okay, say we trust you," Stulken asked. "What is it exactly that you want in return?"

"I want you to take my father down," James answered. "But first I want redemption."

"Redemption for what?" Ellis asked.

"Are you kidding me?" James laughed. "Have you seen my rap sheet?"

"So you're saying you want the law to just forgive you for your crimes?" inquired Stulken.

"No," James responded. "I know that I have to pay for my crimes. Being redeemed is something entirely different."

"And how are we supposed get you your redemption?" Ellis asked.

"Your guess is as good as mine. To be honest, I have no idea. I just know that I want to come clean to God and be made new. I've heard of it, but I've never actually done it. So, I guess you get me a preacher. He should know what to do."

"Drew!" Alyssa said aloud as Drew walked into the sanctuary of First Baptist Church.

Over fifty people had showed up at the church to pray for the community, including the pastor and other ministers. Alyssa was there too, despite the events of the previous night. Her father had told her about Drew when all of the chaos had started down town, but it was all still sinking in.

"How are you?" she asked as she stood and gave Drew a big hug.

"I'm fine," he answered. "Just wanted to stop by and check on you guys."

"We're fine," Alyssa responded. "We're praying for you."

"That's exactly what I need you to do," Drew answered. "Don't stop, whatever you do. How's your head Alyssa?"

"It's fine, thanks to you," she answered with a smile.

"Hiya' kid," said Jim as he approached to shake Drew's hand. Drew ignored the hand and hugged Jim instead.

"How ya' feeling?" Drew asked.

"I'm fine," Jim said. "Listen Drew, I want you to know that I'm sorry. I'm sorry that I didn't tell you about this sooner."

"No," Drew responded. "My Dad told you to wait until the time was right, and that's what you did."

"I know," Jim said. "I just feel like you could have been better prepared if I would have told you a year ago or something."

"You didn't know that this was going to happen Jim," Drew insisted. "You did exactly what my father asked. There's a reason for everything. Just keep praying."

"Mom?" Drew asked with concern. She was crying and had been for some time. "What's wrong, are you okay?"

"I'm fine sweetie," she answered. "Don't worry about me."

"Well why are you crying?" Drew inquired.

"Because you're my son." Drew's mother replied. "It's all just a bit overwhelming right now, but I'm fine. You need to worry about you and keeping yourself as safe as possible right now. Do you still have your Dad's pocket watch that I gave you"

"Yes ma'am," Drew responded. "Right here in my pocket, and I haven't forgot what it means either."

"Can you give us an update on the situation?" Jim asked. "We don't have any televisions here and the radio isn't working. We're all just a bit anxious about what's going on out there."

"Well...," Drew answered. "...the good news is that I have a whole army behind me. I'm getting them settled and situated right now so we can march on the downtown area and take it back."

"Oh, thank God," said Alyssa.

"Right now everyone just needs to stay away from the downtown area and the neighborhoods around it. It's pretty rough out there. I wouldn't put it past any of those men to kill someone that gets in their way. Everyone needs to just stay away from there and pray. The only thing that is going to fix this is the power of God."

XXIV

"Don't even so much as move, not a single muscle," yelled one of the men in a black robe. He had taken his hood off, revealing his identity to his captives in the courtroom. The hostages were being held in one of the courtrooms, the same one where the judge had been decapitated early. His headless body, along with his head, had been taken behind the courtroom and burned along with others who had died during the initial takeover of the building.

Grant Turner was only twenty three years old but had already started a successful business of his own selling sports equipment in the area. Nobody would have believed that he was also secretly a member of Los Ultimos Dias and had been for just over two years now. He was so involved in the group that he had personally financed some of its activities, such as animal sacrifices, in the past. On any given day he was kind and thoughtful, even giving to charities from time to time. When it was time to meet with Los Ultimos Dias, however, his persona changed completely.

Grant and two other members had everyone lying on the floor in the middle aisle and at the front of the courtroom with their hands on their heads. The assailants walked around and throughout them with their guns pointed down at them and their fingers on the trigger. It was as if they were robots carrying out one person's morbid plans to take over.

"Grant," one woman who recognized him said. "Do you remember me? I'm Catherine. You gave to my church a few months ago when we were doing a food drive. Do you remember that?"

"Shut up!" Grant yelled as he rushed over to the woman and pointed his double-barreled shotgun at her.

"You must remember me Grant," she continued.

"Shut your mouth now!" he yelled even louder. "Before I scatter your brain where you lay."

Catherine cried and shook in fear. Still, she felt compelled to try to talk to Grant. Something told her that she might could talk some sense into him, given his reputation as such a good man in town.

"Please Grant," she said as she cried. "This isn't you. This isn't anything like you at all. You are a good man that's been brainwashed and…"

"That's it," he said with the gun resting on the back of her head. "Get up."

"Grant, listen to me, please," she pleaded.

Suddenly the doors of the courtroom flew open and two other members walked in, both carrying firearms. One of them rushed to Grant and handed him a sealed envelope, then walked away. Both of the men then left the courtroom as Grant opened the envelope. It was orders from Bethliel. Grant read the orders and then wadded up the piece of paper and envelope and threw them to the floor.

"You got lucky," Grant said to Catherine, who was still on the floor. "Let's go," he said to the other two men. The three men walked quickly out of the courtroom and out the door, closing it behind them.

After the men left, the hostages were unsure of what to do. Everyone was afraid to stand up until one man finally stood and sat in the front row of the benches. Their cell phones, watches, and jewelry had all been taken from them so they had no way of making any phone calls. The man on the bench, however, had found a way to hide his cell phone so that it wasn't taken. He just told them that he had forgotten his at home. This was his chance to try to reach someone outside, however just as the man pulled his cell phone up to make a call the doors burst open once again. He quickly stuffed his cell phone down his pants and laid back down on the floor with his hands on his head.

This time, instead of just men in black robes, there was a flood of hostages from both the police station and the city hall. There were at least a hundred or so of them, not counting the ones that were in there already. The men and women that were already in the room were made to stand up in order to make room for the rest. Some sat in the benches while most of them stood. All of them were nervous, with some of the women crying out and many praying to God for protection of their lives.

"It's time for us to ready the armies," Eleazar stated to Atheos. Eleazar and his armies were situated at a ball field complex about two miles south of the downtown area. He had sent some of his Warriors Elite in already to put a stop to the raiding of homes and businesses by Bethliel's men. These angels had all become human in order to be able to fight the men under Bethliel's control. The rest of the three legions were assembled and awaiting orders. The fifteen Messengers, the Senior Centurion, and a few of the other warriors had become men as well.

"Call everyone in," Atheos stated to Atzi An, the senior messenger.

Nephuna, one of the Cohort leaders, or Messengers, held a large horn made from what looked like a giant sea shell, and blew it. At the sound of the horn, all of the angels assembled into their formation. Thousands of angels gathered, covering the every square foot of all seven baseball fields and all twelve soccer fields. Angels covered the open fields next to the complex as well. The rows of angels were assembled in perfect squares and seemed to go on forever.

Eleazar's army of angels included right at 80,000 warrior angels, all of whom were considered a "Fidei Defensor", or "Defender of the Faith". They were divided by Unit, then Century, then Cohort, then Legion. Eleazar's Legion consisted of fifteen Cohorts that were led by Messengers. Each Cohort consisted of seven Centuries, led by Centurions. Finally, each Century consisted of seven units that were led by Field Sergeants.

"We're ready sir," Atzi An proclaimed to Eleazar..

"I wanna' send a couple scouts ahead of us, like we did with Xiviche."

"We'll send a couple Warriors Elite," said Atheos. Ilius and Didk Rou. Both are good scouts."

"Sounds good to me," Eleazar replied. "Right now you know this army better than I do."

Eleazar watched as his Warriors Elite returned to the formation one by one. Some were exhausted, others were okay, but overall one could easily tell that they have been fighting. One of them, named Xiviche, returned and headed for the leadership.

"Sir," said Xiviche as he arrived. "They are gathering their forces and shaping a defensive formation around the courthouse downtown." Xiviche took a moment to catch his breath and then continued. "They have taken all of their hostages to the courthouse and are keeping them in one of the courtrooms there. Word is that they're holding them simply for their own protection. They have no demands."

"Thank you," Eleazar said. "Go and rest now before we march."

"Yes sir," Xiviche stated before he flew off towards the fields.

"You will need all you can get," Drew stated.

Eleazar's army was formed and ready to go in just minutes. The angels that had crossed the dimension as a man were below and directly behind Eleazar and Atheos. The rest were hovering above the ground and out of the sight of normal men. All were standing in a ready position to march on the downtown area.

Amongst and around the army, the fog had cleared and the sun was shining through the dark clouds above, sending a ray of light over the entire army. Most of the army wore white armor while the Warriors Elite wore silver. In the front row of each Cohort an angel carried a banner that was white with a silver symbol of a lion on it, which was the symbol of the legion. There was also a Roman numeral on each flag indicating which Cohort it was.

"Are we ready?" Eleazar asked.

"We're ready sir," replied Atheos. "At your command."

Eleazar turned and looked at his massive army. His eyes glowed blue in the gloominess of the area and he had a glow to him, the same that all angels have. He walked towards is forces, and then hovered above the ground himself so that everyone could hear what he had to say to them.

"I am Eleazar, your leader" he proclaimed with a loud voice. "I'm told that I was a great leader. I'm told that I was brave in battle. I'm told that I was a fierce fighter. All these things, I'm told that I was. I am here to tell you that I am still all of these things. I am still your leader and we will find victory."

The angels cheered as Eleazar's voice grew stronger. Before long, his voice could be clearly heard all the way to the back of the formation.

"We are going to march into downtown...," Eleazar continued "...and take those grounds or else I am nothing. We are going to take those grounds because they do not belong to them. We are going to take those grounds because we are angels and they are the fallen. We are going to take them in the name of God Almighty and we will free the grip that evil has placed upon this good town once and for all! Fight with me brothers! Fight with me as you have for ages past!

"March with me!" Eleazar proclaimed. "March with me in the name of God Almighty and His son Jesus Christ!"

"Chief, you're okay," Detective Mark Stulken said into his phone. "Thank God."

Chief of police Robert Davis, the mayor of Adjacent Cove, and two members of the city council had been golfing when the whole incident downtown began. The chief and the mayor, who lived across the street from one another, were now in touch with the news reporter on the inside and plotting out a plan to retake the city from the mayor's home. They were still waiting to hear from multiple police officers that might have made it out before making any moves. Numbers would be key because of the magnitude of the force they were dealing with. There were at least a hundred and twenty-five armed men, maybe more, in black robes and they were not going to send their officers to be slaughtered.

"Yes sir, we called them to," Stulken added, talking about the National Guard. "It's going to be a while though, and things are moving pretty fast here. We need some sort of plan."

"I couldn't agree more," the mayor said. "The problem is that we don't have enough manpower. They're holding a big chunk of our force at the station."

"Yes, I know…," Stulken replied "…but I have some information about Chaos from Control that might interest you. It seems they're not exactly what most people think they are. I've got someone here that has some insight on the situation."

"Oh yea? Who?" the mayor asked.

"Did you ever hear of Los Ultimos Dias?" Stulken asked.

XXV

Detectives Stulken and Ellis had decided to keep James in their own custody until everything blew over because of the information he was continually providing them regarding exactly what was going on in Adjacent Cove. So far, he had given them enough information to know who was involved on a human level and why. They were now at a second makeshift police station, an old abandoned office space on the edge of town, and it was time to dive even further into the truth than they already were.

James' conversion, by this point, had come full circle. After talking with Lucifer and seeing not only his self, but where he was headed as well, he was compelled to convert and follow God. It was then that he was reminded of all the evil he had done in his life and repented. Now, he was helping the police put an end to the chaos that had been gripping the city for many hours now.

"There's another war going on," James began. "One you can't see. Most people think that if there was a war in the supernatural world, it would be between angels and demons. That's not actually true. The war is between man and demons. The angels are the guardians of mankind. They are here to protect men, usually at man's request."

"At man's request?" Detective Ellis asked as she scribbled in her notebook. "I've never requested help from an angel."

"Of course not…," James answered. "…but Christian men and women do pray to God, and how do you think God does His bidding?"

"With the angels," said Stulken.

"With His angels," James replied. "I've studied spiritual warfare for years and I know it's real because I've been on the dark side of it since I was young. I've tried to contact demons in every way I know how but what I never realized, until today, was that they were not with me, they were against me. Every human, no matter who they are or what they've done, is a target to them."

"I'm not big on religion…," Ellis stated. "…and I've never once given thought to the existence of some spiritual world in the skies."

James laughed under his breath. "That world is there, whether you like it or not. It exists in another dimension, a fourth dimension that is usually called the spiritual world. They're fighting up there and down here for God's people. Everything that happens in the spiritual world manifests itself in our three dimensional world."

"Then explain what's going on here," Detective Ellis demanded.

"A demon can possess a man," James started. "With enough time, he can completely overtake the heart, soul, and mind of the man. The man that once was is still there and still conscious, but the demon rules.

"Angels, on the other hand, can come to earth in the form of a man if they so desire. Sometimes it's necessary in order to defeat a demon that has possessed a man. The angel does everything he can, however, to protect the man from any harm."

"There's rumor in the city…" Detective Stulken interceded. "…that there's a man, or angel, going around and fighting off the members of what the press is calling Chaos from Control. Do you know anything about this?"

"I know that the angelic army coming to fight has a leader that has been reborn as a man. He's apparently a commander and fighter like no other. Satan told me this, hoping to make me his number one adversary. You see, my father is the number one contender at the moment. He has been possessed by a demon called Bethliel. Even his physical appearance has changed.

The thing is that he started what they call Impetus Malignus, which means "revolution of evil", way too early because he couldn't wait. His desire is to move up higher in the ranks and he thinks that winning this battle will give him everything he wants."

"Your father?" Stulken inquired.

"Yep…," James replied, "…my own flesh and blood. He is responsible for the scars."

The three were silent for a moment before continuing."

"You must understand," James stated firmly. "There is a war going on here, today. It's going to happen and there's nothing you or we can do to stop it. I might be able to help though."

"How?" asked Stulken.

"My father…," he responded. "I can go to my father and try to find him in that deformed body of his. He's got to be there somewhere. Before he…" James choked up for a moment. "…before he killed my family and tried to kill me, he was a good Dad and I know he loved me. I know he loved all of us. He was just taken over by evil."

"So you think you can get the demons out of him?" Stulken asked.

"I'm not saying I can, I'm not saying I can't. I have no idea, but if anyone should try to get him back, it would be me."

"So, tell us more about that confrontation," Ellis stated.

"He confronted me in the woods about two miles south of here. I was lost and he appeared in a clearing. He promised me an army of my own if I would submit to him and give him my soul. It was then that it hit me. They are fighting against man, and man is unknowingly fighting back, at least most of the men are. He seemed desperate to win this one. So I stood there, knowing full well that I would eventually be possessed, just like my father. If I had accepted, I would be playing a key role in the destruction of my home and more."

"How do you know it was the devil?" Ellis asked.

"Because he told me. He introduced himself as the 'Morning Star' and then 'Lucifer'".

"What happened then?" Stulken inquired.

"I haven't lived the ideal life. I've done nothing but rob and destroy, and I've led others to do the same.

The whole time I thought that I was honoring Satan with what I did. I studied the Bible from front to back and vowed to be the complete opposite of its teachings. The whole time, however, I was Satan's enemy.

"I was just a pawn. I was disposable. I decided I didn't want that life anymore so I turned my back to him and got down on my knees and prayed to God for redemption. Because of His awesome grace, he changed me. He made me realize what I could be with him at the forefront of everything I do. He saved me. He picked me up off of my knees and made me new. I turned around once, but Satan had left. He left because where there is fear, there cannot be love, but where there is love, there cannot be fear."

"Okay, stop," Detective Ellis stated as she abruptly stopped writing for a moment and placed her hand in the air. "I mean, come on Mark. Doesn't this all sound kinda' crazy to you?"

"Well…," Stulken responded. "I don't know. I go to church when I can but we never studied any of this kind of stuff. That doesn't make it not real though. I am a Christian and I certainly believe in angels."

"So you both would have me to believe this stuff? Angels and demons fighting it out in their own dimension and then whoever wins gets control of the courthouse? Is that it?"

"You're simplifying a century's long struggle that can barely be described in words," James stated. "If you had seen what I saw, or even felt the terror that I felt, you might understand."

"It's alright," Stulken stated. "Let's just figure out what we need to do."

Bethliel stood at the top of the concrete stairs leading up to the courtroom's main doors. He used a scope from one of the men's guns to look for the enemy certain to advance on them at anytime. He had his army of one hundred thousand fallen angels ready.

The eager general had all of the men in robes with their firearms and other various weapons out front in the courthouse's lawn. He and the leaders of the four armies under him would direct the battle from where he now stood. The thousands of demons in the spiritual dimension were scattered throughout the neighborhoods and business district downtown allowing them to use a sort of guerilla warfare tactic against the angels.

It wasn't long before Bethliel spotted the first unit of the Angelic Army marching south down Main Street directly towards their front lines of men. In front of the unit were Eleazar and his assistant Atheos. Eleazar was wearing incredible armor that had been given to him just before the march. It was the armor that he had always worn in battle when he was just an angel.

Eleazar's chest plate was pure white with gold trimming and a lion on the front. His arms and legs were covered by pieces of armor that seemed to conform to the shape of them, making him more mobile. Even his fingers were covered by this armor that he wore. He wore a long white robe with a hood covered his jet black hair. The handles of his swords could be seen protruding from behind his head.

Atheos wore armor as well, which was very similar to Eleazar's, except that he didn't wear a robe and he had one long sword sheathed at his side. Behind the two were angels flying banners that were silver and were inscribed with the words "Fedei Defensor", which means "Defender of the Faith", as all angels were called. Another angel three rows back and in the middle held up a large cross that was white with touches of silver lining.

"Impetus Malignus," Bethliel said to himself. "It's time."

"Sir," a scout named Raz'al approached out of breath. "There are a lot of them, but I think they're outnumbered. They all seem to be coming down this one street."

Raz'al was a small demon, only three feet tall, with large wings. He was feathered, like a bird, and looked like a small monkey with wings. He was considered the best scout in the entire world and was coveted by every legion in the Empirical Forces of Darkness. Raz'al was especially good at hiding in places so near the enemy that he could hear them talking to one another.

"How many casualties do we have?" Bethliel asked.

"So far, five men have died while terrorizing businesses and neighborhoods," Raz'al answered. "No worry though, we have more."

Another demon approached, also a scout and also out of breath. Patmus had been flying over Adjacent Cove for hours spying on the enemy. Three times he had to face an angel but he was able to escape twice and defeated an angel once. He was a big demon, resembling a bat, only covered with hair. Scouts were usually smaller demons that could fly fast and get back without detection. Patmus was a scout because of his eyes. He could spot a nickel on the road a mile away.

"What do you have Patmus?" asked Bethliel.

"There are many angels coming as men. There are at least as many as we have, but maybe more. Right now they are spread apart."

Along the front of the lines of demons hovering in another dimension over the courthouse were Mordimec and Wradeon, who were divisional commanders, as well as Naziph and Paroleous, the other two. Mordimec was having his doubts despite their advantage in numbers.

XXVI

"Gabriel," Eleazar called out behind him. Gabriel made his way to the front to see what was needed of him.

"Sir," he responded upon arriving at the front. Gabriel was the senior messenger for Eleazar's Legion.

"I need you to get this message to the angels that are coming as men," Eleazar stated. "Please remember that the men are not our enemy. Defend yourself, and do what you have to suppress them but do as little damage as you can. Free those who are possessed and those who are under Bethliel's curse. I thank you, be well."

"Yes, sir," Gabriel answered and hovered off to do his duty.

As his army approached downtown, Eleazar felt the sudden need to stop. He stepped forward, then turned and placed his hand in the air in front of him. The army did as he commanded and came to a halt. They were only a half mile or so from the downtown area of Adjacent Cove.

"Atheos," he said. "I want to speak to God first."

Atheos smiled. "As you wish, sir."

Both Eleazar and Atheos knelt down to one knee, followed by the front row of the army, then the next, and so on. It looked something like several rows of dominos falling in a wave to the end.

After several minutes of complete silence, Eleazar rose back up to his feet, followed by his faithful assistant Atheos, then the rest of the army. It had been an extremely powerful moment of silence that gave a power to Eleazar's army that could never be possessed by their foes.

Eleazar took a deep breath, and then turned to see an angel approaching. He was just over seven feet tall and had blonde hair and black eyes. He looked magnificent, even pure to the eyes. He wore a long white robe that dragged on the ground behind him and sandals on his feet. As he approached, Eleazar sensed something evil about him. It was a fallen angel, who was there to try to come to terms with Eleazar.

"Eleazar," the angel said in a deep, almost booming voice. "I come in peace. My name is Laimente and I am here to represent Bethliel and his army."

"Why didn't he come in person?" Eleazar asked.

"That is not important," replied Laimente. "What is important is that you hear what I have to say and hear it well. Bethliel has amassed an enormous army, larger than yours. He wishes no harm to any of you, if you turn around and leave this town. If you choose to fight, you will be cast away."

"Now you hear me," Eleazar interrupted. "Go and tell Bethliel that he and his assailants are not welcome in this town and that we will drive them away by the power of God almighty."

"Eleazar," Laimente said. "This is not a matter of good versus evil. This is a matter of domination, plain and simple. Bethliel has already taken this pitiful town and the rest of the county is next. There is no stopping this. If your people were strong enough they could have at least put up a decent fight."

"Stop!" Eleazar yelled. "You have nothing to say about my people. Now go back and tell Bethliel that he can either walk away from this or be driven away, it is his choice. Do you understand me?"

"Eleazar, listen to me," said Laimente.

"Do you understand?" Eleazar firmly stated.

Laimente stood in front of Eleazar for a moment, looking Eleazar in the eyes, then turned and walked away. After walking a few feet, he slowly disappeared as he passed into the spiritual dimension. Eleazar turned and looked over his army.

"I can do all things…," he stated. "…through Christ who strengthens me."

He didn't show it, but Eleazar was growing more nervous by the moment. After all, a few days ago he was the counselor at a junior high school and had no idea who he really was. It was strange for him to have the abilities that he did. They came natural to him, yet he had never even thought of training for such a thing. The angel in him was coming out more and more each hour of the day. According to his new cohorts, he had been in more battles than one could count. He knew that he was ready, but there was an air of anxiousness to it that he was trying his best to shake.

It was already late afternoon, and Eleazar feared that the battle would continue into the night and they would have to fight in the dark if necessary. The time to attack was now. Eleazar turned and raised his arm, signaling Nephuna to blow his horn. The sound of the horn meant to prepare to march. Eleazar turned and began his advance with Atheos at his side and eighty thousand soldiers behind him.

Suddenly, after marching for not even ten minutes, two large balls of fire could be seen in the distance with black smoke trails. They were headed directly for Eleazar's legion. The balls of fire were about the size of a normal man and were traveling at a high speed. Eleazar stood in front of one of the balls and readied himself for its impact but not before commanding the first seven lines of warriors to hold up their shields to protect themselves.

One of the fire balls hit Eleazar square on his chest plate and carried him with it. Eleazar struggled with what was a demon as they flew through the air above the angelic army. Finally, he was able to draw his swords and struck one of the demon's wings, causing the both of them to crash into a street, causing a wide rip in the asphalt for several feet. Before Eleazar could get up, the demon hurried away, unable to fly. The injured demon hid himself in an abandoned building, fearing that Eleazar would capture him and send him away. Eleazar, however, was more concerned about his angels, and took to the sky to return to his post.

The other ball of fire hit the angels with an incredible force, knocking several to the ground. It then turned and headed back to the courthouse and disappeared behind the buildings. Some of the angels were slow to get up, but all of the shields were enough to protect them from any major harm. Being injured in battle was not too big of a deal because injuries to angels healed in a matter of minutes. If an angel was "killed", they did not die, however they were taken from the battle field.

Being killed to an angel or demon was different than what it was to humans. If an angel was killed, he would turn into a fine silver dust that would blow away and then make its way to Heaven. Upon reaching the heavenly realms, the dust would gather once again into the form of an angel. If a demon was killed, he would turn to ashes, which would also blow away but instead make its way to the realms of Hell. There the demon would be mended back into himself. Both processes took a considerable amount of time, usually a few days in our time.

"Everyone here okay?" Eleazar said to his troops. Most of the angels up front had burn marks across their shields from the attack.

"Everyone is okay," Atheos answered. "They're just trying to intimidate us."

At that, another ball of fire, this one much larger than the first two, came out of seemingly nowhere and rumbled towards the angels with tremendous force. The reddish colored ball, leaving a trail of black smoke behind it, was aimed directly at Eleazar and was coming fast. Eleazar dropped to a fight stance and crossed both his swords in front of him as a shield. The fire ball struck him dead on, knocking him off of his feet and several feet behind.

Out of the billow of smoke that was left from the collision emerged a demon that stood at least eight feet tall. He wore only short pants and was covered with muscles that were big even for his size. The beast's body was a light grey color and covered by patches of thin, dark hair. His head look like a bat's with pointed ears and more thin hair on the top. He had small but red and bloodshot eyes and a mouth full of yellowed, razor sharp teeth. The creature's spine protruded from his back leaving what appeared to be a spike going up his back.

Eleazar struck quickly, as soon as he got off of his feet. Atheos drew his sword as well and would have attacked to help out his commanding officer except that Eleazar motioned for him not to. Eleazar thrust one of his swords forward into the beast's gut, but to no avail. The creature let out a horrifying roar and swung his enormous arm at several angels standing only a few feet from him, knocking all of them to the ground. Eleazar struck once again, this time closer to the demon's heart but again without seeming to harm him.

The vicious beast then grabbed Eleazar with both hands, who was still trying to retrieve his sword from its chest. He picked him up over his head and threw him several feet into a telephone pole, breaking the pole in two at the ground and knocking it over. Sparks shot out of the wires at the top of the pole as it fell into the street amongst the angels. Eleazar picked himself up, in obvious pain but relentless determination and looked the creature over while trying to come up with a game plan in his head. His swords were seemingly ineffective, unless he could thrust it in just the right spot to bring the beast down.

Eleazar suddenly ran towards the demon as fast as he could, his swords in hand. Just as it reached out to grab him once again, Eleazar went to the ground and slid under the beasts legs, slicing both of the creature's heels as he passed under. The creature gave out a tremendous yell before falling forward to the ground. Eleazar then quickly approached the beast's head and cut it off with one swift swing of one of his blades. The creature then disappeared into the night more rapidly than it had appeared.

"Atheos, drop back," Eleazar commanded, out of breath. "The first two cohorts will march on with me. You hang back with the rest of the army." One cohort consisted of over five thousand angels and was commanded by a messenger. Eleazar was hoping that by sending only two cohorts initially he could draw out any surprise attacks that the enemy might have been planning. Because they were marching up a narrow street, it would be difficult for the enemy to tell how many were coming at any given time.

The first two cohorts marched forward behind Eleazar, who was being cautious of their surroundings as they went. After marching for a few moments, one of the demons guarding Bethliel at the top of the courthouse stairs raised his sword high in the air and waved it. Almost immediately demons began to attack the cohorts from within and in between the office buildings and home on either side of the street. Some were throwing balls of fire, others were attacking with a variety of swords and knives. Eleazar turned to one the centurions, Ananel, and pulled him in close.

"I want you to go to Atheos," he said. "Tell him to send three cohorts from the back to fight these guerillas and to send the rest up the middle."

The battle thickened as more angels and demons became involved in the urban guerilla warfare taking place in the neighborhoods and business districts north of the courthouse. Meanwhile, over half of Eleazar's army continued to march down Main Street towards the court house. Seeing this, Bethliel placed both arms forward, meaning that the demons should attack. The men hung back to provide further protection of Bethliel.

The bulk of Eleazar's army and less than half of Bethliel's were now squared off against each other on the two way road into downtown. The demons picked up the pace first, hovering just off the ground, followed by the angels. The clash when the two armies met caused thunder to ring out across the area. The angels and demons clashed hard, with Eleazar fighting right along with his army. Bethliel and his lieutenants hung back, on the other hand, watching the battle from afar. Meanwhile, angels also fought in the surrounding areas to fight off the demons that were scattered about. The angels were at a disadvantage in numbers only, as they fought and disintegrated demon after demon.

The mere density of the battle was enough to lower visibility in the entire area for those fighting in the spiritual realm. Still, the angels were gaining the upper hand. Swords and spears swung violently through the air all over as demon after demon was defeated and turned to ashes. The angels suffered casualties as well, but nothing like the demons. On the ground, the angels that were in man's three dimensional realm were fighting hard to defeat and capture the men in black robes. At first, guns were going off, one after another, making the scene sound like one out of war. Eventually, however, the men began to realize that gunshots weren't enough to defeat the angels, whether they were men or not. The angels were now fighting the men in robes hand to hand and were winning. Eleazar was encouraged by the success but still felt driven to capture the demons' leader, Bethliel, who was still standing outside the court house's main doors, unharmed.

"Atheos," Eleazar called out. After clearly gaining the advantage on the battle field, Eleazar wanted some of his men and angels to begin searching for the hostages that Chaos from Control had taken during the ordeal. Before the battle had begun, he had instructed certain warriors to do just that upon receiving a signal from Atheos.

"It's time to find the hostages," Eleazar said to Atheos. Within a few moments, after gaining the upper hand, Eleazar signaled for his men to go and take the court house and Bethliel. Seeing the men approaching, Bethliel sent the men in black robes, members of Chaos from Control, to intercept them. They, too, were overcome quickly as the angels overpowered them and disarmed them, one by one. Bethliel gave out a growl in anger as he pushed his lieutenants forward to join the battle.

Three of the angels that had come to fight as men saw this as their opportunity to attempt to detain Bethliel and made their way to the steps. As they reached the bottom of the steps Bethliel threw his hands in the air and then thrust them forward, sending bolts of lightning towards the angel and knocking two of them to the ground. He then hurled fire towards the third which caught on the ground around him and quickly rose. Two more angels approached, this time a lot faster and made it halfway up the stairs before a great wind began to hold them back.

"Don't you see?" Bethliel yelled. "You can't defeat me! I have the elements themselves under my command!"

Eleazar was trying his best to get to Bethliel himself but had to contend with both demons and men in robes and was finding it difficult to break free. All he could do was watch as the angels under his command were taken down one after another by Bethliel's sorcery. It was important to capture Bethliel and exorcise the demon within him so that he could be held responsible for everything that was going on and so that he would have no power to do any more damage in the future.

Suddenly, out of nowhere, an unmarked police car drove onto the scene containing Detective Stulken and James Walker. The car stopped in front of the court house, obviously unaware of the massive spiritual battle going on about them. James stood from the car and walked towards the bottom of the steps. All of the remaining members of Chaos from Control had now been taken down and subdued by the angels. Police officers in the coffee shop across the street swarmed on the men in order to take them all into custody.

"It's over," James yelled. "You have been defeated."

"This is only a battle," Bethliel replied. "The war has just begun."

Two of the police men and Detective Stulken made their way to the top of the stairs to take Mr. Walker into custody. As they neared him, he suddenly went up into flames and completely vanished with the only trace being a burn mark on the ground.

Meanwhile, the spiritual battle went on. Eleazar's angels had full control, but the demons were not willing to stop without fighting to the very last one. Only a handful of angels fell to the many thousands of demons defeated. Eleazar watched on, out of breath, as his first victory since being reborn as a human being ensued. He quickly gathered himself, however, in order to talk to the detective.

"I don't know how you did it," the detective stated as he shook Eleazar's hand. "But you did it."

"God did it," Eleazar responded. "I just helped."

XXVII

Adjacent Cove was once again quiet and peaceful. Residents were returning to their homes and entrepreneurs to their respective places of business to assess any damage and attempt a return to normalcy. For the most part, the city hadn't suffered too much physical damage, but the loss of life was almost too much to bear. Many good people had lost their lives, and to such senselessness and evil. There was no doubt that residents would morn this day for years to come.

Most of the one hundred and fifty men in black robes had survived the incident and were in custody at the high school gymnasium for the time being. Officers there were working hard to get all of them identified and processed. It was the same story for all of them, they had no recollection of what had transpired. The last thing they remembered was attending a Los Ultimos Dias meeting late at night. James Walker sat in an interrogation room at the police station giving all of the information that he could regarding his father, his following, and the events that took place.

An all points bulletin had been released for both James' father and the man that had broken James out of prison. According to the security tapes that survived, James had not caused any harm to anyone himself, which would certainly work in his favor. James repeatedly stated that he felt as if he was the only person that could bring his father in, but that was, of course, yet to be determined. For now James was going to be held at the county jail in Adjacent Cove and then after a most likely trial he would be sent to another prison in Texas other than Ware State Penitentiary.

Trenton County Hospital was packed solid with the injured and family members. Many of the family members were there mourning the loss of a loved one that had been pronounced dead either before or just after arriving. Doctors and nurses from private practices and other hospitals had come in to help with the load. Many of the patients were being treated in the emergency room's lobby because there was no room for them anywhere else. The most severe cases were being air lifted to Austin for treatment.

News station crew members littered the downtown area, everyone from the local news channels to national ones. The mayor, who had been taken hostage during the assault, was planning a news conference but word had not been released as to what time it would be. With law enforcement officials from the police department, the FBI, and the sheriff's department, and with all the news crews present, there was no way in or out of Adjacent Cove's downtown area.

Ware State Penitentiary was still on lockdown after the escape of James Walker by Saithe. Some of the surveillance video had been destroyed but enough survived to be able to make out exactly what had happened. The FBI had arrived on the scene earlier in the day and were now investigating the incident in connection with what all had happened in Adjacent Cove with the group that the media had named Chaos from Control. They were under the impression, for the time being, that James Walker had broken out of jail, taken control of his group of men, and led them to an attack on the city. This, of course, because they had not had the opportunity to interview any witnesses at this point. After Adjacent Cove was overrun and the governmental seats taken over, the FBI kept their distance, in hopes that there were enough local lawmen to take control of the situation themselves.

The crimes scene investigation unit had finally made it to Thomas Jasper's land, where they could sift through the ashes from the destroyed barn and try to find more bodies. There were still a good hundred or so people missing and unaccounted for and according to Walker, they would most likely be found on this site. It would most likely be several days, possibly even weeks, before everything was tallied up. The cause of the fire was still unknown to authorities, though some speculated the use of an agent such as gasoline to be involved.

Four of Adjacent Cove's uniformed officer and two sheriff deputies were now conducting house to house and business to business inspections to insure that no more of the men in black robes were anywhere in or around the city. Although the inspections would not be overly detailed, this was a process that would take some time and was therefore scheduled to take place over the rest of week. Officials wanted to be certain the men were in custody, especially with so many missing persons still out there.

Drew drove down the road on his way to First Baptist thinking over everything that had gone on in the last couple of days. Just the other day, he was thinking of new ways to reach out to the kids at his school regarding drug abuse, and now he was half man, half angel, working towards the accomplishment of God's will in his entire community. The police were spreading word about the vigilante that stood against Chaos from Control and saved many people from harm and possibly even death. He had already decline interviews with everyone who asked. It wasn't his will to be a local celebrity or to be known or recognized for what he did, because he couldn't have done anything without God. It was by God's strength, God's grace, God's love, and God's will that everything turned out the way that it did.

For the first time, Drew was finding himself comfortable in the new role that God had designed him for. He knew that this was not it and that there were many battles to come, but he also felt more ready for it, especially considering how quickly everything was thrust upon him. Everything that he had ever known about God's will for his life and the simple fact that God had really big plans for him, had come to this.

"Andrew," a voice came from the back seat, startling him. "Or should I say, Eleazar."

"Ah," Drew responded, immediately recognizing who it was. "Alazar of Bethany. It's good to see you again."

"So, it seems you've fit into your new role quite well," Lazarus stated.

"I have so many questions I could ask you right now," Drew responded. "But I think I'll just enjoy knowing what I know for now."

"Well there's nothing wrong with being intuitive," Lazarus replied. "So how do you feel?"

"I feel great," answered Drew as he pulled in to the parking lot of First Baptist. "Not even considering everything I've seen over the last few days. I am doing great and I'm quite confident right now."

"And your abilities have barely begun to come back to you my friend. Your world will never be quite the same again. When Jesus came and brought me out of that cave of a tomb, my world changed drastically. I had died and was brought back to life."

"What did you do with yourself after that happened?" Drew inquired.

"I did what anyone raised from the dead by Christ would do," Lazarus answered. "I worked for God."

"You became a preacher?"

"Yes," said Lazarus. "I lived out the rest of my days preaching God's word and the story of Jesus Christ, and people listened to me because of what had happened. I never told anyone about it but apparently news travels fast."

"Wow," Drew said. "I can't even imagine what that was like."

"Sure you can," Lazarus responded. "The very similar thing has happened to you. You have been reborn and given a great responsibility, one that you will carry for the rest of your life on earth."

"It's all so weird…" Drew stated. "…because I still don't remember much from my angelic life before this one. I remember how to fight, even how to lead, but not much more than that."

"It will all come back to you," Lazarus responded. "Just give it time. You have lived an extraordinary life as an angel and you have found favor in God's eyes and earned the respect of your enemy for being a great warrior." Lazarus leaned forward and put his hand on Drew's shoulder. "And the good thing is…you're on the right side."

Drew was silent for a moment. "Yes it is," he said, turning around to find Lazarus gone. He turned back to the front and took a deep breath before getting out of the truck to go inside.

First Baptist Church had been holding prayer meetings all day that were continuing even now. Drew's mother, along with Jim and his family, had been there for several hours now and had been praying nonstop since their arrival. Drew walked in the back of the sanctuary quietly and snuck up to where his mother, Jim, Cindy, and Alyssa were sitting and sat next to Alyssa.

"There he is," Cindy stated as she looked up to see Drew.

"Hi," Drew said to everyone quietly.

Drew's mother stood up and walked over to Drew to give him a big hug. She had been the most worried, despite Drew's commission, and was quite happy to see him. Alyssa was next to hug him. She was still shaken up by the incident from the previous night and had a large bandage on the corner of her forehead. She was there despite how she felt, however, to pray for support for Drew through this ordeal as well as to pray for her home town and the people in it. Outside of these four individuals, nobody else had put it together that Drew and Eleazar were one in the same.

"Thank you all…," Drew stated. "…for all the prayers. I couldn't have made it through this without them."

"You're welcome Drew," Jim answered. "And thank you for saving our town."

"It wasn't just me," Drew responded. "In fact, I was just a small part of it."

"You never give yourself enough credit," his mother stated. "Adjacent Cove would be in ruins by now if it weren't for you."

"It was all according to God's will," Drew said.

"Let us pray with you," Jim said. As Jim prayed, Drew looked around and for a moment, thought of his father and how much he wished he was there with him. He was grateful, however, to know that his father had known about this before he died. Drew pulled his stopwatch out of his pocket and turned it over to read the words that had gotten him through the ordeal. "Forget Me Not".

"Thank you," Alyssa whispered as she reached out and grabbed Drew's arm, pulling him closer to her.

On the corner of a quiet intersection in downtown Austin there was a small coffee shop. The day was bright and most people were at work but at this particular moment there was one customer. He sat in the corner, wearing a white suit and hat with a black shirt and no tie. His pointed shoes were made from fine leather and were perfectly shined. The man was handsome, well trimmed, and appeared to be in his mid thirties. He wore large rings on both fingers and carried a pearl cane with a solid gold goat head at the top. He sat quietly, drinking his hot tea and reading the newspaper.

Breaking the silence in the shop, a man came stumbling in, an old man that was out of breath. It was Bethliel, and he was obviously aggravated. He pulled his robe back over his head, startling the girl behind the counter, and sat down across from the man in the white suit.

"Master," Bethliel started. "We've been…"

Bethliel was interrupted by the man putting his finger in the air while he finished reading an article about the prison break at Ware State Penitentiary. After a few moments, he folding up the newspaper and placed it on the table in front of him and then gestured for Bethliel to continue.

"Master, we've been defeated," Bethliel said.

"No," said the man in the white suit. "You've been defeated. I, on the other hand, am doing quite well."

"I don't understand," Bethliel stated, perplexed. "This is our plan, our doing."

"This was our doing…," the man answered. "…until you made it your doing by going ahead with the plans before you were supposed to."

"But sir…,"

"Who do you think I am?" the man in the white suit said, slamming his fist on the table and taking off his sunglasses. His eyes were blood red and filled with anger. "You come in here telling me this is *our* doing. Who do you think you are talking to?"

"Master…I…"

"I am Lucifer!" the man yelled. "I am the Morning Star. I was created superior to you and I am superior to you. There is no *our*. This was my plan and you messed it up! This was my evil doing and you went against my will. Do you know what they're doing now in Adjacent Cove?"

"No, sir," said Bethliel with a tremble in his voice.

"They are coming to their senses," Lucifer answered. "They are rebuilding the damage that you caused. Not only that, but now they are looking for you! Humans and angels alike are carrying out manhunts for you. You won't be able to go back to that place for no telling how long."

"I am sorry, sir, I didn't mean to…" Bethliel said.

"To what?" Lucifer interrupted. "You didn't mean to what Bethliel?"

"It just seemed like the opportunity was there master," he answered. "I was being told that the angels' legionnaire barely even knew who he was at the time and I didn't want to give him the opportunity to gather himself before I attacked. The time just seemed right."

"And was it?" Lucifer asked.

"No, master. As it turns out, it was not the right time."

"The legionnaire that barely knew who he was at the time was Eleazar. Did you know that?"

"No master, I didn't," Bethliel stated.

Lucifer leaned back in his seat and took a sip of his tea while looking out the window in an attempt to calm his self down. He was obviously distraught with anger. These were plans that he had been making for many years and now he would have to start over.

"Had I gone on time," added Bethliel. "The result might have been worse."

Lucifer stared out the window in disgust without a response.

"This world is mine," he said. "One day the entire population will see nothing but blood and sorrow and will have no choice but to turn to me. The angels will have nothing left to fight for. When that day comes, I will show the humans nothing but more blood and more sorrow. They will pay for what they are, and so will the angels if they keep getting in my way. One ridiculous population after another, they all will pay."

"For our struggle is not against flesh and blood, but against the rulers, against the authorities, against the powers of this dark world and against the spiritual forces of evil in the heavenly realms." Ephesians 6:12